WHISPERS
of
KITH
and
KIN
a Mystery

KAYE BROWNSTONE

Whispers of Kith and Kin

Book 1 of the Whisper Series

All quotations in this manuscript are from sources in the public domain.

Copyright © 2025 by Kaye Brownstone

Book Cover Design and Interior Formatting by 100Covers.

Fern & Fable
PRESS

Fern & Fable Press
[™2024—Rachel Perkins]

ISBN: 000-0-000000-00-0 (paperback)

For Eliana, Abigail, and Jesse,
who see the world with endless curiosity and wonder.

And El Roi –
the God Who Sees Me and loves me still.

Contents

2024

Prologue

April 26, 2024 - Friday
Lexington, Kentucky

"You know, Spencer, there's whispers he's making a killing. Nobody likes it when somebody's making a killing."

"It's called flipping houses, Lizzy. The question is… is it the legal kind? By chance, have you been to visit your *kin* in eastern Kentucky in the past few weeks?"

"Why would you say that? You know they're not speaking to me—seeing as most of them are dead and all."

"Because you're doing it again. 'Ya' know, he's maykin' a killin'. No-buddy lacks it when sum-buddy's maykin' a killin'."

"First of all, Spencer, I don't talk like that…"

"Oh, yes, you do. You absolutely do." Spencer laughed, the sound carrying a playful note even over the line.

"And second of all…"

But Spencer never found out what was second.

"Jesus! I'll call you back, Spencer. I've gotta call 911."

And those were the last words Spencer Hill ever heard from his friend and fellow real estate appraiser, Elizabeth James. At first he thought it was out of character for Elizabeth to take the Lord's name in vain, but over time he realized: it wasn't said as a curse, but as a prayer.

CR&SO

April 26, 2024 - Friday
Lexington, Kentucky

When Elizabeth awoke that morning, she had no idea she wouldn't be coming home that night, or the next or... well, you get the picture.

While driving last week, she had accepted a request to complete an appraisal for 854 Janson Drive and knew she should have researched it more before she agreed. She always regretted it when she accepted orders on the road. If she were in her home office, she would've checked online public records to find the owner and past sales and looked up current listings and recent photos. However, anticipating a full day out, she Googled the property on her cell when stopped at a light.

There's not a current listing, so it must be a For Sale by Owner. There's an old listing though, showing just a simple ranch-style property. Not the best part of town, but not the worst either.

She clicked the Accept tab, and the order was hers, landing with a ding in her inbox.

It wasn't until she arrived home that Elizabeth realized the property was owned by the Realtor/Renovator/Investor, Thomas

Lassien of T. Lassien Properties, LLC. If she had known this, she would never have accepted it. A previous appraisal she'd completed for him had a whiff of foul smell to it. He bought it well below market value, tacked on the barest veneer of improvements, and flipped it fast for a tidy profit. The numbers looked clean on paper, but she couldn't shake the feeling he was playing both sides, preying on sellers who didn't know what their homes were worth, then unloading those same houses on buyers too green to spot shoddy renovations.

It nagged at her, the thought of him pocketing easy money from both ends of the bargain. Still, the comparable sales in the neighborhood had backed his asking prices. Everything checked out. No smoking gun. No proof of anything shady. Still, the way he worked never sat right with her.

But by the time she realized the house on Janson Drive belonged to Lassien, it was too late; she had already accepted the order. Backing out now would be unprofessional, and while she promised herself it would be the last time she dealt with him, she felt obligated to finish the job. After all, she had no *actual* proof the sales were sketchy. But it had left her feeling unsettled and with a firm conviction to turn down any further appraisal requests where Lassien was the owner.

Okay, just this last one since I've already committed. This last one...

Elizabeth had called Lassien's office to set up the appointment for the appraisal inspection. His assistant had told her the property was vacant, and they kept a key in the mailbox for workers while the property was under renovation. However, Elizabeth picked up a key from the office just to be safe.

The neighborhood around 854 Janson Drive had an air of quiet abandonment. Once a bustling middle-class suburb, the streets were now lined with faded, aging homes—rectangular boxes in various states of disrepair. Rusted chain-link fences sagged between properties, their gaps wide enough to walk through. Ancient trees lined the street, their thick roots breaking through the pavement and creating cracks that snaked along the road.

The house itself was a 1960s brick ranch, built for practicality rather than charm. It stood half-hidden behind dense overgrown shrubs, shrouded in a mess of tangled leaves and branches. A dusty picture window took up most of one side, its view into the house blocked by a dark curtain.

Weeds crept through the cracks in the sidewalk leading to the front porch, which was little more than a crumbling concrete slab. A carport jutted from the side, as if added as an afterthought. This was a home that had long settled into neglect, much like the forgotten neighborhood around it.

Elizabeth sat in her car for a few minutes, looking around the neighborhood and scoping out the house. No cars, lights, or twitching curtains; to all appearances, the house was vacant, as she had been told.

Her cell trilled, and she saw it was Spencer. Friends for a long time, she and Spencer Hill were both real estate appraisers. But they differed in almost every other aspect. He was politically a liberal, she a conservative; he was a city boy, she a laid-back country girl;

he was married, she was single. He was a radical, outspoken extrovert…she was, well, none of these. Yet, he was a skilled appraiser and a loyal friend. She had told him before about her unease with Lassien, and he had urged her to *run hard, run fast*. She would… next time.

Elizabeth cradled the cell between her ear and shoulder as she answered, tucking her iPad under her arm as she got out and locked the car, pocketing the keys. Reaching the porch, she inserted the key into the door's lock and stepped inside. It was a step she would do anything to retract. If this were a movie, she would without hesitation push rewind, and there she would be: removing the key, walking backward to the car in brisk, jerky steps, getting in, shutting the door, reversing out of the driveway, out of the neighborhood, and back to her cozy condo. But life doesn't work that way; reality must be dealt with and lived in and, if not cherished, at least made peace with.

The small living room resembled countless others Elizabeth had appraised—except for the three people lying on the floor covered in blood, hands tied behind their backs. No need to check their pulses. When someone's entire face and head are a raw, pulpy, bloody crater, there's not much doubt as to the possibility of a still beating heart. She disconnected Spencer's call with shaking fingers, intending to call the police, but her eyes couldn't look away. Her shell-shocked mind tried to make sense of what she was seeing.

I can't be seeing what I think I'm seeing. It must be a joke, maybe mannequins from a Halloween haunted house stored here for some absurd reason.

That might seem plausible were it not for the blood pooling on the floor and the horrible stench in the air. She caught a whiff of gunpowder mingled with the coppery smell of blood and sweat and other acrid odors she tried to pretend she couldn't identify. Her stomach roiled, and bile rose in her throat.

How long does gunpowder linger in the air after someone shoots a gun? No idea, but I've gotta get out of here.

Panic clawed at her insides, her heart pounding so hard she could hear it in her ears, and she fought to steady her breath. It was then that Lizzy heard the floorboard creak, and she saw the toe of a black boot come into sight in the doorway between the kitchen and the living room. This was followed by a black-jean-covered leg with a muscular forearm extended downward alongside. On the left hand was a tattoo, and in that hand was a handgun with a finger indexed on the barrel. Time seemed to warp, stretching every agonizing second as she grappled with the nightmare unfolding before her. By degrees an angular profile emerged, black hair, the left cheek covered with a jagged scar.

But Elizabeth didn't wait for the full reveal. She flew out of the door, dropping her iPad but somehow managing to hold on to her cell. She had never been more thankful for her car's keyless entry and push-button start, though how she accomplished either was a miracle considering her body was quaking from her teeth down to her knees.

Elizabeth reversed the car and sped out of the driveway, squealing tires and spitting gravel. She pulled out in front of a car whose driver leaned on the horn, but the sound barely reached her through the rush in her ears. Streaking from street to street, with an eye on the rear-view mirror, her only thought was to get as far away from 854 Janson Drive as possible. Once she hit a major road, a red light forced her to stop. This turned out to be providential, as she scarcely had time to open her door and lean out before she began vomiting. Still shaking and on the verge of hyperventilating, she allowed herself to close her eyes for a fraction of a minute. But then the light turned green, and more horns honked, demanding she move or get out of the way.

You've got to get hold of yourself, woman!

Taking some deep breaths at the next stoplight, she fumbled with her cell, at last getting the password right after many failed attempts, and dialed 911.

A woman's voice answered. "911, what's your emergency?"

"There's three dead men—well, I think they're all men. It wasn't easy to tell, seeing as they didn't have any faces…" she paused, her voice breaking, "…but they're dead. Definitely dead. The no-hope kind of dead, and there's blood everywhere, and…"

The operator's tone stayed steady. "Ma'am, you need to calm down. Can you tell me your name and where you're located, please?"

Lizzy knew the woman had a point. She began again, slower and calmer—at least she hoped she sounded calmer.

"My name is Elizabeth James. I'm an appraiser. I was just at 854 Janson Drive. When I went inside, I saw three people lying on the floor with their hands tied, and they had all been shot in the face—or head—well, both. Someone's still there. I saw him, but I made it out to my car and away before he saw me... I think." The weight of those last two words hit her all at once.

It's strange how a mere thought can cause an actual physical response. Dread and fear and shock churned in her stomach as the last two words and their significance registered in her brain. *Did he see me?* Next came the clamminess, dizziness, and her vision rushing into blackness as she lost consciousness.

ॐ

There are some upon this earth of yours… who lay claim to know us, and who do their deeds of passion, pride, ill-will, hatred, envy, bigotry, and selfishness in our name, who are as strange to us and all our kith and kin, as if they had never lived. Remember that, and charge their doings on themselves, not us.

The Second Spirit, Charles Dickens, A Christmas Carol

CHAPTER 1

November 1, 2024 - Friday
Cowherd, Mississippi

Penelope Fitzgerald was dead twice over. She had been both stabbed in the back and garroted with a Hermès scarf. Adding insult to injury, someone had forced her face into her gravy and biscuits before hacking off her bleached blonde ponytail at the skull—not quite scalped, but pretty close.

It was her cook, Mrs. Rose, who had found her. Just twenty minutes earlier, Penelope had ordered the harassed lady back to the kitchen to make fresh scrambled eggs after she had declared the first batch a "barren wasteland of glutinous, insipid globules, unfit for a shaggy mongrel." Upon this proclamation, Mrs. Rose had scurried back to the kitchen to cook more eggs while searching for her cellphone to Google the meaning of "glutinous, insipid globules."

"Why couldn't she have just said they were dry, sticky, and bland?" Mrs. Rose had mumbled, annoyed. Of course, they were none of these; but trying to satisfy Penelope Fitzgerald was an exercise in frustration. As a writer—or *literary columnist,* as she referred to herself—she had often told Mrs. Rose that she was "determined to educate the poor, ignorant townsfolk," that it was her way of "giving back to society by sharing her multifold wisdom and talent handed down from kith and kin."

"Well, I've known her *kith and kin* since elementary school well-nigh sixty years ago, and I can't say any of them were charitable nor wise," the cook hissed.

When a knock on the back door caused Mrs. Rose to remove her skillet from the stovetop to answer, she'd tried to make quick work of the boy from next door, who was complaining that someone had let his dog out of his backyard, and had she "seen him" (the dog) "or the guy" (the supposed perpetrator)? After a good 10 minutes of assurances to the negative, much tutting, and many "Now, off you go"s, he'd scuttled off to the next house. Mrs. Rose had resumed her cracking and seasoning and whisking, muttering to herself, "I have never served dry eggs. Nor sticky or bland eggs for that matter!" Upon completion, she'd scooped the eggs into a bowl and turned to hustle them back to her employer.

"Shaggy mongrel, indeed! I'll show her a shaggy mongrel…" Mrs. Rose had said under her breath as she delivered the new dish of eggs to the dining room.

But that was then.

CHAPTER 1

Now, we return to the dining room—specifically, to the moment when Mrs. Rose sees the body.

"Oh, my wig and whiskers!" she shrieks, flinging her arms and, hence, the bowl into the air. Knowing what goes up must come down, Mrs. Rose jumps back just in time to avoid being showered with moist, fluffy, delicious eggs. Gravity and comeuppance, they're a lot alike—kith and kin, you might say.

CRBED

November 1, 2024 - Friday
Cowherd, Mississippi

Two doors down from the unfolding drama at the Fitzgerald residence, Lily Jordan, AKA Elizabeth James, throws the local newspaper, the *Cowherd Register*, across the room where it splats against the wall, narrowly missing the mirror with the scarf hiding its face. All the mirrors in Lily's new home are the same; she hates seeing the accusing stranger who morphs into the glass each time she passes.

"Lord, forgive me for my murderous thoughts, but That Woman!"

'That Woman,' *Penelope Fitzgerald*, had visited Lily two weeks earlier and informed her she "felt it her duty to keep the citizens of Cowherd informed of all the latest community hollerins' and happenings via her weekly column."

Well, there's about to be some hollerin' happening over here! thinks Lily, as she darts across the room and grabs the paper to re-read the article, hoping she'd misunderstood or misread. She hadn't.

A Penny for MY Thoughts

All the News I am Morally, Socially and Spiritually Beholden to Report

Unfiltered, Unpasteurized, and Sometimes Unsanitary

By Ms. Penelope Fitzgerald

Friday, October 25, 2024

As most of you know, the house two doors down from mine has been let to a Ms. Lily Jordan. I thought it proper to introduce myself and welcome her to our village. I was hoping to receive some info on her in return to share with my readers. I am sad to say I learned little besides her name and that she is from "up north." She told me she works from home as a writer, although if her writing style mirrors her verbal communication skills, she must be an extremely poor one indeed. She was positively breviloquent! Terse, blunt, and borderline rude. I wasn't on her couch for five minutes before my investigative instincts began to sizzle and fizzle. There's no doubt in my mind—this woman is hiding something.

Every question I put to her, she replied with nebulous non-answers and turned the inquiry back on me. Now you all know I enjoy discussing myself; however, I persevered as a dutiful soldier. After all, that's what you pay me for! I tried flattery, fawning, and all sorts of flummery; I tried outsmarting, out-staring, and outlasting, all to no avail.

Still, I took the high road and, for her welfare, cautioned her about certain individuals and institutions around Cowherd, including which beauticians could provide her with subtle highlights (which I suggested she needed *sans délai*) and which would turn her hair into a green tumbleweed (see my column dated October 11th. You will thank me!). I warned her about which butchers alter expiration dates on their meat and informed her where to find stylish clothing to replace whatever it was she had on (northern haute couture, one may suppose).

I always recommend a religious institution to our newcomers; however, to give her a smidge of credit, she has been attending the Cowherd Baptist Church, for which she always arrives late, well past the shaking hands portion of the service (the best part!) and slips out during the last prayer like a fugitive. She should know people see such Machiavellian behavior as a reflection of someone with a deceitful nature and secrets they are desperate to keep hidden. True, it may be the echoes of poor breeding. But I can tell you without a doubt, she has the smell of a strumpet and the looks of a charlatan.

I'm sure you'll be glad to know I suggested to our new pastor, Brother Carothers, that he pay her a visit. I also plan to pass the same suggestion along to Sheriff Timmons. One cannot be too careful. I certainly shan't, and neither should you.

As a side note, aren't you all just thrilled with our new pastor, Brother Morris Carothers? Once again, a fine addition to our community, for which you can thank *me*. He is the epitome of the type of shepherd we need here in Cowherd: modest, malleable, and eager to please. I can assure you, with him we will not have a repeat of the disgrace and disloyalty of our former *reverend*.

I have offered Brother Carothers specific and inexorable guidance regarding what we here in Cowherd consider proper conduct and counsel from our men of God. You can sleep in peace knowing *this* man will not denounce or disparage you in a sermon or prayer.

Now, on to other news, I know you are eager to hear the latest regarding my daughter… but first let me take a moment to applaud the new dairy in town, of which I am a proud customer. One look at my skin, hair and nails will show you how they can help you too!

Cristo Brothers Dairy

**100% Grass-Fed Cows - Raw Milk and Yogurt
High in Omega-3 & Vitamins A & E & Beta Carotene.
Never Pasteurized or Homogenized
to Preserve Beneficial Vitamins, Minerals,
Enzymes & Natural Probiotics
NO Antibiotics or Hormones
Like our Father's Father - Delivered Direct
from OUR Dairy to YOUR Door
Tomás Cristo, Proprietor**

Now on to my daughter…

Lily closes her eyes and counts to ten, then 50, then tries and fails to say the ABCs in reverse. Every part of her body is burning and hissing with fury—sizzling and fizzling indeed.

Lily looks again at the newspaper. "In the space of four paragraphs she has called me a heathen, a hustler, and a hussy! I wonder if she also knows the definitions of harridan, harpy, and hatemonger?"

Her eyes stray to the top, and with mortification she realizes she'd picked up *last* week's paper.

"So, for an entire week, the community has believed these things about me," she says, looking toward the veiled looking glass.

Still, I'd bet there are countless innocent victims in Cowherd who have been the target of her spiteful diatribes; the poor beautician and butcher can't be the only ones. I think a word with the editor is in order.

But a glance at the editorial page reveals Fitzgerald to be the owner, editor, and publisher.

Fat chance, then, of any defense of my honor. Besides, many people will believe something once it's printed, regardless of how outrageous it is.

Still, she can't deny there is some truth in it. At least one truth. She does have a secret. One she prays this gossip-loving provocateur will never be able to unveil.

CHAPTER 2

November 1, 2024 - Friday
Washington, D.C.

U.S. Marshal Eamonn Kelly tosses the case jacket onto his desk. Lily Jordan, formerly known as Elizabeth James, is coming up on the six-month anniversary of her first WITSEC placement. He has been her designated agent from the beginning, and he remembers clearly the day he was assigned the case.

It was the last week of April when Eamonn's boss had called him about a potential witness in Kentucky. Both local and federal law enforcement had identified this individual as requiring urgent protection.

"Eamonn, you've got a new assignment." His boss' voice had come through with a sense of excitement. The man always had a way of making every task feel like a secret mission straight out of a spy novel. "Not a criminal this time. This one's an innocent person who was in the wrong place at the wrong time. And if the authorities are right, she's in grave danger. She's being treated at the University of Kentucky Medical Center. How fast can you get to Lexington, Kentucky?"

Calls like this always caused Eamonn's adrenaline to spike. He had joined the U.S. Federal Witness Security Program (WITSEC) branch of the marshal service five years ago. His personality and skill set made him a natural fit for the role of a WITSEC marshal. He'd always been a protector, or so his mother claimed. She insisted she'd known this about him since he was in the womb and named him accordingly.

"Eamonn, me wee lad, your name, it means protector, so it does. Sure, and that's your heritage and destiny. The Irish are known for their honor and bravery... loyalty to kith and kin."

He'd taken these seeds of maternal prophecy and planted them in the space where conviction grows. He fed and nurtured them until they had produced a harvest of resolve to keep those he loved, and now those under his care, safe from harm.

Eamonn remembered hearing a quote attributed to da Vinci: "Make your work to be in keeping with your purpose," and he'd taken it to heart as good advice. And so, from childhood to today, he had set out to mesh those two facets of his life.

He recalled his boss' words—that this witness wasn't a criminal. She's just an everyday person thrust into a nightmare. Which meant this case would be unlike anything he'd yet faced in his career. He was used to dealing with informants with murky pasts, but this woman had stumbled into danger by mere chance. Her innocence added a different layer of complexity, one that made the stakes higher than ever before.

And so, he'd booked a flight to Kentucky. He'd never been to Kentucky, but knew it was famous for bourbon, bluegrass music, and basketball. And of course, horses. Still, the McCoys of Hatfield and McCoy infamy hailed from Kentucky too, so it couldn't all be fiddles, whiskey, and roses.

ೞഔ

April 29, 2024 – Monday
Lexington, Kentucky

As Eamonn's plane made its descent into the Blue Grass Airport, he looked down, awestruck. The rolling green hills were so like those of his home in County Down, he felt an intense yearning for old Ulster. The leaves on the trees were just beginning to furl out, and he could imagine the smell of freshly cut grass and primroses. Even from the air, he could see the pink weeping cherry and apple trees.

The millisecond the seatbelt light flicked off, his seatmate bolted up and collected his bag from the overhead compartment. Eamonn observed the chaotic scene as passengers jostled and pushed their way off the plane, oblivious to anything resembling basic deplaning etiquette. Waiting out the fracas, he hoped the shoving and grumbling wouldn't erupt into an outright free-for-all. Staying seated until most of the cabin was clear seemed his safest bet.

On the way from the airport to the Med Center, Eamonn commented to the taxi driver of Kentucky's likeness to his home country.

"Oh yeah? Whar'ya' from?"

"I live in D.C. now, but I'm from County Down, in Northern Ireland."

They made pleasant conversation while the cabbie whipped the taxi this way and that as he managed door-hugging turns and seatbelt throttling stops. Eamonn kept a white-knuckled grip on the door handle, praying for a quick trip. At last, they arrived at the Med Center and streaked into the curved portico at the hospital's entrance. With relief, Eamonn scrambled out of the car. He thanked the driver and gave him a generous tip, whispering, "And thank you, Lord, for getting me here in one piece."

ᘓᘓᘐ

When Eamonn arrived at the front desk, the receptionist directed him to a conference room where the meeting was already underway. Around the table sat representatives from the FBI and DEA, along with a detective from Lexington Metro PD. Two uniformed members of the hospital's security team sat against the back wall. One wore a crisp uniform and the no-nonsense look of a woman who always showed up early; the other looked like he'd just rolled out of bed and into the wrong room. Files, laptops, and confidential documents lay spread across the table. Eamonn was late to the party, and they'd started without him.

"Thank you for meeting with us, Marshal Kelly," one agent began, standing to shake his hand. "I'm Seth Centers with the FBI. This is Agent Hodge from the DEA, and Detective Annie Patterson with Lexington Metro. Officers Jessup and Ortega from the U.K. Med Center security team are in the back."

"Hello, everyone." Eamonn took his seat, his gaze moving across the room. "I've read the official file in route, but I'd like to hear everything from your perspectives to be sure I haven't missed anything."

"Of course," Centers replied, nodding. "Please stop me if you have questions. We're dealing with a high-priority witness, Elizabeth James, who walked into the aftermath of what appears to be a cartel execution.

"Ms. James is an appraiser, and in the course of her job, she arrived at 854 Janson Drive here in Lexington this past Friday, April 26th. When she walked in, she found three men with their hands bound behind their backs. They were all shot in the back of the head at close range."

"How did she access the house? Was it unlocked?" he asked, frowning slightly.

"The house is owned by an investor named Thomas Lassien. Ms. James picked up the key from Mr. Lassien's assistant; however, she was told that there had been renovations going on in the property and that workers may have put a key in the mailbox." Agent Centers again referred to his notes. "After seeing the dead men, Ms. James saw a man with a gun, the supposed shooter, enter from a back room. She ran from the house and called 911. Detective Patterson, would you like to take it from here?" Agent Centers turned his attention to the Lexington Metro officer.

"Of course. Ms. James fled in her car and called 911." Detective Patterson opened a file on her laptop and played the 911 call.

911, what's your emergency?

There's three dead men—well, I think they're all men. It wasn't easy to tell, seeing as they didn't have any faces...but they're dead. Definitely dead. The no-hope kind of dead, and there's blood everywhere, and...

Ma'am, you need to calm down. Can you tell me your name and where you're located, please?

My name is Elizabeth James. I'm an appraiser. I was just at 854 Janson Drive. When I went inside, I saw three people lying on the floor with their hands tied, and they had all been shot in the face—or head—well, both. Someone's still there. I saw him, but I was able to get out to my car and away before he saw me... I think...

"At this time in the call, she became involved in a traffic accident." The detective stopped the recording and referred to her notes. "Witnesses at the scene reported she appeared to have blacked out, which caused her foot to slip off the brake. Her car coasted into the intersection, where a cement mixer broadsided it on the rear driver's side, causing the car to spin and catapult onto the berm. Seconds earlier, and the truck would have t-boned the driver's door. It's unlikely she would have survived the collision.

"The emergency responders took Ms. James from the crash scene to the emergency room here at U.K. Med Center. Exam and CT scan revealed a concussion, broken nose, and arm and facial burns from the airbags. Her nose doesn't need surgery, but after the swelling subsides, the doctor will manually realign it. Despite her protests of being in jeopardy, they admitted her to a regular inpatient floor because of the concussion and injuries." Detective Patterson cast a stern look at the security officers at the rear of the room.

"Any doubts as to the veracity of her perceived threat vanished later that night when a nurse walked into Ms. James' room to find a man dressed in scrubs and a surgical mask holding a pillow over the patient's face. Unfortunately for the would-be assassin, the nurse had just started jujitsu, and what she lacked in skill, she made up for in passion. Her outcries and clamor coming from the room alerted the staff, who ran to assist." Patterson's expression tightened, emphasizing the gravity of their oversight.

"She screeched like an angry peacock!" Officer Jessup's voice boomed across the room. "The man barely escaped with his clothes on!" He exploded with laughter, oblivious to the critical glances from those gathered at the table.

Patterson shot a disapproving glance at the officer, her lips pressing into a thin line. "Yes. The assailant bolted. They have now moved Elizabeth to a more secure ward and have stationed a guard outside her room."

Eamonn's jaw tightened. He referred to his notes. "My files show that the information she imparted in the 911 call had already led authorities to suspect she was in danger, which was relayed to U.K. Med Security before the ambulance had even arrived at the hospital. And then she herself expressed a fear for her safety. So why did the security department neglect to protect her?" Eamonn glanced up, leveling accusing looks at Jessup and Ortega.

"I'm sorry, sir, I wasn't on duty that day." Ortega sat straight and composed as she cast an accusing side-eye toward her colleague. "You'll need to ask Officer Jessup."

Eamonn looked at the other officer with raised eyebrows. "Officer Jessup?"

"Well…" Jessup squirmed in his seat, his gaze darting around the room. "I weren't sure the woman was rational. I mean, she kept goin' on about there being blood everywhere. Wailing that 'it was a scene too horrific to put into words,' even though she sure had plenty to say about it. I doubted she was in her right mind. But hey, better late than never, right?" He ended with a crooked grin.

"I'm not sure that adage applies when one's life is at stake." Eamonn narrowed his eyes, his expression serious.

Jessup had no response to this, but Eamonn could see his words, as well as his look, had struck a nerve.

Eamonn turned his attention back to the table. "Regardless, our priority today is to assess risk and determine if we need to place Ms. James in WITSEC." His eyes swept the group, steady and sharp. "I assume this group believes this to be the case, else you wouldn't have called me. What information do we have that supports this opinion?"

Agent Centers turned to the DEA agent. "Agent Hodge, would you like to communicate this?"

"Of course," said Hodge. "Elizabeth's description of the assailant at 854 Janson stated he was Latino. He had black hair and a scar on his left cheek. He was left-handed and had a tattoo on the back of his left hand. She was too far away to discern the tattoo image, but she thought it was a bird with something in its mouth. This description exactly matches Prieto Bautista of the Bautista Cartel."

Eamonn's inner alarm ramped up several degrees. He knew the name well. Prieto Bautista and his brother, Raúl, control the Bautista Cartel under the heavy hand of their father, a notorious drug lord known as Padrino Diablo.

"This syndicate has its headquarters in Los Fiera, Mexico, and has a pipeline running from southern California, cross country through Kentucky, then up the east coast before heading west to Detroit," added Centers. "They're the chief supplier of millions of dollars' worth of heroin that passes through the U.S. yearly. We believe they are responsible for the heroin laced with fentanyl that killed close to 1,400 people last year in Kentucky alone."

Hodge nodded. "As you probably know, this cartel is notorious for its ruthless tactics. Ms. James placing Prieto at the execution scene puts her in immediate danger, as the attack in her room has proven. It's the DEA's opinion that we must act without delay to protect her. Experience has shown that this organization is determined to do whatever it takes to avoid implication, including a willingness to target witnesses outside their own country. We believe that Ms. James' testimony is crucial in our efforts to cripple the cartel and bring the key players to justice. They've slipped prosecution multiple times and pose a dire threat, not only to Ms. James but to the public as well."

Yes, thought Eamonn. *They're involved in everything from money laundering to human trafficking and worse—devils who terrorize, maim, and murder. They're one of the richest entities in the world, as well as one of the most savage.*

"But why would Prieto make the hit himself?" asked Eamonn. "They have plenty of hired killers in the syndicate. He's a co-lieutenant, along with his brother Raúl. Why would he take the risk?"

"We think Prieto is making a power play. While he and his older brother, Raúl, both hold the position of co-lieutenants in the Bautista syndicate, it's Raúl who their father has groomed to inherit the family empire," answered Hodge.

Eamonn nodded, his mind working through the implications. "If Prieto is trying to prove something to his father, that would increase the risk considerably. Is the witness willing to cooperate?"

"We haven't gotten that far," admitted Agent Centers, leaning back in his chair. "We're painfully aware that entering WITSEC is a significate and life-altering decision, and we first wanted to weigh the threat against potential consequences to Ms. James."

"Okay, to summarize," Eamonn said, leaning forward and placing his clasped hands on the table. "We have a credible witness who faces an imminent threat from a ruthless drug cartel. Her cooperation is vital to the investigation and identification of a key member of the Bautista syndicate. Based on the risks, resources, and contingent upon the witness' willingness, are you all in agreement that WITSEC is our best option?"

Those gathered around the table all nodded and murmured in agreement.

"Yes, we believe WITSEC is the most effective way to protect the witness and preserve the integrity of our investigation," Agent Hodges asserted.

"I concur." Eamonn also nodded, his expression resolute. "Our priority is the witness' safety, and WITSEC offers the best chance for ensuring this."

CHAPTER 3

April 30, 2024 – Tuesday a.m.
University of Kentucky Medical Center
Lexington, Kentucky

"For the tape, it is April 30, 2024, 0800 hours. Hello, Ms. James…" Eamonn began.

"Miss."

"Miss? Pardon, Miss James, I am the marshal assigned to your case."

"Hello, Mr. Marshall."

"It's just Marshal."

"Marshall?"

"Yes, Marshal."

"Your name is Marshall?"

"It's fine if you just call me Marshal."

"Your first name is Marshall?"

"Well, you can call me Marshal. I'm a marshal."

"So, your name is Marshall Marshall? What kind of parent does that to a child?"

"Nurse, is she on something?"

"Yes, sir. She's on some powerful painkillers. The doctor realigned her nose this morning."

"Interview terminated April 30, 2024, 0801 hours."

CR&O

April 30, 2024 – Tuesday p.m.
University of Kentucky Medical Center
Lexington, Kentucky

Later, hoping to set a different tone than before, Eamonn began, "For the recording, this is U.S. Marshal Eamonn Kelly. The date is April 30, 2024, 1430 hours. I am with Elizabeth James and Officer Mark Jessup from the University of Kentucky Medical Center Security. Also present is RN Shelly Abney."

"Miss James, I am the U.S. Marshal assigned to your case. I have reviewed your 911 call, as well as conferred with the local police, FBI, and other various agencies, and we are all in agreement that you are in considerable danger."

"Yes, thank you! I tried to tell the doctors, the police, the janitors…They all just gave me the Big Dumb Woman Look."

"The Big Dumb Woman Look?"

"Yes, you know, the *Big Dumb Woman Look*. The look that can only be translated as, '*Honey, don't worry your little head about it. And by the way, why aren't you home raising some man's babies or barefoot and pregnant?*' I know you know that look."

"I'm sorry, I do not."

"If you truly do not, then please don't be sorry. It's demeaning and bigoted and ignorant."

"And downright vile and ungodly."

"For the record, that last comment was from Nurse Abney, and the rude spurting and snorting noises are from Officer Jessup."

Eamonn smiled at the look Jessup shot him… Big Dumb Man.

But his smile faded as he thought again of what he must convey to Elizabeth.

He'd had this conversation before, more times than he could count, with criminals desperate to cut a deal, men who'd flipped on their crews to avoid prison or worse. They knew the risks. They'd made their choices. The relocation, the new identity, the long silence—it was the price for staying alive.

But Elizabeth James wasn't one of them; she hadn't asked for any of this, nor had she made shady deals or run drugs across state lines. She wasn't a fixer, a snitch, or someone who'd spent years lining her pockets through organized crime. She hadn't laundered money, moved product, or buried secrets for the people who kept cities in fear; she was just a woman who showed up to do her job and opened the wrong door at the worst possible moment. And now she was the only person alive who could identify the monster behind the massacre.

Explaining to this innocent person that she must leave behind everything she has, everyone she knows, and live for an extended time, possibly the rest of her life, as a person wanted dead or alive by one of the most aberrant and bloodthirsty organizations on the planet... well... it felt downright vile and ungodly.

Eamonn took a deep breath, knowing the weight of his words would be felt keenly by the woman before him. "As I said, we feel there is a credible threat to your life, and it's crucial that we take quick steps to ensure your safety."

Elizabeth's eyes darted up, then away again, uneasy. Her fingers fidgeted with the edge of her blanket, betraying the anxiety she sought to hide. It was a brave front—but only just—and she blinked rapidly, though it couldn't quite mask the shimmer in her eyes.

"What type of steps?" Despite the quaver, her tone remained calm.

There was no easy way to say it. "We feel the best option for your safety is for you to enter the Witness Security Program. WITSEC."

Elizabeth reached up to tuck a tendril of golden hair behind her ear. "WITSEC. You mean...I have to disappear? As in leave everything behind?"

Eamonn nodded, his expression solemn, noticing the tight set of her shoulders as she watched him. His heart ached thinking of the difficult journey that lay ahead for Elizabeth. "I'm afraid so. We'll provide you with a new identity, a new life. It won't be easy, but I know no better way to keep you safe."

The words hung in the air, and to Eamonn it felt like the oxygen was being sucked from the room, as if dread and fear and grief had blown in like a cyclone, rattling the windows and echoing against the sterile walls.

Likewise, a whirlwind of emotions swept over Elizabeth's face, and he could see her mind was struggling to comprehend the enormity of what he was suggesting. A furrow appeared between her brows, a subtle indication of the inner turmoil threatening to overwhelm her carefully constructed defenses. Eamonn watched as a single tear escaped, tracing a path down her cheek.

He leaned forward, fighting the urge to place a reassuring hand on hers. "I know it seems impossible right now, but I promise you, you're not alone in this. I'll do everything I can to ensure your safety. Unless you go into Witness Protection, there's a strong likelihood that you'll face the same fate as those men you found executed. Or worse."

Eamonn saw the conflict etched on Elizabeth's face. She faced a grim reality: a stark choice that felt like a zero-sum game, where every gain came with a significant loss. If she entered Witness Protection, she would secure her survival, but that choice would sever all ties to her past: her family, her friends, everything she held dear.

The silence stretched, thick with unspoken fears. Eamonn could sense the battle raging within her as she considered her options. He felt a profound concern for her well-being. The path he was suggesting felt harsh, as if he were forcing her to trade one form of suffering for another.

Elizabeth's eyes shifted from wall to floor to ceiling, seeking a comfortable place to rest where the future didn't seem so bleak. He could see her grappling with the implications of each choice, the reality that staying meant facing the threat of a violent death. But the alternative was equally daunting—embracing a new life as a stranger, haunted by the ghosts of what she had to leave behind.

After a moment, she straightened. "All right. If this is the only way. If this is what it takes to stay safe, I'll go into Witness Protection." Eamonn heard a newfound resolve in her voice. "I'll find a way to adapt… to start over. I have to."

CRSO

May 2, 2024 – Thursday
WITSEC Safesite and Orientation Center
Washington, D.C.

Eamonn and Elizabeth arrived at the WITSEC Safesite and Orientation Center in Washington, D.C., on May 2nd. The building stood stark and unassuming amidst the bustling city, a plain facade deliberately designed to blend into its surroundings, much like the witnesses sheltered inside would soon learn to hide in plain sight.

Throughout the next week, she underwent exhaustive psychological evaluations, designed to assess her current mental state, as well as prepare her for the emotional toll of permanent disconnection. The doctors asked careful questions, some straightforward, others that seemed to circle around things she hadn't expected to talk about. The answers mattered- that much was clear, even if no one said exactly how. She answered the best she could, aware that somewhere behind their measured nods and quiet notes, decisions were being made about what version of herself might survive this.

Next came medical exams: bloodwork, reflexes, vision. The usual stuff. The doctors were thorough, and Elizabeth understood it was about making sure she was healthy enough for what came next. They explained there would be travel, stress, constant change, and possibly danger, and no one wanted unexpected medical problems slowing her down or drawing unwanted attention. They were hoping to predict any health issues that might cause trouble once she was relocated—illnesses that could flare up without proper treatment or conditions that might hold her back.

One wrong move, one hidden problem, and everything could unravel. This isn't just about hiding or starting over. It's about controlling every piece of my life, down to the smallest detail, to make sure nothing from my past can catch up with me. Oh, how fragile this new life truly is.

During one of these exams, a nurse glanced at the file in her hands and smiled. "So, you're about to become a WISPER?" she said, the term delivered like a joke shared among insiders.

Startled, Elizabeth replied, "A whisper?"

The nurse smiled. "It's just a nickname we use among the staff here. WISPER—Witness Intelligence Security Protection

Enforcement and Regulation program. It was one of the proposed names for the program before they decided on just plain WITSEC, as in Witness Security. The story goes that someone once said, 'WISPERs can't even be *whispered* about.' It caught on, and so we call our residents WISPERs, not in a joking way, just to make things more colorful."

Is that what I am to become? Elizabeth wondered. *A whisper— like an ethereal melody swept up by the wind that dissipates into the heavens. As King David lamented:*

As for man, his days are like grass; he flourishes like the flower of the field; for the wind passes over it, and it is gone, and its place knows it no more.

She had to admit, in theory, there could be no better candidate for a WISPER than herself. No parents, few close friends, no romantic entanglements, no binding commitments, no remaining family. Or nearly none. No one from her past who would storm hell to find her, not resting until she's found. No one except for the one she cannot speak of. He would do exactly that, which is why he must never find out.

ᘓᘏ

May 16, 2024 – Thursday
WITSEC Safesite and Orientation Center
Washington, D.C.

Elizabeth's first briefing with Marshal Kelly and other field agents to establish her backstory reminded her of a quote from a favorite fairy tale she'd memorized long ago:

> *"The past must be reckoned with; it is seldom as far behind us as we wish; it is more often in front, blocking the way and the future trips over it just when we think the road is clear and joy our own."*

"Okay, first, a few points of interest that need clarification." Marshal Kelly had said as he opened the discussion. "Miss James, can you please explain your relationship with Garrett Elliott?"

This had gotten the attention of every agent in the room, and all heads had shot up. The silence that followed was deafening.

Elizabeth's fairy tale had also told her,

> *"There is nothing more terrible than silence. Shame grows in that blank, or anger gathers there, and we must choose which of these is to be our master."*

But to Elizabeth, that was an impossible choice. Many times, shame and anger become wedded in an unholy matrimony. One is embedded in the other, and it is vain and hopeless to think it possible to sunder the union.

CHAPTER 4

November 1, 2024 - Friday
Cowherd, Mississippi

Lily's doorbell rings just as sirens fill the air, and her heart flip-flops, fluttering in her throat like a moth trapped in a spiderweb. Tiptoeing to the door, she closes one eye and squints through the peephole to see a man standing on the stoop, his body angled to the side. Still, Lily knows who he is: the forewarned and aforementioned Brother Morris Carothers, no doubt come to caution her that heathen hussies who hustle in Cowherd will not be tolerated.

Convicted of her unkindness, she whispers a quick prayer for forgiveness as she opens the door. Brother Carothers turns startled eyes and gaping mouth toward her, pointing with a trembling finger down the street. Lily steps out onto the porch and sees that blue flashing lights have surrounded the house two doors down—the Fitzgerald house.

What's the woman done now?

People driving in the street stop and gather with nosy neighbors congregating on the next-door neighbor's lawn. Lily sees a man sneaking through the un-monitored police tape and creeping over to the Fitzgerald house to peek into the windows. It doesn't take long to hear what she's done now: she's gone and got herself murdered.

The little boy from the house between Lily and the Fitzgerald home bounds toward her, his dark brown eyes wild with excitement. He'd been by earlier begging for information about his lost dog and now fancies himself Lily's best friend.

"Did ya' hear? Someone strangled her with a handkerchief!" He makes a twisting motion with his hands across his neck, then flops his head to the side, squelching out a grotesque gurgle.

"Weren't no handkerchief, boy!" a man from the crowd informs them. "It was a scarf! A silk scarf!" he clarifies, pursing his lips and pointing a "gotcha" finger at the boy, followed by a wink and a sharp nod.

"No, you idiot! Didn't you hear Mrs. Rose saying the poor woman had smothered in her gravy and biscuits?" says a stout lady wearing a purple housecoat and pink curlers in her hair. "Smothered in her gravy and biscuits... Why, I never heard the like!"

This brings a round of cackles and guffaws from some men whose wives are quick to smack various chests, arms, and bald heads.

"Naw, woman! I looked through that window myself. The old girl was scalped! Can't mistake something like that," continues another neighbor.

"I heard the deputy say she got stabbed with scissors," says another.

"Woooah! Stabbed *and* scalped *and* strangled *and* smothered in her gravy and biscuit? This is the most exciting thing to happen in this town in my entire life!" says the dogless boy, running off properly impressed.

The preacher recaptures Lily's attention as he drops onto the porch step. He's hyperventilating and mopping sweat from his face. He's pulled the fingers of his other hand back through his red hair until it's standing on end like a legionnaire's plume. Frightened he's having a heart attack, Lily offers a glass of water, startling the man from his shocked stupor, and he pops up like a jack-in-the-box. Thrashing his head in the negative, he spins and dashes to his car, diving inside and starting the engine. He inches his car up the street, eyes fixed on the paramedics wheeling a stretcher in through the front door. The entire time on Lily's stoop, the man had not uttered a single word.

As Lily watches Brother Carothers weave through the cars idling in the road, she notices a man standing on the open door frame of a pickup truck parked at the curb with his forearms resting on the roof, glowering at the Fitzgerald house. His face is long and angular, his countenance not unlike a grouchy camel. A fierce grimace furrows his eyebrows, causing his bulbous eyes to narrow and his lips contort into a snarl. Realizing Lily's notice, he hops off the door frame and spits tobacco juice on the ground. He then climbs into the truck, slamming the door before screeching away.

Shaking her head in wonder, Lily remembers she's supposed to be keeping a low profile. She goes back inside for some sweet tea and retreats to the back garden, vibrant with scarlet asters, goldenrod, and purple coneflowers. A rustle in the hedge separating the houses causes her to jump, tea sloshing over the rim of the glass and onto her jeans. Relieved, Lily lets out her breath when she sees it's the boy from next door. Earlier, when he'd come around asking about the lost dog, he'd introduced himself as James Chaney Bridges— "but everybody calls me Chaney. I'm ten and three-quarters. I'm named after James Chaney. He was a friend of my great grandfather. Can you believe my great-grandfather was a Freedom Rider and walked with Martin Luther King in Alabama? Anyway, the Klan killed James Chaney before my daddy was born. My daddy's named after Percy Greene. Percy Greene was a newspaper columnist and then *owner* of the *Hattiesburg Advocate*. My great grandpa was a journalist, and my grandpa became a journalist, too. Until a couple months ago, my dad owned and wrote for the *Cowherd Register*." The words tumbled out in a rush until he paused and gasped for air.

"Nice to meet you, Chaney," Lily had said. "And your last name is Bridges?"

He had puffed out his chest a bit. "My great-grandfather and Ruby Bridges' grandfather had the same grandfather. She's like my 20th cousin, fourteenth removed."

Lily had tried to follow that logic but failed. Suffice it to say, this young man was a relation of that brave little girl, Ruby Bridges, and was rightly proud of his heritage.

So now he's burst through the tangle of leaves, wearing a dazzling grin that lights up his brown face, and Lily can tell he's eager to share something.

"Hey, Daisy…"

"It's Lily."

"Lily, Daisy, same thing…guess what? You know how that old man said he snuck up to the window to hear what was going on? Well, I did too. Just before the ambulance people put her on the stretcher and took her away. Man, I was just like a ninja! Anyway, you want to hear what I saw?"

Lily would indeed like to hear, but Chaney continues before she can answer.

"There was that woman, face flat down in her gravy and biscuit, just like the lady said. At the side, you could see this piece of fabric sticking out the side of her neck, the hankerscarf…"

"Silk scarf."

"Right, that. But you want to know the wildest thing? I'll never forget this as long as I live. Someone had hacked off her hair right to her scalp, and there was red stuff all over her head. I thought it was blood, but then the deputy picks up a ketchup bottle from the table and takes a whiff. Then leans kinda' close to her head and sniffs. He raises his eyebrows and puts the bottle back on the table. It was ketchup! Someone had poured ketchup all over her head. Besides the ketchup bottle, on the table there was a half-drunk glass of milk, a half-eaten platter of bacon, some white gooey glop in a small bowl with blueberries on top…"

"Yogurt?"

"Yeah, I guess. There was also something silver sticking out of her back. And all her long white hair that was hacked off was scattered evra-where and what looked like scrambled eggs on the floor. She was sitting at her dining room table right across from that front window, and behind her was a French door open a little. I'd guess that was the killer's escape route," he says with a serious nod of his head.

Chaney sits down on the porch beside Lily, helping himself to her iced tea, causing Lily to smile.

It's ironic that this is the most comfortable conversation I've had since I arrived in Cowherd almost six months ago.

The day in May when she had pulled into the drive of this Lilliputian cottage, the dogwood trees in the front yard were over-flowing with white blooms, and the peony buds along the stone path to the door were beginning to burst open. When she followed the path where it forked and meandered into the backyard, her breath caught as she walked into a heaven of color. Flowers rioted through the back garden: bluebells, purple iris, velvety lamb's ear, red roses. Massive oaks and sugar maples hemmed the sides and most of the rear yard with bright, new leaves, and sassafras trees sported green balls on their bony branches. Tall boxwood hedges intermixed with an understory of yellow forsythia and still green burning bush flanked the sides. When Lily had seen the Bleeding Heart and Lily of the Valley tucked under the trees, she fancied for a moment they were promising a healing balm from her pain and welcoming her home. However, like a zealot, reality elbowed and kicked its way to the fore of her mind, barreling over whimsy and forcing fantasy to flee.

Today, the backyard has been transformed by autumn's arrival. The burning bush looks like a wildfire closing in. Sugar maples and sassafras trees whisper in the wind, their leaves dancing in swirls of gold and red and yellow. The oaks give a serene backdrop of green, as they are just beginning to show tinges of fall color.

Chaney props an elbow on his knee and rests his chin on his palm. "Lily, I think me and you can solve this case. We can be like those English dudes, Sherlock Holmes and Watson, in those books I stole from my Pops. I'm Sherlock, of course," says Chaney.

She smiles, "Oh, really?" *He'd be a fine Sherlock. It's clear he's smart and curious. Not sure how good a Watson I'll be, but it could be a helpful distraction.*

Chaney continues, "We just need to study all the clues and talk to the suspects. Now, that's going to be a *long* list. That woman was just about the meanest female I've ever met. My daddy wouldn't even let her come into our yard. I think she's got kin in the Ku Klux Klan. No kidding!" he adds when Lily gives him a startled look.

"Chaney, I think it would be alright for us to decipher the clues, but I don't think it's our place—not to mention safe—for us to talk to suspects. That's the sheriff's job. And I believe your dad might ban *me* from your yard if I encouraged you to do that."

He gives Lily a solemn look, yet there's mischief hidden there.

"Okay," he says with a roguish smile. "I bet the sheriff'll be coming out to talk to his deputies any minute. I'm going to creep up behind the car and see if I can hear what they say. See ya' later, Watson."

And just like that, he crashes through the shrubbery and is gone, leaving the bushes quivering, sticks and leaves raining to the ground.

"Well, if I'm to be a good Watson, I guess I need to record the clues," Lily says with a sigh and goes inside. She wishes she had a whiteboard, but her eyes light on her sketchbook, and she grabs it, opening it to a blank page.

"Okay, the clues," she mumbles and begins her list.

Clues at crime scene:

1. Strangled with silk scarf.

2. Head pushed into gravy.

3. Hair lopped off at the scalp.

4. Head covered with ketchup.

5. Shorn hair strewn over floor and table.

6. Something silver in or on her back.

7. French door behind the victim was ajar.

8. Left on the table are a half glass of milk, a bottle of ketchup, yogurt with blueberries, a half-eaten platter of bacon, gravy and biscuit, and scrambled eggs on the floor.

She tears the page from her sketchbook and grabs a roll of tape from a drawer. With a few quick strips, she sticks the list to the kitchen wall. She steps back, trying to make sense of the mess.

"Mercy! It's like farm-to-table served with a dash of terror and a side of madness."

CHAPTER 5

November 1, 2024 - Friday
Cowherd, Mississippi

The doorbell rings for the second time that day. Moments later, the pounding begins—urgent, relentless, and impossible to ignore. A furtive peep out the window reveals a flamboyant female in retro attire. She looks out of place but harmless, so Lily opens the door.

"Hello, I'm Bourgeois Fitzgerald, but you can call me Bougie. You're not as plain as my momma—late momma—said. God rest her soul," she says, holding out her hand.

"Well, thanks, I guess," Lily says, extending her hand, wary but polite. "I'm sorry about your mother."

I mean, I am sorry.

"Yes, what a shame," Bougie replies without a hint of remorse in her voice. Then, she positions her hand on her hip, twisting and curving her body into a pose somewhat reminiscent of a model. She flashes a huge smile and fluffs her hair but says nothing. She turns her head to the right and then left.

What in the world is she doing? Modeling? Is she waiting for a compliment?

Lily takes stock: a long, makeup-caked face with rouged cheeks, eclipsed by a sharp elongated nose; protruding eyes smudged with bright green eyeshadow from lid to eyebrow. Her red hair had gone full frizz, though it was hard to tell if that was the goal or just a lousy hair day. Her dress is neon green with a wide, flared skirt sporting huge pink watermelon slices on it. She holds a pink straw purse in the shape of a watermelon.

"What an interesting dress. Very vintage," Lily stammers.

"Oh, thank you! I bought it at a little boutique called Classic Fifties. I just love the 50s and 60s, don't you? The clothes were so fashionable, and life was wholesome and simple. Everyone was so kindhearted and cheerful. Those sure were the good 'ole days," she says, hugging herself, closing her eyes, and smiling.

Lily thinks about her recent conversation with Chaney… about the man he was named after… about Ruby Bridges and the Freedom Riders and the Ku Klux Klan.

"The problem with thinking about the *good 'ole days* is that what was heaven for some may have been the exact opposite for others. I doubt many African Americans would describe the '50s and '60s wholesome, simple, *or* kindhearted," Lily says, her voice tight.

From Bougie's expression, it's clear she despises correction. She puffs out her chest like Chaney did earlier. But where his was pride, hers is pure anger.

Her chin lifts in challenge. "Well, if they were so unhappy, they should have just gone back to where they came from. It's not like they were slaves anymore. They had the freedom to leave."

Lily's eyes widen, and her mouth drops open. She cannot believe what she's hearing, but the Fitzgerald woman hardly notices, or maybe it's just that she hardly cares. Regardless, it doesn't slow her toxic rant.

"A lot of people would have been happier if the whole lot had just packed into one of those ships they came over in and shoved off into the wide, blue yonder," hissed Bougie, theatrically thrashing her arms, presumably toward her estimation of wherever *yonder* may lie.

Lily feels her face heat, and her heart begins pounding as if it wants to burst from her chest and scratch this woman's eyes out. And what's worse, she sees Chaney out of her peripheral vision slipping around the house. Had he just heard all this venomous, soul-sickening vilification of his ancestry?

Oh Lord, I know I'm called to love and show grace and mercy and turn the other cheek, but even Christ cleared the temple in righteous indignation. How could I have ever imagined her to be harmless? This woman is a demon raised by a devil! This and much more she wants to say to Bougie but is afraid once she begins, she won't be able to stop. Plus, how many times have the marshals warned her to keep a low profile?

Lily swallows the bile rising in her throat. Through gritted teeth, she leans toward Bougie and says, "You need to leave right now. I never want you to set foot on my property again. You are a hateful person, and you are not welcome here."

But Bougie just smiles this sly, slow smile and says, "Well, that's just the thing. The very reason I came here was to tell you to leave *my* property within the week. But seeing as you're being so spiteful, you have an hour to vacate this house. It was my mother's, and now that she's dead, it's mine."

Lily feels her breath catch. This is news to her. She thought the cottage belonged to the government. *Eamonn Kelly has some 'splainin' to do.*

"I have a six-month lease, and I intend to stay the full time. When the lease is up, I will leave with pleasure," Lily replies.

"A lease can be broken, and I'm breaking it. I'm evicting you. Get out, or I'll call my lawyer," Bougie snaps, taking a threatening step toward Lily.

"I think that's an excellent idea. And while you're doing that, I'll call mine," Lily retorts, placing her hands on her hips and taking her own step toward Bougie.

"I see the sheriff is still over at mother's. I think I'll just skip the lawyer and have you forcibly removed," Bougie says, tottering off on 6-inch red stilettos Lily had somehow failed to notice. They sink into the ground at every step, causing her to twist and toddle to keep her balance. But Bougie's bellowing had already drawn the attention of the sheriff, and he meets her halfway. Lily sees them conferring in hushed voices, Bougie's arms flailing, fingers pointing. The sheriff takes out his cell and confers with someone on the other end. Ending the call, he turns to speak to her again.

Bougie's face turns beet red and contorts into an infantile pout. She turns and shimmies off to her car, righteous indignation radiating with every step.

Lily lets out a long breath that catches as she sees the sheriff heading her way. He's a beefy man whose shirt buttonholes are agape and straining against his round stomach. *My word! He's the living image of Boss Hogg from the Dukes of Hazard. Let's hope he's not as crooked.*

Just shy of the porch, the lawman stops and assumes the stance of an old-time gunslinger, with feet braced and hands on hips. As if by accident, his left hand casually pushes his jacket back, revealing his firearm. But Lily doubts this man does anything by accident. He looks like someone who is used to intimidating. And likes it.

"Hello, Ms. Jordan. I'm Sheriff Timmons. I see you and Bougie haven't exactly hit it off," he drawls.

Yep, just like a gunslinger.

Lily nervously bites her lip before answering. "You could say that. She's trying to evict me, saying this house belongs to her now that her mother has passed away."

"Well, it seems there's been a little confusion on that score. Her mother did own this house, but she sold it six months ago, according to her lawyer. So, you're in the clear as far as that goes."

"As far as that goes? Is there another problem, Sheriff?" Lily knows her face is overreacting. Her eyes are so wide her eyebrows feel like they're about to fly off her face. She takes a breath and tries to get her face under control.

"I'd like to speak with you about the death of Mrs. Penelope Fitzgerald. Do you think we could step inside?" asks the Sheriff, taking a step toward Lily.

Lily takes a step back. She thinks of the clue list taped to the kitchen wall, and her heart skips a beat.

"Am I a suspect in her death? I don't know how that could be. I'd met her only once for a very brief visit," Lily responds. *Stop talking so fast and shifting from foot to foot; you look suspicious. Steady yourself, woman!*

"Maybe so. But she had a definite opinion about you. It was all down in black and white. Now, I've never been one to consider things in her column as gospel, but I did notice you acting all furtive and sneaking into church after the service had started and slipping out during the closing prayer. Is that so people can't talk to you? It's a fact that you've been spurning our stores and places of business, not attending community events, or getting to know your neighbors, and most of all, refusing to share anything about your past. Well, if that right there don't smell of secrets, I don't know what does. And it just gave me a little squiggle in my gut. My gut is an excellent judge of people, Ms. Jordan. And I'd have to agree with Penelope, God rest her soul, it appears you've got something to hide."

"There's a difference between being secretive and being private, Sheriff," Lily explains, raising her chin.

"Maybe so, maybe so. Still, with you living practically on the Fitzgerald doorstep, I'd be a fool not to get a witness statement and any pertinent info you have. So how about a glass of iced tea?" he asks with a toothy smile, taking another step toward Lily.

Lily crosses her arms. *I hope this makes me look confident instead of a desperate attempt to hold myself together.* "Sheriff, after all you've just said, I think it's obvious you view me as a suspect. Considering this, I feel I must claim my right to have my attorney present for any statements or questioning. I will be happy to talk with you as soon as a lawyer can accompany me."

Sheriff Timmons' jaw clenches, and he tilts his head, then narrows his eyes as if taking her measure. "All right. But just so you know, I am going to have deputies posted at every exit route in town. Don't be trying to escape on me now, Ms. Jordan." And with that, he turns on his heel and saunters away.

With deliberate steps, Lily goes inside, closes the door, and triple-locks it. Grabbing her cell, she dials a number she'd memorized but prayed she'd never have to use. A soft brogue answers, "Eamonn Kelly."

"Marshal Marshall, my neighbor has just been murdered. And I'm a suspect."

CHAPTER 6

May 16, 2024 - Thursday
WITSEC Safesite and Orientation Center
Washington, D.C.

The silence in the room pulsed in Eamonn's ears as he opened the file his boss had given him the previous night. He'd spent hours stewing over the information, weighing how best to handle it. He knew the story from his training at the Academy, but until last night had no idea it would apply to this case.

At 9:30 a.m. on August 6, 2012, Kentucky District Judge Garrett Elliott was found in his McCoy County, Kentucky, home with a claw hammer buried in his skull. The Elliott's cook had arrived for work and couldn't find her employer, so she summoned Miles Fairchild, the Judge's assistant, to the home. After an extended search, Miles suggested checking the detached garage, where the two found the judge dressed only in his robe and pajamas. He was lying face down on the concrete floor with the hammer protruding from the back of his head.

The McCoy County Sheriff arrived at the scene within minutes and alerted the coroner. Forensic specialists were called to collect physical evidence. It was clear from the beginning that this was a murder.

Judge Elliott was a "widower" as his wife, Erin, had vanished in the middle of the night eight years ago and was subsequently declared legally dead. The judge lived with his 13-year-old daughter, Grace. He also had an older son, Jackson, who was serving in the Navy. An interview with the Judge's assistant revealed Jackson had been home on a short leave. Neither Grace nor Jackson could be immediately located.

Deputies later found Grace at two in the afternoon in a hunting cabin on the far side of the estate. Having spent the previous day sketching in the woods, she informed the sheriff that she had slept there the night before. She reported that she had no knowledge of what had occurred at her home the night before. She was so distraught at the news of her father's death that she had to be sedated by the family doctor.

Jackson was never found. However, the judge's garage was bursting with evidence of Jackson's presence, including his very clear fingerprints on the hammer handle.

As the U.S. Marshal Service, in addition to WITSEC, is responsible for protecting Supreme Court justices and federal and district judges, they were called in to investigate and apprehend Jackson Elliott. But no one ever saw him from that day on.

It was a huge black mark for the service, and the agents on that case became as infamous as Jackson Elliott himself. Whenever they walked the halls, their peers would call out, "Hey, Captain!"—a cutting nod to Moby Dick's elusive nemesis. Jackson Elliott had become the agency's great white whale. He had been reborn into legend.

Which explained why everyone in the WITSEC Orientation briefing had been speechless when Garrett Elliott's name had been mentioned, but none more so than Elizabeth.

"Miss James, this will not be the first time your name has been legally changed. Am I correct?" asked Eamonn.

ᘓᘔᘒᘗ

It wasn't Elizabeth's intention to be rude. She simply couldn't make her brain and her mouth work at the same time, and for the moment, her brain was working in overdrive. *How does he know this? How could I have thought he would not know this? And how am I going to get out of this without breaking a sacred promise?*

"Miss James, again, would you please explain your relationship with Garrett Elliott?"

"Marshal, that has nothing whatsoever to do with the situation I am in now."

"Please answer the question, Miss James."

Elizabeth took a deep breath and gathered her thoughts. Her mind cautioned her tongue to keep itself under control, to just answer in the most direct and brief manner possible. But Elizabeth was worried because her tongue rarely obeyed her mind.

"Garrett Elliott was my father. My birth name was Grace Elliott."

The other agents in the room looked awkwardly at their neighbors, expressions frozen in disbelief. The air was thick with tension, and many shifted uncomfortably in their chairs or swallowed to keep from expressing their astonishment.

"And why did you change your name, Miss James?" asked Eamonn.

"My father was murdered in 2012. The identity of his killer remained a mystery. My maternal grandmother felt I would be safer if I changed my name. My mother's maiden name was James, and my middle name was Elizabeth, so I became Elizabeth James."

"And what can you tell me about your brother Jackson's whereabouts?"

"I have not seen Jackson since the time of my father's death."

"Have you spoken with him since that time?"

"I have not."

Keep eye contact. Stick to the facts. Stop trying to break your own fingers. Don't forget your promise.

"You told the authorities Jackson did not kill your father."

"He did not."

"And why do you believe this?" Eamonn leaned forward, his brow furrowed in curiosity.

Uh oh. Elizabeth's face was composed and calm, her upper body straight as a flagpole. But under the table, her hands again clutched each other in a deathlike grip, and her legs were trembling as if itching to make a run for it.

"Miss James?"

"If Jackson were going to kill my father, he would have done so long before that night."

Where did that clichéd response come from? It's the pressure talking. Or maybe it's those magnetic brown eyes of his—hypnotic, perceptive, and dangerous.

"If you believe your brother didn't kill your father, you must have an impression of who might have?"

"If you're asking me who would have wanted to kill my father, I can assure you the list is lengthy and diverse."

"That's not what I asked. I asked, who do you think killed your father?"

Elizabeth was silent, yet knew the silence wasn't empty. It was full of answers. Marshal Kelly's glare said he knew it, too. For a long moment, they held their ground, neither willing to give way nor disturb the tense silence that stretched between them.

Finally, Eamonn let out a slow breath, rubbing a hand over his dark, cropped hair, and continued, "Okay, let's move on, for now, and review the Memorandum of Understanding, which I will from here on refer to as the MOU. This document is to ensure you know your responsibilities as a witness and what the federal government's responsibilities are toward you.

- "You agree to cooperate fully and truthfully with law enforcement agencies, including providing testimony, information, and/or evidence as required in connection with the incident you witnessed at 854 Janson Drive, Lexington, Kentucky, on April 26th, 2024.

- WITSEC agrees to provide you with protection, including but not limited to relocation, change of identity, including any needed official documents, and any necessary security measures. Likewise, you agree to accept said protection.

- You agree to maintain strict confidentiality regarding your participation in WITSEC and any sensitive information disclosed to you.

- WITSEC affirms to take reasonable measures to protect your personal information and identity.

- Either party may terminate this MOU by providing written notice, and you are aware that termination may result in the discontinuation of protection and support provided by WITSEC.

- As a participant in WITSEC, you are required to pay your own expenses after six months in the program.

"This last item doesn't appear to be an issue for you. A review of your financials reveals you have substantial reserves in cash, bonds, and investments, as well as a large, albeit unmaintained and deteriorating, estate in McCoy County, Kentucky."

"I can't use that money." Elizabeth shifted in her seat, her gaze dropping to her fidgeting hands. "It's not all mine."

"Pardon?" Eamonn's brow furrowed as he looked at her, confusion plain in his expression.

She raised her eyes to his with quiet resolve. "At least half of it belongs to my brother. I won't use it. He may need it someday."

Eamonn's eyes narrowed. "So, you think your brother is alive?"

"Do you think he's alive?" she countered. She heard the hopeful lilt in her voice.

Eamonn hesitated, his expression inscrutable. Then, without breaking eye contact, he reached into his messenger bag and brought out a packet of cards tied with twine. He dropped them onto the table with a smack, rattling the table and Elizabeth. "Can you explain these cards, which were found at your home?"

Great, he found them. Stop underestimating him, you twit. He's a U.S. Marshal, after all. Yes, these cards are the reason I'm sure Jackson is still alive.

Twelve postcards…twelve birthdays remembered…twelve single hearts the only message, whispering his love and continued existence. I was fourteen when the first one arrived. It was a mystery, and I had laughed it off as a joke. Grandma thought it was from a secret admirer.

When others arrived on subsequent birthdays, I felt hope unfold inside me. Jackson. There was no other explanation. Each card came from a different location: Denver, Vancouver, San Antonio. I decided that after I graduated, I was going to go wherever the next card was postmarked from and find my brother. It was to be a holy pilgrimage.

But it wasn't until after Grandma's death years later that I was able to set out on my crusade. That year the card came from Savannah, and so that's where I traveled, only to later realize I had no idea how I would find him. Loitering on a bench on Broughton Street or rumbling through Savannah by trolley, my eyes were never still as they studied every face that passed. I became numb to the beauty around me as day after day my hopes melted away like candy floss. It had been a child's fantasy and a fool's journey.

"Miss James?" asked Eamonn, startling her from her thoughts. "Do you know who sent these cards?"

"As you can see, the cards are unsigned. I cannot tell you who they are from because I do not know," she replied.

At least I don't know 100%. Still, there's no one else living who cared for me like Jackson had. The cards followed me through various address changes. I'm not sure how he accomplished that and remained a ghost, but it's always made me feel watched over and protected, just like he had always done before.

"Marshal Kelly, if you are going to charge me with a crime, please get on with it." Elizabeth shifted in her seat, her gaze steady on the marshal. "Yet still under oath, I will testify that I do not know who sent those cards."

"That's enough for today." He closed his file with a thud, clearly frustrated. "We'll resume tomorrow at 0900 hours." Standing, he gathered his notes and the cards and exited the room without another word.

CHAPTER 7

May 17, 2024 - Friday
Washington, D.C.

Eamonn watched Elizabeth take her place at the table across from him, reaching up to twist a lock of blond hair behind her ear. *I hope today goes better than yesterday, when every word she spoke sounded as if she was imparting state secrets. As Da would say, she never missed a good opportunity to shut up.* Still, as exasperating as she was, Eamonn couldn't help but admire her unconquerable spirit. It will serve her well.

It was on his superiors' orders that he had pressed the line of questioning from yesterday. He's always believed Jackson Elliott to be dead; in today's world, it would be the feat of a Greek god to remain in hiding for twelve years. Of course, Jackson Elliott was not your average Joe, and he was no ordinary sailor. He was Navy Intelligence, so that stretched the realm of possibility.

Still, I've made the attempt, which will have to satisfy my boss. For now, at least.

He had met Elizabeth at breakfast in the cafeteria this morning, and she had agreed to use a portion of the money in the joint account with her brother for her living expenses, along with what she had in savings. Still, she needed at least a part-time job to avoid unwanted attention; being a lay-about or a lady of leisure is especially noticeable in a small town.

"Good morning. Today we will review the highlights of your employment and backstory," began Eamonn. "You are now legally Lily Jordan from Cincinnati, Ohio. You are 28 years old. Your parents are deceased, and you have no siblings. An aunt and uncle on your mother's side raised you. As you studied literature and English at college, we have arranged for you to work remotely as a part-time writer for LitPages, analyzing and summarizing 18th and 19th century literature. You've worked for them for the past four years. You hold degrees from Washington and Lee in English and literature.

"A safe house has just become available in Cowherd, Mississippi, a small town with a population of around 35,000, thirty miles east of Natchez." Eamonn paused when he noticed her chewing her bottom lip. "Is something wrong?"

"It's just… that's a lot of lies. I hate lies."

Eamonn leaned forward, laying a hand on the stack of documents in front of him. "Your name has been legally changed, and it will reflect as such on your new birth certificate, driver's license, and social security card. It's no different from when you changed your name when your grandmother adopted you."

"Yes, that's true, but that didn't feel like lying. Elizabeth was my middle name, and James was my grandmother's last name, my mom's maiden name. I moved to my grandma's home in central Kentucky, and none of my classmates knew anything about my parents except that they were both dead. If anyone tried to pry into my past, I told them it was too painful to talk about, which it was."

"Miss James, excuse me, *Miss Jordan*, it's vital you have a solid backstory. Your life is still in grave danger and will likely be so for many years. I know it's hard to hear, but it's the truth. I understand you hate lies. So do I, but you really have no choice. Well, I suppose you do, but the other choice is a deadly one."

The tears gathering in her eyes didn't escape Eamonn's notice; he could see her trying hard to maintain her composure. He felt a lump form in his throat, and his heart ached at her vulnerability. She looked fragile and fearful... and altogether lovely. For a moment, he wanted to reach out to her, comfort her. *Catch yerrself on, lad! This is work and nothing else. Stop being an eejit!*

Eamonn cleared his throat. "Miss Jordan... I'm just going to go ahead and call you Lily. I know you're a Christian, and the thought of lying goes against everything you believe to be right. Do you know the story of when King David pretended to be insane to save his life? While he was with the king of Gath, he was terrified of him, and so he acted like a madman, which was a lie. Still, David is called a man after God's own heart. Missionaries who go into dangerous places often have a backstory for their safety and the safety of their families back home. Your new name and new job, that much is true. Just start with that. I hope you will be able to come to terms with the rest."

"I'll do my best," Lily whispered.

"Good. Tomorrow, you will have your makeover, and then next week we will leave for Cowherd. I will accompany you on the airplane, and when we land in Natchez, there will be a car waiting for you registered in your new name. You'll travel to Cowherd alone. The house is ready, stocked with linens and food. The agency has purchased a new wardrobe for you, which is already packed and waiting in your room."

Eamonn could see Lily was overwhelmed again. It was a lot to take in. Yesterday she was exasperating, defiant and obstinate. Unconquerable. Today she's withdrawn and dispirited, and she looked utterly defeated. He much preferred the former.

"Will I be able to take any of my own things with me?" she asked.

"We have put the contents of your condo in long-term storage. There aren't many personal items we can allow you to take." He leaned to the side and fished a bag out from under the table. "They retrieved your Bible and this book from your nightstand," he said, as he removed the items from the bag. Seeing the books, a look of surprise washes over her, causing her eyes to widen. Despite her usual attempts to hide her emotions, he can discern a glimmer of relief etched on her face.

"So, this book," he said, picking up the green hardback with frayed edges and creased spine. "*Irish Fairy Tales* by James Stephens, I wholeheartedly approve. I read this book from cover-to-cover dozens of times over when I was a wee lad in County Down. To be honest, I still read it. Yours looks well loved."

"Yes, it was my grandmother's. She's also Irish. She came to the States as a child with her parents. It was the last gift *her* grandmother gave her before she left, and it was special to her. She gave it to me, and I cherish it, not just because it was hers. I love the stories."

"Where in Ireland was your grandmother from?"

"She was from Northern Ireland, County Armagh."

"Ah, I'm from the next county over. Which is your favorite fairy tale?"

"It's hard to pick a favorite, but *The Story of Tuan Mac Cairill* has a special place in my heart."

"The boy who became a stag, a boar, a hawk, and a fish and then a man. That story is brilliant."

"I think what I love best about it is the Abbott Finnian determined to convert Tuan to the One True God. His response when he is rebuffed is priceless."

"'Finnian could not abide that any person should resist both the Gospel and himself,'" quoted Eamonn with a crooked grin, which made her smile.

"What's your favorite?" she asked.

"Well, like you, it's difficult for me to choose a favorite. Though I think it may be *The Enchanted Cave of Cesh Corran*. I've never read a characterization as mesmerizing and ghastly as how Stephens described the Conaran's four daughters. I used to color pictures of them and label them with my sisters' names. Then I'd have to go find a good hiding place or get thrashed." He laughed. And despite her anxiety over her new life, Lily couldn't help but laugh too.

ᏣᏇᏉ

May 18, 2024 - Saturday
Washington, D.C.

Lily looked in the mirror and saw a stranger. The stylist had dyed her honey blond hair a deep brown and clamped in long, wavy hair extensions; she said they were made of real hair, which to Lily seemed more creepy than impressive. The clothes the agents had purchased for her were a bohemian style with bright colors—just the opposite of her normal wardrobe, which was the point, she supposed.

Last night she re-read the account of King David with Achish, the King of Gath. Eamonn was right in that David had played the madman, even to the point of allowing spit to dribble down his beard. *Still, I'm not convinced he was following God in that charade. David wasn't always honorable before God or man. He was a sinful wretch, just like me. Still, God called David a man after His own heart. Though I think that had a lot more to say about God's character than David's.*

She picked up the fairy tale book and turned to the story of *The Enchanted Cave of Cesh Corran*, the tale of when Fionn mac Uail and the Fianna, his band of Irish warriors, encountered Conaran, the fairy king of the Shí of Cesh Corran.

This Conaran had four daughters. He was fond of them and proud of them, but if one were to search the Shí's of Ireland or the land of Ireland, the equal of these four would not be found for ugliness and bad humour and twisted temperaments. Their hair was black as ink and tough as wire: it stuck up and poked out and hung down about their heads in bushes and spikes and tangles. Their eyes were bleary and red. Their mouths were black and twisted, and in each of these mouths there was a hedge of curved yellow fangs. They had long scraggy necks that could turn all the way round like the neck of a hen. Their arms were long and skinny and muscular, and at the end of each finger they had a spiked nail that was as hard as horn and as sharp as a briar. Their bodies were covered with a bristle of hair and fur and fluff, so that they looked like dogs in some parts and like cats in others, and in other parts again they looked like chickens. They had moustaches poking under their noses and woolly wads growing out of their ears, so that when you looked at them the first time you never wanted to look at them again, and if you had to look at them a second time you were likely to die of the sight.

"Yes, that would enthrall a *wee lad* from County Down," she said, and laughed like she hadn't in weeks.

CHAPTER 8

May 26, 2024 - Sunday
Washington, D.C.

Over the course of the next week, Eamonn and the staff worked to introduce Elizabeth to her new home, new self. Her new life. They quizzed her on the details she'd need to remember in order to be convincing. Every day brought something different: scenarios to rehearse, backstories to memorize, quiet reminders that none of this was temporary. This was her new reality. Days melted into one another during that intense week, and soon enough, it was time to face what lay ahead.

Upon arriving at the airport, they hurried through the crowds, passing through security ahead of the general boarding call for Natchez, Mississippi. The boarding agent gave Marshal Kelly's ID only a cursory glance before waving them through. Lily stepped onto the plane behind him, the name Natchez echoing in her mind like a distant drumbeat. As the first wave of passengers boarded, the usual bustle of traveling, the steady rhythm of footsteps, the strained sighs and polite excuses felt muted, almost surreal. She sank into her seat beside Marshal Kelly, her heart pounding as she fought the urge to glance nervously over her shoulder. Eamonn's eyes never settled, shifting with practiced alertness as he discreetly scanned the growing stream of passengers.

The plane's lights flickered as Lily placed the seatbelt across her lap, anchoring it with a resonant chink, the noise meant to reassure and calm. But to Lily it spoke of finality, as if she were hearing the snick of flint striking steel and a madman inside her screaming, *'Girl, that way madness lies!'*

With a deep breath, she tried to quiet her manic thoughts and brace herself for the journey ahead. Lily knew her life was about to change forever. About this there could be no doubt. Hadn't Eamonn said as much countless times? He'd cautioned Lily that this path she was setting out on would be a rough one; yet she knew the alternative meant no future at all.

She cast a side-eye at the marshal, taking his measure. He radiated a quiet confidence that belied the gravity of their situation; he also looked like someone you didn't want to mess with. He would ensure her safety at all costs. She'd only ever fully trusted one person before, so it surprised her how easily she trusted Eamonn. Still, the truth of her past taunted her, accusing her, reminding her of her secrets—and the promises she's made to protect those secrets.

I do trust Eamonn; I can't deny that he makes me feel safe. The kind of safe I haven't felt since Jackson went away. He's willing to put his life on the line for me...

The hum of the engines roared to life, and her seat trembled. She clenched her jaw to stop her teeth from rattling.

...but no matter how secure Eamonn makes me feel, I can't betray those promises... I can't betray Jackson.

From her window seat, Lily saw the ground crew dart about readying the runway for departure. A crewman with a lighted baton directed the pilot as he maneuvered the plane into position. As the aircraft rolled forward and gained speed, the world outside began to blur, by degrees morphing into a dizzy chaos of motion and color.

He hasn't mentioned my dad's murder or Jackson since Friday, but I can sense the unasked questions simmering just beneath the surface.

The aircraft shuddered and quaked as it continued to gain speed, like water with heat gains energy, swirling and rippling... moving faster and beating against each other as the temperature rises.

You must protect Jackson. And yourself.

Like water molecules churn and increase pressure until they escape in a spew of steam, with a surge of acceleration, the plane propelled into the sky, pinning Lily to the seat. She closed her eyes and tried to calm her breathing.

Keep the crazy in, woman!

But Eamonn must have sensed her distress, as he reached out a hand, resting it gently on her forearm, offering silent support. Startled, she opened her eyes and exhaled sharply. Looking at him, she felt a surge of gratitude—and relief that he couldn't hear the rest of what raced through her mind.

"Are you alright?" Eamonn asked in a low voice.

She nodded, "I'm okay. Just feeling a little unsettled."

"It's natural to feel that way," he assured her. "But you're safe with me. I'll get you to your new life, away from danger."

His sincerity brought another surge of gratitude. And guilt. Still, she found herself relaxing back into the seat. She *knew* she could trust Eamonn, and also knew he would do whatever it took to keep her safe from the present danger, but can he protect her from her past? Especially when he's so keen to open all the closets and expose the skeletons rattling around the place?

"Thank you, Marshal Kelly, for all you've done."

Eamonn nodded, his expression serious. "It's my job. And I take it seriously."

"Tell me about your family." She needed distraction and was desperate to divert attention from her own truths. She had found that most people like to talk about themselves, and asking questions was the best way to avoid having to talk about yourself. "You still have a slight Irish accent, but I would have thought that a U.S. Marshal would need to be an American citizen."

"Yes, you're right. I actually hold dual citizenship. I was born in Ireland. Da's Irish, and my mother is American. She came to study abroad and fell in love with my dad and Ireland and never left."

Lily's smile softened as she leaned forward with genuine curiosity. "And so, you grew up in Ireland, hence the accent," she remarked. "You mentioned sisters the other day. How many do you have?"

"I have four sisters, all older than me. My mother is a romantic and named us strategically. The oldest is Brighid, but we call her Bridie. Her name means the exalted one, and she's spent her whole life proving Mam named her properly." His laugh was warm.

Lily laughed too and felt her tense muscles start to relax.

"She and her husband have two daughters, Aisling and Ayleesh."

"And do those names hold special meaning?"

"Oh, yes, Ma passed down her romantic heart to all her kids, bless her. Aisling means dream and Ailis means noble and kind."

Here's a man not embarrassed to show his love for his family… and he sure is handsome. Stop it! He's only here to do his job. A job he takes seriously, as he just pointed out.

"The next oldest is Muriel, which means bright sea. Mam went into early labor with her when they were on vacation at the seaside. Muriel has a daughter called Erin and a son, Finn. He's the only grandson and a real corker, he is.

"Then comes Rosaline, who has three daughters: Ciara, Úna, and Talulla. Rosaline is meant to mean rose, but my brother read somewhere that it meant gentle horse in German. So, you can imagine that wasn't the most pleasant discovery for her, nor for Declan when she finally caught up with him. And then my youngest sister is Eilish, which means God is my oath."

"God is my oath… that's beautiful. Are your parents Christian?"

"Yes, all of my family are. Well, all except for my younger brother, Declan. He's a troubled soul." He glanced downward, his voice taking on a somber tone.

She could sense it was a hurtful subject for him, so she was relieved when the flight attendant stopped at their row offering nuts and a drink. Lily accepted a ginger ale and salted peanuts, hoping they might settle her stomach. Afraid of any awkward silences and what questions he may put her way, Lily continued her query.

"And how did you end up in the U.S. and become a marshal?"

"I studied in Dublin at Trinity College and then transferred to Cornell to study criminal justice. After I graduated, I spent four years in the Marines before joining the Marshals. Lily…"

"Yes?"

"Are you trying to keep me talking about myself to avoid talking about yourself?"

Too observant, by far….

"There's not much more I can tell you about myself, Marshal Kelly." Her voice was soft, and her gaze dropped to her hands.

"You mean there's not much you *will* tell me?" Something in his tone made her eyes rise to meet his. She wanted to look away. But those eyes were causing all kinds of jitters in her stomach.

"Lily, I'm not trying to push you to relive the past. I just think it will be safer for you if we can find out who killed your father. You say it wasn't Jackson, so then who was it?"

Do they really stock brown bags under airplane seats for airsickness? Or possibly hyperventilating and/or hyper-crazed fliers? 'Cause I'm about five seconds from diving under my seat to find out.

He must have noticed her distress, as he quickly apologized, and let it go. They spent the rest of the trip in silence—outwardly at least. Inside her mind roared, refusing to be silenced.

ଓଃଇଠ

November 4, 2024 - Monday
Cowherd, Mississippi

Lily had had a frightful night, full of dreams of being placed in stocks and Bougie Fitzgerald throwing scrambled eggs, bacon, and yogurt at her before dousing her with ketchup. Thankful for the morning, Lily takes her coffee and Bible out to the back steps. Before her, the dew glistens on the grass, and the trees form an arch over the entrance to the rear meadow. Filtered sunshine plays and dances on the jeweled leaves, causing them to sparkle in kaleidoscopic prisms like the windows of a chapel. The shiny green path below and the encircling trees above form a vestibule, drawing one into a cloister beyond the gate into what must surely be a holy place. Lily is grateful for the peace it brings. Turning to Psalm 143, she prays:

"O LORD, hear my prayer, listen to my cry for mercy;
in your faithfulness and righteousness come to my relief....
Let the morning bring me word of your unfailing love, for
I have put my trust in you."

A whisper of leaves shushing as they beat against themselves breaks the sacred stillness. Lily sees the hedge shuddering, and Chaney pushes his way through.

"Morning, Watson," he greets her with a beaming smile, which easily takes up half of his face. He's wearing a t-shirt about two sizes too big, sporting the logo of the *Cowherd Register*—the name of the newspaper encircling a graphic of a black and white spotted cow chewing a newspaper—across its baggy front. He's carrying his breakfast with him: a cold slice of pizza.

Lily closes her Bible. "Good morning, Sherlock," she says, nodding towards his shirt. "Nice shirt."

"Thanks, it was my dad's. He had it when he owned the newspaper. Ya' know, Lily, I've been doing a lot of thinking, and I've got a plan to get our investigation going."

"Oh, yeah," replies Lily, suspicion filling her voice. "And what would that be?"

"I'm going to get the supplies we need for a murder board. I've seen them on TV," he says with a roguish grin. "We better set it up at your house, though. We shouldn't bother my dad. He's had a not so good night."

"What was not so good?" Lily asks, taking a sip of her coffee.

"Well… " She can see Chaney is uncomfortable as he moves to sit beside her. He fidgets with the hem of his shirt before continuing. "After Mrs. Fitzgerald stole his newspaper from him and fired him from the reporter's job she had 'graciously' let him keep, he started drinking…a lot. That's why my Pops moved in with us, so he could take care of me. And dad, too, I guess."

"Oh, I'm sorry. Is your mother around?" Not sure why she hadn't asked him before.

"She died when I was little. I don't remember her much."

"I'm so sorry. You said the Fitzgerald woman stole your dad's newspaper from him. How exactly?"

"I guess she didn't actually *steal* it. Dad had to borrow a lot of money to take care of my mom when she was sick and couldn't pay it back right away. Mrs. Fitzgerald bought the newspaper from him before his creditors sued him, but it wasn't near what it was worth, and then there was something about back taxes. She let him keep writing for the newspaper until she got mad at him and just up and fired him one day. No warning or nothing."

"Does he know why?"

"She said she had to cut costs, and that one journalist was enough for the paper, meaning herself—even though she was just a glorified *gossip* columnist. But Dad says it's because he was researching something called 'Air Rights'. She didn't want him reporting on it, but he thought she had something to hide, so he didn't give up. Then she fired him. That's when he started drinking during the day."

"It sounds like something we may need to check out." Lily glances at her watch. "But this morning I'm going to the sheriff's office to give my statement."

"Whoa! I never gave a statement before. Whatcha' going to say?" He takes a large bite of his pizza and wipes his mouth on his sleeve.

"That I had only met the victim once, and I have no idea what happened at her house on Friday. I mean, that's all I can say. He seems to think I have a motive after what she wrote about me in her column."

"Well, it was pretty bad, you gotta' admit." Chaney shrugs in the matter-of-fact way only a kid can muster.

"It was very unkind and judgmental. She knew nothing about me."

"And she did kind of admit that before she laid into you. So, there's that," Chaney says between chews.

"Which is why she had had no business speculating about me. I need to leave for the Sheriff's Department, Chaney, and you need to go to school. We can talk afterward. Would you like to warm up that slice of pizza before you go?"

"Why would I do that? Breakfast pizza is always ate cold."

CHAPTER 9

November 4, 2024 – Monday
Cowherd, Mississippi

Eamonn had promised Lily that a lawyer would meet her at the sheriff's office on Monday morning. He had suggested relocating her that day, but she insisted she couldn't leave with a cloud of suspicion hanging over her head. If she disappeared, everyone would believe she was the guilty party. Plus, she had just made a friend and didn't want to cut off that relationship abruptly. She didn't mention the friend was only ten and three-quarters. He'd agreed with great reluctance but clarified he hadn't abandoned the idea of pulling her out. For now, they would see how things progressed.

As Lily takes her first step through the entryway of the sheriff's office, an involuntary shiver runs down her spine. *They must keep the temperature below 60 degrees; the place feels like a crypt.* Her shoulders loosen a fraction when she spots the lawyer, just as Eamonn had guaranteed.

Dressed in a dark green pantsuit and sharp, white-collared blouse, the Honorable Patricia Jennings looks polished and professional. Her brunette hair is pulled into a side bun, and her gaze is confident and unmistakably alert. Lily had expected someone older and bald who would intimidate and talk down to her. *Thank you, Lord—and Eamonn.*

"Hello, Miss Jordan. I am Patricia Jennings from Jennings and Wilder in Natchez. Marshal Kelly has informed me of the specifics of your situation. Before we go meet with the sheriff, I would like to ask that you answer no questions without my consent. Provide concise responses that only address his specific questions. It's in your best interest if you refrain from volunteering any extraneous information."

Lily nods as they walk up to the clerk's desk. "Of course."

They sign in, and a clerk escorts them to a windowless 12 x 16-foot room, even dingier and colder than the lobby, which Lily didn't think was possible. The chairs are hard plastic, wobbling and scarred, and the table is ringed with ancient coffee stains. A sour smell wafts from the trash can, and an overflowing ashtray in the center of the table announces just how little this station has evolved from the '70s. *Not exactly the most welcoming of places.*

As if to herald his self-importance, the sheriff makes them wait fifteen minutes before appearing with a deputy trailing behind. He places two plastic bags on the table, one with a scarf and the other a pair of scissors. There's no recorder in the room, which may or may not be to Lily's advantage. If she were a betting woman, she would lay money it bodes ill for her. She's thankful, therefore, when Ms. Jennings takes her phone out and informs the sheriff she plans to record the questioning. She stands her ground despite Timmons' spewing and sputtering.

"Very well, have it your way," he grumbles, his voice tinged with irritation. "My memory is like an elephant, and I have no need of any recording devices, but I am aware there are few who share my skills. Therefore, I'll allow it." With a pointed look, he turns toward Lily. "So, Miss Jordan, can you tell me where you were on November 1st?"

Ms. Jennings gives a slight nod.

"I was at my house. I had been… " she begins but stops short at a slight shake of the lawyer's head.

"You had been… "

Just then the door opens, and a deputy interrupts the sheriff, handing him a folder. He opens it to read the contents and then raises his eyebrows and hisses an anemic whistle between his teeth.

"Well, well. The coroner's results are in, which clears up the cause of Mrs. Fitzgerald's untimely demise. You see, at first, we all thought someone had strangled her with the scarf, pushed her head into the gravy, and then skewered her with the shears. The lack of blood splatter and minimal blood spreading told us she was already dead when she was stabbed. We hadn't considered the gravy as the cause of death, and the coroner confirmed there was no gravy in the nasal cavities. Hence, our conclusion was that the old girl had been choked to death. Then we received a call from the coroner, who informed us that there were no signs of… uh… pet-eh-chee… pet-ek-ee-uh…" The sheriff stops to squint at his notes, muttering the word under his breath once or twice before trying again. "P'teekia—those tiny red dots from burst blood vessels—in the whites of her eyes, thus wrecking the strangulation theory. So, we were a little stumped. But now the old doc is claiming someone poisoned her. You know anything about poisons, Miss Jordan?"

"Absolutely nothing," she said, her eyes widening in astonishment at the news.

"We won't know for a week to ten days what type of poison, but it was some toxicant that did her in."

Lily had noticed it seemed the Sheriff liked the sound of his own voice and being the center of attention, so she says nothing, hoping he will spill more details that are doubtless confidential. He doesn't disappoint her.

"So, here's how I see it playing out." He stands, dropping the envelope on the table. "The killer enters the house through the French doors, finds Fitzy face down in a plate of gravy and biscuit... no, no that doesn't work," he trails off, rubbing his chin, thinking. "He finds her sitting ram-rod straight in her chair. He or *she* twists the scarf round the neck, thinking to choke the life out of her, but it was too late. She was already dead from poison, stone-cold-dead—maybe not cold yet, as Mrs. Rose had just been told to start over with the eggs—but stiff as a corpse. Then, either out of pure meanness or just to be sure they'd done a thorough job, the killer shoves her head into the gravy, takes the shears and hacks off her ponytail, strewing hair over the table and floor, before thrusting them into her back."

Throughout this impassioned soliloquy, the sheriff has been unconsciously acting out the hypothetical assault with the flair of a seasoned thespian, while Lily and the lawyer watch spellbound and speechless. Upon the final plunge of the scissors, Timmons awakens as if from a trance; he clears his throat, straightens his clothes, and smooths his sparse hair across his shiny pate.

"The killer then pours ketchup over her noggin and escapes out the French doors," he ends with a feeble attempt at professionalism. "According to Mrs. Rose, she had only been out of the room twenty minutes at the most; therefore, there was premeditation that bled into improvisation," he says, chuckling and plopping back into his chair. "Bled into, get it?"

Lily stares, amazed she had ever feared this man. "Sheriff, are you insinuating that there may have been two killers?"

"That's not what I said. That makes for an interesting theory, though…" His thoughts trail off as he scratches his head, and Lily wonders just how deep his stash of wild theories could go.

"Sheriff Timmons, do you have anything to ask that is relevant and applicable to Miss Jordan? Such as what she saw or heard on the day of the murder?" asks Ms. Jennings.

"Good question!" The sheriff leans forward and slaps his palms onto the table. "What did you see or hear on the day of the murder, Miss Jordan?"

"I saw nothing and heard nothing until your sirens and lights alerted me that something was amiss at the Fitzgerald residence."

"Nothing unusual happened previous to that?" He leans forward, his eyes narrowing in suspicion.

"Nothing except a lost dog."

"A lost dog? Whose dog?" he asks, abruptly straightening up.

"The dog belonged to Chaney Bridges."

"Oh, Chaney Bridges' dog, was it?" the sheriff drawls out the words with a sly smile. "You mean that yapping, howling, can't-walk-by-the-fence-without-fear-of-dismemberment dog? The very one who would normally broadcast an ear-splitting warning that someone was in the next-door neighbor's backyard? Well, I find that suspiciously interesting."

And Lily suddenly feels she's volunteered far too much.

⊂⊃⊱⊰

November 4, 2024 – Monday
Cowherd, Mississippi

On the way home, Lily spots Bougie Fitzgerald stepping out of a tanning salon called Ritzgerald Gold, a cell phone pressed to her ear. Bougie bursts into an exaggerated laugh, then pauses mid-stride. Without missing a beat, she lifts her arm to snap a selfie, tilts her head with a beguiling grin, quickly sends the photo as a text, then returns the phone to her ear and resumes her call. People on the sidewalk skitter around, shooting her angry looks and sideways glances.

What does the woman do all day? Does she have a job? And who is she talking to that she's so thrilled to send a selfie? With a smirk like that, it must be a boyfriend. If so, is he a local?

Bougie continues down the sidewalk, still talking and preening. She has boutique shopping bags hanging from the crook of her right elbow, and they bounce against her hip with each step. Dark sunglasses hide her eyes, but the expression on her shiny, red-painted lips leaves no doubt as to the image she wants to project: posh, privileged, and prosperous. *More like spoiled, snooty, and smug. Undoubtedly, I've formed a very unfavorable impression of her, but is it entirely fair?*

But then Lily remembers Bougie's visit following her mother's death and the offensive comments she made while on Lily's doorstep. With a mother as hateful and vindictive as Penelope Fitzgerald, is there any wonder Bougie would be any different?

Still, Bougie Fitzgerald might have been raised with a sense of entitlement, self-righteousness, and an over-inflated view of her own importance, but there should be a time in all our lives when we realize we can no longer blame our actions or attitudes on our parents or our upbringing—a time when we accept responsibility for our own choices and behavior. I should know this well. But do I? And do I really have any right to judge this woman?

She Had It Coming

THE DEVIL WEARS HERMÈS

My mother said I wasn't smart enough to make it on my own.

Well, here I am—back in the house she tried to erase me from like I was some bad memory. Everything comes back to me. That's how inheritance works.

Do I miss her? Sure. The way you miss a stone in your shoe— the kind you walk on for years because you're told it's your fault it hurts.

She was my mother. She gave me life, then spent the next several decades mocking what I did with it. Every haircut, every friend, every decision—I was a walking punchline in her column. She even gave me a shout-out in her speech at the country club, calling me her "cautionary tale." Got a laugh, too. I smiled... like I was supposed to.

She said I stole her Hermès scarf. I didn't. I just borrowed it. But sometimes I'd wrap it around my neck and wonder how it'd feel to wrap it around hers instead—tighter and tighter. It was a delicious thought. She kicked me out of the house over that silly misunderstanding. But even starving on the street sounded better than another second trapped under that roof.

People think rich means comfortable, but they've never lived as a Fitzgerald. In that house, you smile when you're breaking, laugh when it hurts; you swallow the screams long enough to not ruin the family portraits. I was trained like a dog to perform. But even the tamest lapdog will turn on its master when it's been kicked enough times.

So now she's gone, and everyone looks at me like I finally went feral.

If I *did* do it, would I use *that* scarf? Then again, maybe I used it *because* people would think I'd never be that stupid.

Speculate all you like. But the truth is, she had it coming.

They say blood is thicker than water, but money is thicker than both. And now, it's all mine.

Bougie Fitzgerald

CHAPTER 10

November 4, 2024 – Monday
Cowherd, Mississippi

Upon returning home, Lily hears a commotion and looks out her back door to find Chaney coming up the steps. He has a roll of newsprint sticking out of an open backpack. As he crosses the threshold, she looks inside and sees it contains tape, a brown envelope, a pair of blunted scissors, and some markers. He has a vintage Polaroid camera hanging around his neck.

"So how was it? What did he ask? What did you say? Did he put you in handcuffs? Is he going to charge you? Was the jail really cool?" he asks.

"Yes, in fact, it was cool. The foyer and interrogation room were, anyway, about 60 degrees."

"Interrogation room? Whoa!"

Lily recaps the sheriff's questioning, assuring him no handcuffs were involved—much to his disappointment—and as far as she knows, no charges are going to be filed. She leaves out the part about the dog for now. She has to admit it seems curious.

"And while I was there, the coroner delivered the cause of death," Lily says. "She wasn't killed by the scissors or strangulation or being smothered in the gravy. She was already dead before all of that. She was poisoned."

Chaney's eyes light up, wild and curious. "Poisoned? How? With what?"

"The sheriff didn't disclose how the killer introduced the poison, and he said it would take a week to ten days to identify the specific type. There was another thing he said that I found interesting: he never referred to the scissors as such. Every time he said anything about them, he said shears."

"Is there a difference?" asks Chaney.

"Well, shears are much sharper than regular scissors. They're sharp enough to cut through a ponytail. Barbers and hairdressers use them."

"That's a valuable clue. We need to start on this murder board on the double." Chaney tosses his burden onto the kitchen table. He grabs his scissors, cuts off a swath of newsprint, and tapes it to the wall next to Lily's clue list. Opening the envelope, he produces a newspaper photo with the panache of a magician.

"First, our victim, one Penelope Fitzgerald," Chaney says, taping the photograph in the center of the newsprint. He grabs a marker and starts to write Penelope with a large P, then pauses, as if unsure how to spell her name.

"Watson, since I'm the brains of this outfit and you're the brawn, I'll let you handle all the clerical details." He hands Lily the marker with a gesture akin to a nurse passing a scalpel to a doctor.

"Penelope Fitzgerald," Lily repeats as she prints the name under the photo.

Chaney then reaches into the envelope and brings out a Polaroid of a palm held up like a stop sign, with red frizzy hair spilling out on either side of it, and tapes it to the paper.

"Suspect Number One: Bougie Fitzgerald, daughter of the victim. As you can see, she resisted having her photo taken. She screeched, 'Get away, you little paparazzi!' I gotta say, it amazed me she even knew the word."

Lily suppresses a smile. "And where'd *you* learn that word?"

"I dunno," he shrugs, scratching the side of his neck. "Maybe from that time the mayor got mad when I tried to take his picture eating cotton candy. Yeah, that was it. I asked Pops about it later, and he said it meant annoying people with cameras."

Lily gives a small laugh and nods, her eyes twinkling with amusement. She writes Bougie Fitzgerald under this photo, wondering why someone would name a child Bourgeois.

"I saw her earlier today," she informs Chaney.

"Oh, yeah? What was she doing?"

"Primping and posturing and spending money, from what I could tell."

"That doesn't surprise me. She can spend all she wants now that she's come into her mama's money."

"They say most murders are committed by someone close to the victim, and money is always a motive for murder. I know people handle grief in different ways, but when she visited me soon after the sheriff told her that her mother was dead, there were no tears or even what appeared to be sorrow. In fact, she preened like a peacock on my doorstep." Lily felt unkind saying it. Still, truth is truth.

"Which is why she's my number one suspect."

He takes another Polaroid from his envelope, clasping it against his chest, and whirls around to place it on the murder board.

"Suspect Number Two: Miss Lily Jordan."

"What!" Lily squeaks out. The photo was of her sitting on her back porch. It appeared Chaney had taken from the bushes, as leaves framed her profile.

"Well, I don't think you did her in, but the sheriff does, so we need to know why, don't you think?"

"His only justification is that he feels I've been secretive. I explained that I'm just a private person, but he thinks what she wrote about me would be motive enough for me to kill her. I admit I may have theoretically had murderous thoughts, which I would classify more like imaginative, or maybe more like fantastical."

"So, you're saying you fantasized about murdering her?" Chaney asks with an impish grin.

"What? No! I mean, not really. I couldn't, wouldn't. Not in this case," she stops, raises her eyes to the ceiling, and growls. "For heaven's sake, I'm a Christian. True, being a murderer and being a Christian aren't mutually exclusive. But… "

"Lily!" interrupts Chaney, laughing as he holds up both hands like a referee. "Relax! I know you didn't do it. I just meant we need to think like the sheriff. Okay, moving on. We need more suspects. I mean, my money's on Bougie. She's just a clone of her mama except with worse clothes."

"That scarf found at the crime scene… I wonder who that belongs to? The sheriff had it in an evidence bag and laid it on the table during the interrogation. I could see it was high end and definitely silk. It cost several hundred dollars, maybe more."

"*Several hundred!*" exclaimed Chaney. "A tiny thing like that?"

"I might be wrong, but I think it's a Hermès scarf. I saw a documentary about them. This scarf had rolled edges, which are a distinguishing feature. Did Bougie have money like that before Penelope's death?"

"Not likely. Her mama had cut her off."

"Cut her off?"

Chaney nodded. "Word around town is she gave Bougie an allowance until a few months ago."

Lily's eyebrows shoot up in surprise. "Penelope gave Bougie an allowance? The woman is at least forty-five. What self-respecting adult would take an allowance from her parent?"

"One that's lazy and thinks she's too good to work. And even if she wanted a job, who'd hire her? She ain't got any 'marketable skills,' as my daddy once said. Plus, she's rude and bossy and has that great big head."

"You mean she's egotistical?" asks Lily.

"Well yeah, but you gotta admit, her head is pretty big with all that hair sticking out evra where."

Lily laughs, but then her expression sharpens as she narrows her eyes, trying to make sense of it. "Why did she cut her off?"

"I don't know. I just heard Bougie was asking people all over town for freebies and telling people her mama had stopped giving her 'what was rightfully hers'."

Crossing her arms, Lily takes a step toward the board. The photo of Penelope looked as if he had clipped it from Penelope's newspaper column, and under the photo it read:

A Penny for MY Thoughts
All the News I am Morally and Socially and
Spiritually Beholden to Report

"Hmm. I'll be right back, Chaney," Lily hurries into the living room and returns with the newspaper in which she had been disparaged, dishonored, and disgraced. *Okay, so maybe I'm still a little bitter. Lord, I'll forgive her eventually… I hope.*

Lily runs her finger down the article and begins reading aloud what she had earlier skipped in her anger.

"Now on to my daughter… I'm sure you've all seen the atrocious mess she's made of her hair. I'm embarrassed to even be near her. The dye job was awful enough—I mean fire engine red! It blinds a person to look at it in a bright light—but then she spent

money she certainly doesn't have for a perm!
A perm! No one has perms anymore, at least
not like that. I mean, did she hold up a
photo of a circus clown and say, 'I want to
look like this'? I had warned her about that
beautician. You know of whom I speak. But as
usual, she doesn't listen to me. As a side
note, I'm missing a lovely Hermès scarf. I
hate to call my own daughter a thief, but
everyone knows her bent toward kleptomania.
She sure didn't get that from *my* side of
the family."

"Now that's a mama nobody needs right there." Chaney shakes his head in disbelief. "And you were right that it's Errmeeze. So, Bougie stole the scarf that was found around Mrs. Fitzgerad's neck at the murder scene?"

"There's no proof she stole it." Lily sets the newspaper on the table. "Nor that she kept it if she did. If she needed money, she could have sold it. But it's a line of inquiry. Then there's the part about the beautician. We need to get a copy of this column she referenced, October 11th. Chaney, the more I think about it, the more I think her columns could hold the answer to who murdered Penelope Fitzgerald. I don't suppose your newspaper has progressed beyond microfiche, has it?"

"I don't know what micro-fish is, but my grandad has a copy of every *Cowherd Register* since 1968. They're in the room above the garage. I don't think he'd let us just waltz up there and root around, though. Plus, he keeps it locked, and he's on a motorcycle trip out west right now."

"Okay, let's just keep that in our back pocket. She also mentions a butcher and a former pastor. Do you know anything about that?"

"Nothing about the butcher, but the preacher? Oh, man! It was something awful."

"What happened?"

"Pastor Meadows called her out from the pulpit. I'm not kidding!" he said, seeing Lily's shocked face. "He was preaching about gossip, how it's like a fire, calling it a world of wickedness and said we shouldn't associate with gossips and busybodies. He tried to keep it general, but evra body knew who he was talking about. That woman should have 'busybody' written on her tombstone. Then, in his prayer, he sealed his fate by asking the Lord 'to convict those members of the congregation who gossip and abuse their office by attacking others with their words, whether spoken or written in black and white'."

Lily's eyes widen. "He didn't!"

"He sure did. I think he'd just had enough. Every week she had something mean to say about somebody in town, most of it lies. Well, if he thought she had set fires with her tongue before, he was about to walk into a blazing inferno. The next column was so bad my Pops hid it from me, and he and Dad would only talk about it in whispers. But the people in town weren't so careful about being quiet around me. Mrs. Penelope wrote some awful things about Pastor Meadow's wife. All lies. His wife is just about the kindest woman I've ever met. Mrs. Fitzgerald kept on for eight or nine weeks, slamming them both until he left the church, but he didn't leave his wife. He knew who she was, and she weren't no floozie or Jezebel nor woman of ill repute, whatever that means. I was right sad to see him leave. According to my grandad, this Brother Carothers can't preach his way out of a wet paper bag."

"Sadly, I'm inclined to agree with that assessment. Did you know Pastor Carothers came to visit me the day of the murder? He showed up just as the squad cars arrived, and he was acting bizarre. I thought he was having a heart attack right on my porch stoop. He was hyperventilating and sweating. He didn't say a word but just pointed to where the sheriff and deputies were getting out at the Fitzgerald house."

"So, Brother Carothers was in the neighborhood at the time of the murder? That alone might be enough to consider him a suspect, but when you add how he was acting, that definitely puts him in the running. Write him up there, Watson."

"I think, in all fairness, both reverends should be up there. I mean, Brother Meadows' motive seems even stronger than mine," says Lily, picking up the marker.

"I suppose you're right." Chaney nods half-heartedly. "Okay, write Morris Carothers and Stanley Meadows up there. Oh! And the beautician and butcher she trash-talked in her column."

"Alright," says Lily, "so we have…

1. Bougie Fitzgerald
2. Morris Carothers
3. Stanley Meadows
4. The beautician (name?)
5. The butcher (name?)"

"And don't forget yourself," Chaney adds, his eyes full of mischief.

Lily sighs, "And number six, Lily Jordan."

"What about the housekeeper, Mrs. Rose? She could slip the poison into her food easy enough."

"Good point." Lily adds Mrs. Rose to the list. "Seven suspects…"

"So far," says Chaney. "If we get into those articles, that list could reach out into the street."

"You're right. I think we need to focus on these seven first, and I promise you, we can eliminate number six right off." Lily decisively marks out her name. "Now we've already made progress. We're back down to six suspects."

"Why don't you go visit that beautician tomorrow and see if she says anything incriminating? I don't know nothin' about hair, and yours looks pretty good to me, but at least one person thought it needed help." There's an impish twinkle in his smile.

I had warned Chaney not to interview the suspects, but now that I'm under suspicion myself, I'm beginning to reconsider that advice—at least when it comes to me. Still, getting a haircut could be tricky with these hair extensions. "I'll stop in to get my nails done."

"And I'll ask my grandpa when he calls in about the butcher. This is a great start. The game is afoot!" declares Chaney, rubbing his hands together.

"You're fantastic at this, Sherlock."

"I am a brain, Watson. The rest of me is a mere appendix."

She Had It Coming

THE UGLY TRUTH

I never named her—not from the pulpit. I preached the Scripture, same as I always did. James Chapter 3: *The tongue is a fire. A world of wickedness.*

I prayed for conviction for those who gossip and use words to wound others. I could see she knew I was talking about her. I guess everyone did.

She took it as an attack and declared war.

Every week after that, one column after another, she wrote lies and half-truths, things she twisted to appear scandalous. She didn't come after me. Not directly. She came after my wife, Serena. The sweetest person I've ever known: gentle, kind, merciful. A woman who loves her enemies and prays for those who curse her.

I'd have stayed if it were just me. But it wasn't. When someone hurts someone you love, the wound is deeper and more septic than if it had been directed at you.

So we left. We packed up our home and started fresh in another town.

But some wounds follow you, no matter how far you go.

I'd be lying if I said I never wondered how it'd feel to see her finally reap what she sowed. Biblically, I know that feeling should be sorrow. But that wasn't my first emotion. It was peace. *Lord, help me. It was peace.* The kind that settles after a storm has ravaged the land.

Maybe it's a sin to say she had it coming, but there it is. Sometimes the truth is ugly.

But God can handle our ugly. He's not even surprised by it. After all, that's why He sent His Son. Because, down deep, we are all just sinful and ugly. *Thank God for forgiveness.* We all need it. I know I do.

Reverend Stanley Meadows

CHAPTER 11

November 5, 2024 - Tuesday
Cowherd, Mississippi

Lily has to admit Sheriff Timmons did get one thing right about her—well, one besides the whole having secrets thing. She is guilty of "spurning our stores and places of business." Except for driving through, she had not visited downtown during the entire six months she's been here. She did her shopping, banking, and any other retail or commercial transactions in Natchez when she went for her monthly hair color touch-up. It's just easier; people in big cities don't ask as many questions, and she doesn't have to work so hard to avoid lying.

When she arrived in Cowherd, she'd told herself she would just bide her time, keep a low profile as instructed by the marshals, and *no* new friends. *Friendship at this time in my life is a luxury I can't afford. New friends mean probing questions and even more lies. Not to mention trust. Something I can neither give nor expect because trust requires truth. I've made it almost six months before violating my goal of remaining friendless. Fortunately, Chaney's preoccupation with the murder investigation has prevented him from inquiring about my personal life or history. It's been a relief and a blessing, this friendship God has placed me in with this young man.*

Tuesday afternoon, Lily decides to walk downtown to the beauty shop. She knows she's at risk of either having to a) pretend she's mute (hey, a similar thing worked for David), b) be rude, or c) lie a lot. *I'll just try to avoid eye contact*, she thinks. Except of course, for the beautician. Getting her to talk is the one and only objective for this covert op. *Goodness! Chaney's rubbing off on me.*

Lily is grateful for the chance to stroll in dappled sunshine. Fall is her favorite season; it has a smell unlike any other time of the year. Yes, some people may call it rot and decay, but to Lily it smells of peace and home. Kicking the swirling leaves on the sidewalk, she's filled with memories of the woods behind her grandmother's house. She had always loved to scuttle and shuffle through the forest duff or just sit with her back against a tree and sketch. A peace would fill her heart, and she would linger and cherish the solitude she found there.

Walking from her cottage, she passes the Fitzgerald house and slows her pace, looking at it closely for the first time. It's easily the largest house on the block, probably the largest in the town: Georgian-style, symmetrical with three stories, a pitched roof with double balustrades along the roofline. Two multi-paned windows flank each side of the covered entry porch supported by round columns and balcony above. Five windows grace the second floor, and five pedimented dormer windows round out the third floor. The meticulously landscaped yard resembles an English manor house, with perfectly trimmed hedges and vibrant flower beds.

Lily can imagine a corps of gardeners on their knees with scissors trimming each blade of grass.

Lily has found that houses often reflect the owner's personality. This one speaks of pretension and pride and pomposity. It shouts of generational wealth of kith and kin. Lily wonders what the house whispers because every house whispers.

The Fitzgerald legacy echoes through the town, as well: The Fitzgerald Hotel, Fitzgerald Five and Dime, the Fitz and Ritz Boutique, Penelope Aromatherapy, and of course, the *Cowherd Register* also brandishes the Fitzgerald name in gold letters above the newspaper's logo. Downtown is literally a town "square" with all the shops, establishments, and courthouse framing a grassy common area. A three-tiered fountain, adorned with intricate details, dominates the middle of the green. A plaque on the base reads: "As a tribute to the esteemed Fitzgerald family, this fountain perpetually flows as a reminder of their wisdom, generosity, leadership, and legacy for generations to come." *At least they're predictable.*

Lily doesn't know the name of the salon and clearly can't ask anyone or risk questions and prying. She doubts this one will also be a Fitzgerald enterprise, and she isn't wrong. Turning the corner, she spies her destination alarmingly named "Dye! Dye! Dye!" Gilt lettering on the window indicates the shop is "Owned and Operated by Norma Jean Badger" and, happily for Lily, confirms "Walk-Ins Welcome."

A bell tinkles when Lily pushes open the glass door. As she steps inside, the sharp reek of acetone and nail polish rushes at her, sharp enough to sting her eyes. A breath later, the acrid bite of bleach catches her off guard, burning the back of her throat. But threaded through the harshness is a faint sweetness from the shampoos, just enough to soften the mix.

The salon is small, with just two cutting stations to the left, a manicure table at the rear with a door leading to the back of the shop, and a counter to the right. Over the counter there is a sign stating, "At Dye! Dye! Dye! you'll leave with a killer look!" Along the front windowed wall are three vinyl straight-backed chairs and a coffee table with hairstyling magazines spread across it, overflowing onto the floor.

A woman with ebony black hair caught up in a clip emerges from the back. Lily must have caught her at break time; she has a Dr. Pepper in one hand and a white powdered donut in the other.

"Mornin'!" she says, bringing her hand to her mouth as she struggles to swallow the donut. "Welcome to Dye! Dye! Dye! What can I do for you this morn…oh, you're that new girl from up north! I'm Norma Jean. Nice to meet you," she continues in a thick Southern accent.

"Yes, that's me," Lily says with an awkward laugh and a nervous, twitching smile. "I'm Lily."

"What can I do for you?" Norma Jean asks, draining the rest of her Dr. Pepper and tossing the can into the trash.

"I'd like a manicure, if you have time." Lily tucks a loose strand of hair behind her ear, glancing at the colorful array of nail polish.

"Honey, all I got is time. Go pick you out a color, and we'll fix them nails right up."

Moving across the room, Norma Jean settles herself at the manicure station and assembles her supplies. Lily looks over the color selections, most of which are neon or have glitter in them. She settles on the one sedate color on the shelf: Seashell Pink. Sitting down in the chair opposite Norma Jean, Lily's taken aback when the woman sprays something all over her hands and arms, causing her to cough and choke on the fumes.

"Just a spritz of anti-bacterial spray," explains Norma Jean, leaning forward with a smile. "You can't be too careful." Lily suppresses a grimace. *I didn't see her wash her hands after licking the powdered sugar from her fingers. So much for sterilization.*

Norma Jean picks up an emery board and begins filing the nails on Lily's right hand, swiping out from the base to the tip. Somewhere along the line, she had popped in some gum and is now chomping on it like she's trying to set a record.

"So, how do you like our little town?" she asks Lily.

"It's quaint, when someone's not getting murdered, that is," Lily says, watching for a reaction. The swishing of the file halts for half a heartbeat but swiftly resumes. Norma Jean's lips compress until they're white, but the corners of her mouth curl upward a tic.

Is she trying to avoid talking or trying to hide a smile... or both?

"Did you know the victim?" Lily asks.

"Everyone knew Penelope Fitzgerald. She was someone you couldn't ignore if you wanted to. She nearly ruined my business. You're my first customer in days," she says, switching to the other hand.

91

Lily lifts her eyes to meet Norma Jean's. "How did she do that?"

"That newspaper column of hers: 'A Penny for My Thoughts.' She backstabbed and flat out lied like Satan in that thing. She was a scandalmonger who didn't have a care who she hurt so long as she could make her opinions known. A spiteful, deceitful, greedy brute. I could go on and on, but I won't waste my breath. She's gone, and I say good riddance. The killer did the town a huge favor," she says with a wild sweep of the nail file that would make a concert violinist proud. "She considered herself the savior of this town and that newspaper, her pulpit. But the gospel she spread was far from godly, more like the bellowing of the Beast from Revelation."

Lily hardly knows what to say to that. *Norma Jean definitely stays on the murder board.*

"She took a swing at me in her column, too," says Lily. "She didn't even know me. I think she must have had a fickle relationship with the truth."

"She was a pathological liar with a narcissistic complex," says Norma Jean, leaning forward in a conspiratorial manner. "Her husband was even worse. He thought he owned the town, just like his daddy and his grandfather before him. And if you got on either of their bad sides, well, I'll just say that was a dangerous place to be."

"How so?" Lily asks.

"All I know is, anyone who stood against a Fitzgerald would either forever regret it or find themselves incapable of regretting anything ever again."

"What do you mean, incapable of regretting anything ever… you mean they killed them?" asks Lily in a high-pitched voice.

"I've said too much already," says Norma Jean, dropping the nail file and picking up the cuticle cream. She squirts a dot of cream on each cuticle of Lily's right hand, grasps her pinkie finger and wrangles it like she's milking a cow.

Lily lets it go for now. *That's something that begs looking into, though.*

"I heard Mrs. Fitzgerald had a daughter. Do you know her too?" Lily asks.

"Me and Bougie used to be best friends until her mother decided I wasn't good enough for her, which is saying a lot considering the low opinion she had of Bougie. But we still talk some. And Bougie lets me do her hair, much to her mother's vexation, which was the point, I guess. She was just in here last Thursday for a trim even though she didn't need it," says Norma Jean, getting up to go into the back room.

So, Bougie was in here the day before the murder. Could she have slipped out with a pair of shears? Did she make an unneeded appointment just for that purpose? Or were the shears wielded by this bitter woman?

Norma Jean returns with a bowl of warm, soapy water and places Lily's right hand inside. She then picks up Lily's left hand, repeating the cuticle process with the same enthusiasm.

After a quick rinse, Norma Jean swaps hands, plunging the left into the warm water. She grabs a towel to dry Lily's right fingertips and then resumes her work, applying more cuticle cream with a determined focus. *At this rate, I'm going to have the softest cuticles in all of Cowherd.*

"I think Bougie may have had a premonition that her mother was going to kick the bucket," says Norma Jean, pinning Lily with intense blue eyes.

"Oh? Why's that?" asks Lily.

"At that last appointment she told me, 'One day real soon I'm going to get what's coming to me, and I'll pay you and everyone else every penny I owe.' She runs a tab for my hairdressing services. I try to tell her no every time, but she always talks me into it. She's very persuasive when she wants to be."

More like manipulative, Lily thinks.

"I know I could use what she owes me, and I'm sure there are others who could, too," continues Norma Jean. "Maybe a good Samaritan helped things along. That person would be a hero in many locals' eyes, Penelope Fitzgerald was just that evil. No different from an assassin taking out a ruthless dictator," she says with a nod, picking up a beveled-edged cuticle stick.

Just then the door jangles, and Chaney blazes in with a rush of air. He snaps a Polaroid and shoots back out without a word.

"Why, the little devil!" screeches Norma Jean. "What's gotten into that child?"

Lily takes this opportunity to inform Norma Jean she isn't feeling well—*which isn't a lie after thinking of all the damage that torture stick could do*—and she must go home. She offers to pay for the entire manicure, which she does, leaving a large tip and an astonished manicurist. Then she trails after Chaney, thanking the Lord for a merciful escape.

She Had It Coming

YOU CAN'T FIX MEAN WITH MOUSSE

She used to sit in my chair twice a month, acting like I should thank her for the privilege. Like I needed her business. I didn't. Back then, I had a three-week waitlist.

Then came the column.

"Unless you want to look like a circus clown or see your hair fall out and sail away like a green tumbleweed, you'd be better off going to Natchez for your beauty needs."

That's what she wrote. No names, of course. But everyone knew. That's how she operated. She could ruin you without ever saying your name.

My bookings dropped to almost nothing in a week.

Of course, I wasn't the only one. She humiliated her own daughter just for sport.

That newspaper column, *A Penny for My Thoughts*, should've been called *A Knife in Your Back*. She called herself the voice of the people, but all she did was lie and backstab and ruin good folks.

But I didn't cry. I didn't beg. I held my head up and kept working. Well... mostly. There comes a point when dignity won't pay the bills.

I've been holding my tongue a long time, but since you're asking... yes, I hated her. And no, I'm not sorry she's gone.

Here's something no one can deny: whoever did it couldn't have staged a better exit for Penelope Fitzgerald. Hair hacked off, dignity in tatters. It was poetic. And I don't feel bad saying it.

Do I have shears? Of course I do. I cut hair, don't I? But plenty of folks do. The real question is, who had enough reason to use them? She gave a dozen people a motive before breakfast most days.

You want to know if I did it? I'll tell you this: I thought about it. Plenty of nights.

Norma Jean Badger

CHAPTER 12

November 5, 2024 - Tuesday
Cowherd, Mississippi

Arriving home, Lily finds Chaney at his normal perch on her back stoop laying out several Polaroids. Besides Norma Jean, who's brandishing the cuticle stick like a dagger, he's caught Brother Carothers eating a sandwich at the local deli, eyes wide and cheeks bulging, with lettuce hanging from his mouth. Next is one of Mrs. Rose taken through the kitchen window at the Fitzgerald house, looking like she'd seen a ghost. *What is she doing there so soon after the murder?* Finally, he produces a photo of what must be the Reverend Stanley Meadows, which looks like he had clipped from a church directory.

"Well, you've been busy," says Lily.

"My mind rebels at stagnation! Give me problems! Give me work!" he exclaims, quoting Holmes and gathering the photos as Lily unlocks the door. Once inside, he tapes the suspects' photos to the murder board.

"So how was the nail thingy?" asks Chaney.

"Agonizing. My fingertips will be sore for days. Thankfully, you saved me from further torment with your well-timed blitz," says Lily, absently rubbing her fingers.

"Did you get any useable intel?"

"Norma Jean had some intense opinions about Penelope Fitzgerald. Let's see, she called her a backstabber, a liar, a scandalmonger, greedy, spiteful, and narcissistic. And I believe she called her both Satan and the anti-Christ."

"Dang! That's harsh, but perceptive," says Chaney. "Okay, I think we need to go over the clues again. Lily, grab that marker…" He stops at Lily's raised eyebrows. "Please, would you grab that marker so we can add any new info we have? Clue Number 1: Strangled with a silk scarf. Write beside that 'Not cause of death, no pah-tee—what was that word the sheriff used?"

"Petechia—small red or purple spots in the whites of the eye caused by hemorrhaging," says Lily. "I looked it up," she adds, shrugging when she sees Chaney's crooked smile.

"Okay, so write 'Not cause of death. No petite-cha-cha. Expensive scarf. PF thinks BF stole it'. Anything else we should add to that one?"

"If Bougie did steal it, she may have sold it to pay off debts. According to Norma Jean, she owes everybody in town. So, it could have ended up in anyone's hands," Lily says.

"Good point, we should add that," says Chaney.

Lily writes, "Possible BF sold scarf to pay debt; anyone in town could have it."

"Clue Number 2: Head pushed into gravy. Also not the cause of death, the Sheriff said they could tell that right away. But that would have been cool, wouldn't it?" asks Chaney.

"Chaney, we need to remember that, as unlikeable as Mrs. Fitzgerald was, death by murder is an unholy thing. I've felt convicted that, despite all the evidence that she was a thoroughly ungodly person, we need to speak of her with more sensitivity and respect," says Lily.

"You're right. I just get carried away when I remember some things she did and said. I'll do better. As my granddad says, 'There but for the grace of God go I.'"

"Amen," agrees Lily. "Now, next clue: hair lopped off at the scalp and head covered with ketchup. This could be a symbolic expression of rebellion by Bougie toward her mother's micromanagement and criticism of her personal choices."

"I don't follow any of that, but I think if Bougie did it, I think she was thumbing her nose at her mom and saying, 'I'll do what I want and now that you're dead, you'll do what I want, too! Enjoy your new 'do.' Straight up revenge," says Chaney.

Lily nods. "Yes, perfectly expressed."

"And you know what they say about revenge?" asks Chaney.

"It's best served cold?" Lily replies with a twinkle in her eye.

Chaney raises one hand into the air and places the other on his chest.

"*If you prick us, do we not bleed? If you tickle us, do we not laugh? If you poison us, do we not die? And if you wrong us, shall we not revenge?* It's Shakespeare. And guess who said it? A dude named Shylock!" says Chaney, laughing.

"James Chaney Bridges, just when I think I've got you figured out..."

"I just know stuff. Brains passed down from kith and kin," he says with a shrug, causing Lily to laugh too.

"Norma Jean seems to think Bougie had a premonition that her mother was going to die. At her appointment last Thursday, she said she would soon get what's coming to her and could then pay back everyone who she owes money to," says Lily. "Inferring Bougie planned to kill her mother and would get her inheritance soon. Norma Jean also said something in passing that I think may be significant. She said Bougie came into the shop for a trim on Thursday even though she didn't need it."

"The day before the murder," Chaney confirms, springing up onto the countertop, legs dangling.

"Yes. She could have gone for the sole purpose of stealing the shears."

"It's possible," says Chaney. "Okay, what else?"

"You know, it also could be someone trying to make it *seem* like it was Bougie, taking advantage of what Penelope said in the article," Lily replies.

Chaney leans in, eyes bright. "A frame job."

"Right. But I don't think we should rule out Norma Jean. That woman has some deep-rooted bitterness. She called the murderer a hero and a good Samaritan who did the whole town a favor. She said the killer was the same as an assassin taking out a ruthless dictator. Those were her exact words," says Lily. "She also alluded to Mr. Fitzgerald, Bougie's father, being at the very least a criminal and at the worst a murderer himself."

"Whoa! I'll have to ask my Pops about that when he comes back from his motorcycle trip. I talked to him on the phone last night and asked him if we could get into the garage to look through the past articles, but he took the key with him. So, we'll have to wait until he gets home in the middle of the month. I also asked him about the butcher. He said Penelope claimed some meat from his shop was old and gave her food poisoning. She warned everyone in town about going there. It hurt his business for a while, but he's the only butcher in town, so everyone got tired of going to Natchez for their meat and started going back to him. Even Mrs. Rose sneaks in there to buy meat for the Fitzgerald house from him," says Chaney.

"I wonder if the bacon that was left on the table came from there?" asks Lily.

"Most likely. And Pops said his bacon isn't pre-packaged. He gets pork from the Cristo farm and then cures and smokes it and will cut it as thick or thin as you want…"

They jump as the piercing sound of sirens echoes through the air. Startled, Lily looks out the kitchen window and sees blue lights flashing through the trees.

"That's MY house!" yells Chaney, jumping from the counter-top and streaking out the front door.

Lily runs after him, and they hurry across the lawn. Sheriff Timmons is pounding on the Bridges' door shouting, "Open up! It's the sheriff."

A deputy sees Chaney and Lily and holds up a hand for them to stay back. Lily puts her hand on Chaney's shoulder, but he tears away from her. He reaches the porch just as his father opens the door. It's the first time Lily has seen Percy. He's a tall, thin man with a distinguished bearing and a scholarly manner.

"Percy Bridges, I'm taking you in for questioning regarding the murder of Penelope Fitzgerald…" begins the sheriff.

"What? Are you crazy?" screams Chaney, pushing to get between Timmons and his dad. "He didn't kill nobody!"

"Chaney…" Percy says, reaching down to calm Chaney.

"Get back, boy, before you get hurt," shouts the sheriff.

"You're the one who's going to get hurt if you don't get away from my dad. And don't call me boy!" says Chaney, still pushing and landing a hard kick to the sheriff's shin.

"Ow! If you don't get back, I'll have you restrained!" yells the sheriff, dancing backward and rubbing his shin.

"What proof do you have?" asks Chaney, leaping from the porch and turning to face Sheriff Timmons, splaying his arms between him and the sheriff's cruiser.

"I'd like to know that myself," says Percy, raising his chin and folding his arms across his chest.

"Well, it's like this… everybody knows about the feud between you and the deceased. This morning the bank president came in to inform me about an altercation between you and Miz Fitzgerald in his bank two days before the murder. Then yesterday, this lady here," says Timmons, hitching a stubby thumb toward Lily, "told me that your dog had gone missing right before the murder. My theory is that someone shooed him off so he wouldn't bark himself crazy when the murderer walked into the Fitzgerald home. Now we all know the only people who will allow that dog near them without risking grave bodily harm are you," he says, pointing to Chaney, "your dad, and your granddad. Well, *Granddad* left on his Harley on a tour of 'Merica on the 31st of October, so he has an alibi. And you—why, you're too scrawny to skewer the woman, so that leaves your dad."

"That's all circumstantial, Sheriff, and you know it," says Lily, crossing her arms.

"You do your job, little lady, and I'll do mine," says Timmons, turning toward Lily and pointing an accusing finger.

"Plus, if Percy murdered Mrs. Fitzgerald, why would he need to shoo off his own dog? That makes little sense," says Lily.

"It doesn't rule him out as an accomplice," says Timmons, now aiming his finger toward Percy.

"Chaney, it will be okay." Percy walks down the steps and kneels to look his son in the eye. "I didn't kill her, so there's nothing to be afraid of. You go call your Pops and tell him what's happened. He'll be back before you know it." Standing, he turns his attention to Lily. "I take it you're the Lily Chaney's been talking about. Can Chaney stay at your house until my father can get back from his ride?"

Lily brushes a stray hair behind her ear, nodding. "Of course. He can sleep on the couch for as long as needed. I'll be sure he gets to school, too."

"Good, that's settled," says the sheriff. "Now move along. We also have a warrant to search your house, which my deputies will complete straightaway." He grabs Percy's arm and drags him along to the police car, making a wide pass around Chaney, mindful of his shins.

With reluctance, Chaney moves to stand by Lily as they watch the sheriff put Percy in the back of the squad car. But as soon as Timmons puts the car into gear, Chaney takes off after it, running alongside in tears. The sheriff notices him in the side-view mirror and guns the engine, thus further entrenching Lily's opinion of him as an immature bully. The thought that they are all at the mercy and whims of such incompetent and imbecilic law enforcement is terrifying. She sighs and whispers, *"Against stupidity, we have no defense."*

Chaney continues to race behind the car until it turns off the street. Jolting to a stop, he falls to his knees and buries his head in his hands in anguish and defeat. Lily moves to sit on her front porch to allow Chaney time to grieve in peace, even as her own spirit is in a state of awe. Such a testimony of love between father and child is something she thought only existed in fables and folktales. It was certainly not something she nor her brother had ever experienced with their father. It left her feeling she had just witnessed something magical and miraculous in the midst of misery.

She Had It Coming

BREAKING NEWS: I'M STILL MAD

When my wife got sick, I did what any husband would do: took extra work, borrowed what I had to. I thought I'd be able to pay it back quickly, but the bills came in faster than the payments went out. Before I knew it, I was drowning.

That's when she swooped in, offering to buy the paper. She said it'd help keep me afloat. And it helped. Sort of. Just not for long. It wasn't near what the *Register* was worth, but she knew I didn't have time, or stamina, to negotiate. I was trying to save a life.

She let me stay on as a writer for a while. Until she didn't like what I was working on.

It wasn't some exposé or scandal, just something I saw in a folder on her desk once. It didn't seem like anything special. Until she caught me looking. She slammed it shut and whisked it away like it was radioactive. You don't do that unless you've got something to hide.

Then one day, with no warning, she fired me and changed the locks.

She said it was budget cuts. One journalist was enough, she told me, meaning her. That's how she saw herself, I guess, even though she was really nothing more than a glorified gossip columnist.

And every time I passed that building with my name still faint on the glass, I remembered who I used to be. And what she took from me.

People ask if I hated her. I don't answer that. Some things are better left between a man and his prayers. Let folks draw their own conclusions. That's what they always do anyway.

I never set out to be the story. But when the one holding the pen gets silenced, you have to find another way to be heard.

Sometimes, the silencer must be silenced.

Percy Bridges

CHAPTER 13

November 5, 2024 – Tuesday
Washington, D.C.

Stacks of files clutter Eamonn's desk, closing in on a half-full coffee mug that's long gone cold. Sunlight slices through the partially drawn blinds, creating bold stripes that dance across the floor. Mugshots and maps plaster a bulletin board on the wall, reminding him of investigations that still demand his attention.

He ends his call with the lawyer, Patricia Jennings, uncertain whether to feel relieved the Sheriff has no evidence against Lily or terrified by the ineptitude, unfitness, and unprofessionalism in the Cowherd's sheriff's office. Mix that with shoddiness, ham-fistedness, and stupidity, and you've got an unstable compound. Wondering if he's got the right analogy, he pulls up his dictionary app on his cell.

Unstable Compound: a component is said to be unstable if it can corrode, decompose, burn, or explode under the conditions of anticipated use or normal environmental conditions.

Yes, that's the phrase I'm looking for.

He's still unsure if he did the right thing in not pulling Lily out immediately. He can understand her reluctance. Everyone will believe she's guilty if she just takes off, and that doesn't sit well with her. He would feel the same. Still, despite his best efforts, he's found it impossible to disregard the uneasy sensation that washed over him as she casually mentioned her new "friend" and her hesitancy to end the relationship out of the blue. He'd noticed that she had used gender neutral pronouns when informing him of this "friend"; therefore, he has no clue whether this "friend" is male or female. *Not that it should matter. It's just that she doesn't seem the type of person to pursue a romantic relationship without being able to tell the truth about her identity and past.*

No doubt Da would ask whether this was uneasiness or just plain jealousy. If I'm honest, I'd have to admit it may be both. But honest feelings have no place in WITSEC, and I'll just have to make peace with that.

Honest feelings were something Da could always pry out of me. He knew just the right questions to ask... how I miss the man. Mom and the girls, too. And Declan.

He rubs his forehead to ease the tension building there and pulls his fingers back through the short crop of hair atop. He smiles, remembering his mother's reaction the first time he'd returned from the barbershop with a crew cut.

Despite her American roots, Mam could always imitate Da's rich Irish lilt when she wanted to wax poetic. Ever the romantic, she had clasped her hand over her heart, saying, "Och! Would you look at me handsome lad! He's traded his brown curls for a new look that would make the angels jealous. And won't all the lasses be fallin' for him?"

"Eamonn!" Declan had squawked, looking up from his calculus book. "Is it yourself? Was that barber out of his tree? He's gone and made a dog's dinner of your head! The girls will take one gander at 'ya and run the whole road home, they will."

"Declan, I'll be thankin' you to stop actin' the maggot. Yer brother looks fierce good, so he does."

"Mammy, don't be giving him notions! He'll get him a swelled head, like."

"None of that begrudgery, now. Eamonn, don't be listenin' to him."

"I never do. He's a mad eegit, altogether." I'd said with a smile.

"Aye, right!" Declan had whispered. "Ye've gone mental. I'm scarlet for ya," he'd continued, shaking his head while circling his finger around his ear.

"And you're away in the head…totally barmy." I'd whispered back, giving him a punch on the shoulder.

"Still an' all, yer a good skin. A dead legend. I'm just slagging you," he'd said, returning the punch.

"Sure look!" Mam had continued, her eyes lifted toward the heavens. "He's the splittin' image of a young Sean Connery, so he is! He's made his mammy swoon, and that's the truth."

"Sean Connery's Scottish." Declan and I had said in chorus, looking at each other with wry grins. It was an old family joke, and we knew what was coming.

"*Come here till I tell ye, his grandad was…*" Mam began.

"*An Irish Traveler!*" Declan and I had blurted together. And the lot of us had laughed, as always. Mam was for good and all mad for Sean Connery.

Now, just what sparked those thoughts? Had the thought of what Da might think of my "non-feelings" for Lily led me down this tour of memory lane? Or had the actions and incompetence rampant in the Cowherd Sheriff's office reminded me of Da's stories of The Troubles, when a person couldn't tell the difference between the good guys and the bad guys? Good and evil should be plain to see and easy to discern. But according to Da, those lines had constantly blurred like an ever-shifting mirage.

Okay, enough reminiscing. Back to the job at hand.

He picks up the report from his colleague at the Lexington district office. Lily's condo had been cleared for sale, and there was an open house last Sunday. Once it was over, the realtor contacted the lawyer she believed was handling Lily's estate. She mentioned an attendee whose behavior she found suspicious. The man had asked questions about the former owner, why she was selling, and where she had moved. The realtor explained that one of her fiduciary duties was confidentiality, so she couldn't provide him with that information.

However, a meddlesome neighbor informed him that men had loaded the furniture onto a moving truck either in the first or second week of May. She said there were rumors that the previous resident had passed away in a car accident. This information seemed to fluster the man. He gave the neighbor his name and number before leaving, asking her to please contact him if she found out any concrete information. Before the realtor could ask about it, the neighbor had left, and the realtor was unaware of the neighbor's name.

Eamonn's colleague had reviewed footage from the Lexington traffic cameras and didn't locate anyone matching the realtor's description of the man entering or leaving the condo development. He then sent an officer to knock on near neighbors' doors under the ruse that there had been a hit-and-run accident after the open house, and he was seeking information on the attendees. The guy got lucky on the third knock when a Mrs. Enid Jefferson informed him she had spoken to a man who "seemed a little sketchy." He'd given her his contact information, but her husband had thrown it away, telling her to "stop poking her nose into other people's business." The man's name was Elton something, and she was pretty sure he was a private investigator.

I'd say there's more than a strong chance that someone connected with the drug cartel had sent the man to track her. We had stopped Lily's mail soon after the accident, and she had few personal friends they could interrogate. She had been self-employed, working as an independent contractor. Hence, there are no co-workers or bosses to question. The physical trail would be reaching a dead-end.

These cartels also use hackers to follow online leads by crowdsourcing a person's personal information, physical description, photographs, and social media check-ins. We had wiped out all of Lily's email, social media, and cell accounts, leaving her with no online presence whatsoever. But they won't give up. The government security operations center analysts, AKA our team of legal hackers, have been monitoring computer searches for Elizabeth James on the dark web.

I know the cartel is looking for her, but they won't find her. Elizabeth James no longer exists.

Eamonn had cautioned Lily to avoid having her photo taken, especially by someone who may want to put it on social media. Drug cartels have millions of dollars and near limitless resources, and they use a large array of techniques to find people, including facial recognition. He prays she heeds his warning and exercises caution, for this would likely be the only means by which one can find any trace of Elizabeth James.

☙❧

November 5, 2024 – Tuesday

Washington, D.C.

Eamonn arrives at his apartment on Penn Street NE just after 6:00 p.m. Although he grinds his teeth when paying the ridiculous rent, he's willing to shell it out for the prime location near the Metro Station and Union Market on 5th Street. On the way home from work, he had grabbed takeout from the Vietnamese bistro—pork bánh mì and garden spring rolls. He's now ready to settle down with his newest after-hours project, which has gradually grown from a self-appointed work assignment to a slow-burn personal crusade: discovering the sender of the anonymous postcards taken from Lily's house. Twelve postcards with single hearts as the only signature and no return address.

With a map of North America tacked to the wall, he's the flagged cities from which the postcards originated, noting on the flags the year received, and Lily's age at the time, and the city it was postmarked from. Next, he drew arrowed lines, tracing the path of the sender.

- 2013 – Denver – age 14
- 2014 – Vancouver – age 15
- 2015 – San Antonio – age 16
- 2016 – Seattle – age 17
- 2017 – Miami – age 18
- 2018 – Virginia Beach – age 19
- 2019 – Savannah – age 20
- 2020 - Chicago – age 21
- 2021 – Boston – age 22
- 2022 – Montréal – age 23
- 2023 – Kansas City – age 24

He then made a list of what he could deduce from these dates and locations.

1. Only U.S. and Canada—no passport needed if entry by land or sea.

2. All are large cities—a person is better able to blend in.

3. He followed her through various address changes, tracking her. Was he stalking her or watching over her?

4. The person was persistent, methodical, and dedicated—and still alive as of May 2023.

And... that's about it. No card for 2024 because the execution and Lily's wreck were on April 26th. The agency stopped Lily's USPS mail after her accident, but on what date? If it was before her birthday on May 4th, the mail carrier would have sent it back to her local post office as undeliverable. USPS forwards mail that seems valuable to the Mail Recovery Center in Atlanta; if it seems to have no value, it's destroyed. A postcard that is unsigned and blank, save a single heart, would most certainly not be considered valuable. However, USPS scans and photographs all mail. He had hoped this would be an avenue for viewing this year's birthday postcard.

But a two-minute call had dissolved that hope: the post office keeps mail scans for a minimum of 7 days to a maximum of 30 days. Although the postcards' provenance had been worming around in his mind since the time of the interviews, it was only a month ago that he decided to undertake this study. Therefore, the images would have been destroyed by now.

It's just as well. Explaining to a judge that I needed a court order for a postcard signed with a single heart would have proven embarrassing.

USPS would have sent images of Lily's mail to her email if she had Informed Delivery set up. Is it worth getting IT involved to retrieve that data? Possibly, as it would establish the most recent location of the sender. I'll not rule that out yet.

Eamonn has spent just about every night the past month looking at this board…just looking and feeling sure he must be missing something and, at the same time, feeling positive there is nothing else to know.

There is only one person who would have that kind of loyalty, persistence, and devotion—Jackson Elliott.

CHAPTER 14

November 6, 2024 - Wednesday
Cowherd, Mississippi

Lily's cottage isn't really what folks would call "tiny house," although the part she uses comprises only about 600 square feet. She's started calling it Lilliputian Cottage in her mind; she loves it for its coziness and charm. It's a far cry from what she had feared: a seedy apartment on the scary side of town.

Just inside the front door, an open staircase curves upward, its handrail worn smooth by generations of use. To the left, sunlight pours through a large window looking out over the front yard. A small fireplace sits against the left wall, flanked by windows and anchored below by bookcases which were—much to Lily's delight—filled with classic novels and poetry.

Straight through from the living room is a small kitchen with a round table tucked into a bow window on the left wall. A window above the farmhouse sink looks out on the rear garden, and a door to the right leads to the back porch. Overall, it was one of the happiest and homiest kitchens Lily has ever seen.

When she first arrived, Lily had explored the second floor, which was accessed through a heavy door at the top of the staircase. This floor appeared to have been unused for many years. It was just one large room with knee walls meeting a slanting roof and two dormer windows at the front, where little light fought its way through the dirty panes. Peeling wallpaper covered the walls and ceiling, while cobwebs hung over everything. The room was gloomy and dank smelling, making you feel that if you stayed too long, you might meet Mrs. Havisham floating around in her tattered wedding dress. This spook factor, along with the dust that had made Lily sneeze and cough, convinced her there was no need for her to return.

After Chaney had contained his distress last night, he and Lily went to his house for clothes and toiletries. When they returned to Lily's cottage, he had gone to the murder board, taken a picture frame from his overnight bag and removed the photo of his dad, which he taped to the wall. He took the marker and wrote "Percy Bridges," crossed it out and wrote "Dad—innasent bystander." Lily smiled at the misspelling but didn't correct him. The suspect list was again up to seven names. Lily had updated the list to note the beautician's full name and the relationship of the suspects to the victim.

1. Bougie Fitzgerald—daughter

2. Morris Carothers—current pastor

3. Stanley Meadows—former pastor

4. Norma Jean Badger—beautician

5. The butcher (name?)

6. ~~Lily Jordan~~

7. Mary Rose—Fitzgerald cook and housekeeper

8. ~~Percy Bridges~~ Dad—innasent bystander

Chaney had reached his grandad on his cell, and Mr. Bridges Senior was now on the journey back home. However, as he and his traveling buddies had already reached San Francisco, it will be next week before he returns. After Lily had explained the condition of the upstairs, Chaney was all too happy to camp out on the sofa.

"I don't do creepy," he had been quick to inform her.

Lily had phoned the sheriff's office this morning. A deputy had told her they could hold Percy for 96 hours before they must either charge him or release him, which wasn't much time to prove Percy's innocence. *Considering Timmons' unpredictable and contradictory tactics—a strange combination of laissez-faire and tyrannical dictatorship—time is of the essence.*

That morning, Lily began researching air rights on her laptop, trying to understand why Percy's investigation provoked such a fierce reaction from Penelope.

I remember studying this in my appraisal classes. It means a property interest in the "space" above the earth's surface.

Her teacher often emphasized the Latin phrase: *Cujus est solum, ejus est usque ad coelum.* "Whoever owns the soil, it is theirs up to Heaven and down to Hell."

So, air rights originally meant from a point below the ground and extending indefinitely upward.

Lily clicks a web link and begins reading…

People have used the term "air rights" as far back as medieval Roman law, and later in common law in the *Commentaries on the*

Laws of England by William Blackstone. In the U.S. the FAA regulates airspace, and the U.S. Government has "exclusive sovereignty of airspace in the United States."

So today, the FAA only allows air rights that cover the airspace directly above the land that is reasonable for individuals or entities to use it in relation to the land. And a homeowner can sell the air rights above their land.

Why would researching air rights cause Penelope Fitzgerald to be angry enough to fire Percy? Was she planning on building a skyscraper in Cowherd? That hardly seems plausible. But what else can it mean?

Lily leaves to pick up Chaney from school at 2:45 and right away realizes she should have left earlier. The pickup line wraps all the way around the block. Inching her way toward the student queue, she wonders if the teachers will allow Chaney to go with her, since she's not on his records as an authorized adult for pickup. But they not only allow him to jump in her car, they wave goodbye with goofy grins, eager to get all the kids home so they can go home as well. *I shouldn't have worried; this is Cowherd, and they do things differently here.*

After last night, Lily feels Chaney needs a treat, so they stop at the ice cream parlor and each get a cone. The sun casts a warm glow on the vibrant autumn leaves, which crunch underfoot as they step outside. They find a table beneath a large tree, where a cool breeze sends a swirl of color dancing around them. The air carries the crisp scent of fall and the sweet aroma of the ice cream shop.

"So how was your day?" she asks.

"Nothing special," he murmurs with downcast eyes. "Some guys tried to pick a fight on the playground, calling Dad a jailbird. I should have known everyone in Cowherd would know. It's a gossip town, after all."

"What did you do?"

"There were a bunch of them, but they were all younger kids, so I just stood there and stared 'em down; didn't say anything or move toward 'em. It freaked them out, and they ended up skulking off."

"Wow, I'm impressed. That was a wise choice." Chaney shrugs, but she can tell he likes the compliment.

As they enjoy their cones, tables around them fill up. From just behind them, a voice mentions a name that snaps Lily and Chaney to attention. They lock eyes when a woman mentions someone on their suspect list.

"Did you hear about Brother Carothers? He's taken off." The woman speaks with sly relish, savoring her chance to be the first to share juicy gossip.

"You mean he just up and left?" her friend asks, disbelief sharp in her tone.

"Packed up and left in the dead of night." A brief, amused chuckle escapes her. "And that's not the worst of it!"

"What's the worst of it?" the friend presses, eagerness creeping into her words.

"He's left town with some of the church's money! It seems Penelope Fitzgerald had convinced the church treasurer months ago that there was no need for him to miss his Sunday roast every week. She assured him that the new pastor could handle taking the money from the offering plate straight to the bank on Monday mornings. So, today the treasurer had a look at the bank account, and Brother Carothers had deposited only a piddlin' amount of cash."

"He stole it!" she exclaims, her voice part shock and part wicked amusement.

"Yes, indeedy!" The words are thick with satisfaction.

"Do you think Penelope knew what he was up to?" Her question drips with knowing suspicion.

"You know the Fitzgeralds. That family has had its hand in every pot in town since before we were born. I not only think Penelope knew what he was doing, I think she put him up to it and was taking a cut herself."

The women toss their trash and stroll off, and Lily and Chaney gather their own trash, toss it in the bin, and sprint to the car.

CHAPTER 15

November 6, 2024 - Wednesday
Cowherd, Mississippi

Chaney hops in Lily's car, slamming the door, and shoots her a look that's all fire and curiosity. "Did you hear that?" he says, strapping in like he's joining a high-speed chase.

"I sure did," Lily nods, starting the car and pulling from the curb. "I'd like to say it's hard to believe, but it's not. He was in the neighborhood around the same time as the murder, and his response to seeing the police seemed irrational."

"So, she had Brother Carothers under her thumb the whole time he was here. Remember what she said in her article? The town could thank her for him being here. She said he was 'modest, malleable, and eager to please'. What's malleable mean?"

"It means someone who can be easily influenced or manipulated," says Lily, maneuvering her car around the town square. "Combine that with someone who's 'eager to please,' and you've got somebody that's exploitable."

"And a person who is exploitable is...?"

"It's someone you can push around or take advantage of to get what you want, usually not in a good way."

"Like telling a preacher what he can and can't say from the pulpit and using him to rob the church so you can profit from it?" Chaney's eyes widen as he speaks, his astonishment clear in his voice.

Lily shakes her head. "We don't know for sure she told him to take the money, or that she profited from it. It's just a guess and gossip at this point."

"Yeah, but an educated guess seeing all we *do* know about her." Chaney points out the car window as Lily pulls into the cottage's drive. "Look! It's Pastor Meadows!"

Chaney jumps out before Lily can even come to a complete stop. Lily sees an older man, with the height and bulk of a grizzly, sitting on her front porch. He stands but then kneels to accept Chaney's bear hug. It's easy to see they are both happy to see each other. Breaking off the hug, Chaney grabs the man's large hand and drags him over to Lily.

"Pastor Meadows, this is my good friend, Lily Jordan. Lily, this is the preacher I've been telling you about." Chaney grins widely, his eyes sparkling with delight as he shifts his gaze between them.

"Very nice to meet you, Lily. I'm Stanley Meadows." The big man extends his hand, his grip warm and firm.

"And you, as well. Chaney has told me a lot about you," Lily replies, shaking his hand. She smiles at his curious look and adds, "All positive, I promise."

"Well, that's good to hear." Brother Meadows returns her smile, his eyes crinkling at the corners.

"Whatcha' doin' here?" Chaney's brow creases as he squints up at the man.

"I heard about what happened to your dad, so I went to visit him at the jail. He told me where you were staying, so I thought I'd check in on you."

Lily glances at Chaney, then back at Pastor Meadows. "Would you like to come in for some iced tea?"

"That'd be real nice, thank you," he says, stepping forward with an appreciative nod.

As they make their way in, Lily remembers the murder board. The one with this man's face on it. Chaney hasn't forgotten, though. In fact, he's eager to show it to him, and he drags the preacher by the arm into the kitchen.

Chaney's words spill out. "Me and Lily are investigating the Fitzgerald woman's murder. We got this murder board with all the suspects we've identified so far." His expression shifts into a grimace. "Sorry, your name's on it. But that woman was plenty hateful to you and Mrs. Meadows. Some people would carry a grudge and might decide to pay her back. I know you wouldn't. I've been meaning to tell Lily we can cross off your name," he says, giving Lily a withering look.

"Well, I've never been on a murder board before, that's for sure. Don't take my name off just yet. I think it's kind of exciting to see it up there," says Brother Meadows, grinning. "I see the other reverend has earned a spot on it as well."

"Did 'ya hear what he did?" Chaney asks.

"You mean running off with the church funds?" Brother Meadows nods. "Yes, I heard that. It's a terrible thing to steal from the Lord."

"So, since he's gone, and she's gone, can you come back and be our preacher again?"

"No, I'm sorry. I'm the pastor of a new church over in Seaton. If I hadn't already accepted their offer, I would have loved to come back. I pastored Cowherd Baptist Church since I was just out of the seminary. Those were good years."

"Tell me what happened at the jail. Is my dad okay? Is he wearing an orange jumpsuit? He ain't got into any prison fights, has he?"

"Your dad is doing pretty well, considering. He's still wearing his own clothes and isn't in the prison, so no fights, either," Brother Meadows says with a chuckle. "They've placed him in what they call a holding cell. He said the Sheriff hasn't talked to him again since he put him in there. There's only a bed in the cell, so he said he's spent most of his time just pacing and sleeping and thinking about you. They can hold him three more days, and then they'll let him go if they don't find enough evidence to charge him with her murder."

"They won't find any unless they fake evidence, 'cause he didn't do it." Chaney's expression is serious, his jaw set in determination. "Plus, we're going to find out who did… hopefully before they charge him."

Pastor Meadows walks closer to the board and studies the faces and names on the suspect list.

"I can fill in that question mark for you. The butcher's name is Niles Gibbons." He turns to Lily. "So why is he there?"

"We think we may find the answer to who murdered Penelope Fitzgerald in her columns," says Lily. "She wasn't indiscriminate on who she dragged through the mud. From what I've read so far, the only people she had anything good to say about were Brother Carothers and the Cristo brothers."

"Cristo brother," clarifies Brother Meadows. "Tomás runs the farm by himself now. His brother, Luís, was killed in 2010."

"Killed!" exclaims Chaney.

"Some cows had escaped after someone left a gate open, and a car hit Luís while he was herding them across the road. Hit and run in broad daylight. To this day, there have been no charges filed against anyone involved."

"Now that you mention it, the advertisement said *Tomás* Cristo, Proprietor," says Lily. "Do you know where his farm is?"

"Why, right behind you." Brother Meadows walks to the window over the sink and points out. "Your backyard backs up to the farm. See that gate in the back there? That leads to his south meadow. In fact, this house used to be part of the farm, and both it and the farm used to be three times the size as it is now."

"Really? How?" asks Chaney.

"Why don't we take the tea out to the garden and let him tell us the history of this house and the Cristo family," says Lily, opening the back door.

CHAPTER 16

November 6, 2024 - Wednesday
Cowherd, Mississippi

"The Cristo family moved to Cowherd in the 30s, long before my time," Brother Meadows begins, settling in an Adirondack chair with his sweet tea. "They owned 450 acres on this side of Raven Ridge Road and around 250 acres across it. They built the dairy and delivered milk in glass bottles to the folks in Cowherd. The patriarch was Carlos, and his wife was called Elena. I've heard that she was the sweetest lady ever to have lived in Cowherd. She always helped the poor, and evidently there were a lot of poor people here in the 30s. They had a son, Mattias, and a daughter, Mary. She's Mary Rose now."

"Mary Rose, the Fitzgerald's housekeeper?" Lily asks.

"The very one. She married Sam Rose in 1978, the year I came to preach at Cowherd. I performed the ceremony. It was the first one I'd ever done. I guess I did okay, seeing as they're still married." Brother Meadows chuckles, his eyes twinkling with amusement. "Sam's a commercial soybean farmer. Their place is on the outskirts of Cowherd, going toward Seaton.

"Mattias married a lady named Camilla Saunders. It was before my time, but there were whispers he had a brief marriage prior to Camilla. He didn't want to speak about it, so I didn't push. But I'll tell you one thing: I have never met a man more honorable than Mattias Cristo. Mattias' parents raised him to believe all people are equal and loved by God, regardless of the color of their skin or the balance of their checking account. And he lived it. His wife, Camilla, was just about as close to an earthly angel as I've ever met.

"Anyway, Mattias and Camilla had two sons, Luís and Tomás…"

"Tell us about the house. How did it shrink?" asks Chaney, who's lying on the ground looking up through the leaves. From somewhere, he's retrieved a baseball and is tossing it up and catching it in a steady rhythm.

"It didn't exactly shrink," the pastor says. "This house and your house, Chaney, were all one big farmhouse. It was the largest house I'd ever seen, with a porch that wrapped all the way around. Those stairs you see when you first come in Lily's door were stairs to the servant's quarters."

"They had slaves?" Chaney rolls to his stomach and stares wide-eyed at the preacher, the baseball dropping forgotten to the ground.

"Oh no. They had paid help who were free to live at the farmhouse or live with their families. Men who worked at the dairy and farm could also live there if they chose. And the Cristos paid them all well."

"Okay, well that's okay, I guess," says Chaney. "So, what happened to the middle part of the house between Lily's and mine?"

"In 1995, there was a fire that started in their kitchen that killed Mattias. The fire investigator from Natchez was certain it was arson, but the investigation failed to locate the arsonist. The damaged portions of the house were removed, allowing for the construction of two separate houses. Despite Camilla's confidence that they had insurance coverage for the house, they weren't able to locate the policy. After that, the family had set back after set back. Camilla had had the two houses built on credit, because she was sure there was insurance money coming, both from the house and from a life insurance policy on Mattias. But guess what?"

"Both were lost!" Chaney and Lily say together.

"That's right. The Cristos could find proof of neither. There was only one insurance company in Cowherd, and Frank Fitzgerald, Penelope's husband, had purchased it a year prior. He had just fired several employees, saying they wrote fake policies and pocketed the payments, although they denied it. He also owned the construction company that did the work on the two new houses, *and* he was the Chairman of the Board for the local bank. So, now Camilla was broke, had two young boys, and owed a lot of money to the most ruthless man in town. He *very graciously* bought all their property except for 150 acres of farmland and this house, which Camilla moved into. They moved the farm's office to the second floor, as they could no longer afford any paid help.

"The brothers did a nice job with the farm, adding beef cattle and pigs. They were just about to expand into soybeans like their uncle, but then the older brother, Luís, was killed. He had life insurance, but only enough to cover his funeral expenses. Three months later, Camilla died of a heart attack. Tomás said it was more like a *broken* heart.

"So, Mary and Sam moved into this house, but it didn't take long for Fitzgerald to raise the hatchet again. Camilla had gotten behind on the mortgage payments, and the bank was threatening to foreclose—with the urging of the Chairman of the Board, of course. Thankfully, Tomás and Luís had separated the working part of the farm and this house into two separate parcels and, therefore, two different mortgages. Frank Fitzgerald told them he'd buy this house, contents, and lot for what they owed the bank, around $30,000, which was only about a tenth of what it was worth. It was the only way to save the farm, so they accepted.

"But Fitzgerald put a stipulation into the contract: nothing except personal items belonging to Mary and Sam were to be removed from the property, and that had to be done within an hour of the closing."

"Why would he do that?" asks Chaney.

"Likely meanness, but I have always thought there was something in the house Frank wanted, documents or such from the office. He stood guard in the house, along with the sheriff, to enforce the edict. All furniture, books, kitchen items, rugs, and linens were to stay, and the rush meant there was no time to remove the farm office paperwork from the second floor. No amount of arguing by Mary and Sam would sway him or the sheriff. They considered taking legal action but lacked the financial means and were aware that they would surely lose, given that the judge was also under Fitzgerald's influence.

"And so now, except for his aunt, Tomás is the last Cristo left. I see he's started doing unpasteurized milk and yogurt. The yuppies are really into that *holistic health benefits* craze now. When I was growing up, I was taught unpasteurized milk would kill you."

Pastor Meadows drank the last of his sweet tea and set down his glass.

"Well, I need to be going. The missus will be expecting me. Chaney, hang in there. It will be okay. Call me if you need me; my cell number is the same. Can I say a quick prayer with you before I go?"

"Sure, Pastor," says Chaney, and Lily nods.

"Lord, here's your child, Chaney. He's rightly worried about his dad. I ask you to put your arms around him and comfort and love on him. I ask that you bring Percy home soon, and that the sheriff finds the true murderer and brings them to swift justice. In the name of our Savior, Amen.

"Lily, it was delightful to meet you, and thank you for the iced tea," says Brother Meadows, standing.

"You are very welcome, pastor. It was nice to meet you, as well."

"Thanks for coming and for going to see my dad."

"You're welcome. I'll stop by again in a few days to see how things are going."

"Great!" Chaney looks at Brother Meadows, a smirk on his mischievous face. "Preacher, I got one more question though… what's a yuppie?"

ⓒᔥᔍ

After dinner, Chaney and Lily again sit on the back porch, Chaney with his legs dangling over the sides. The cool autumn air brushes against their faces, carrying the crisp scent of fallen leaves; they gaze through the yard to the meadow beyond, each thinking of the sad events in the Cristo family.

"Lily, can a person really die from a broken heart?" Chaney asks, his expression heavy.

Lily glances at him. "I've heard of Broken Heart Syndrome. So, it's possible."

"There sure were a lot of things piled up on Miss Camilla. First, a fire kills her husband and destroys part of her house, then all the money troubles." Chaney pauses, his eyes distant. "So, if the fire was arson, and someone killed Luís by hit and run, I wonder if it was the same person who did all that?"

Lily leans forward, resting her arms on her knees. "The deaths were 15 years apart. It would be a long time to hold a grudge but sometimes anger and bitterness fester. The person hated the Cristos enough to set their house on fire, although we don't know for sure that they knew Mattias was inside. Luís' death could also have been an accident. But if it was premeditated, then someone deliberately opened the gate to let the cows out and waited for him to be in the road, herding them home."

"Like someone opened the gate to let my dog out the day of the murder?"

"Exactly so." Lily nods, then glances toward Chaney's yard. "I see he's back now. How did that happen?"

"Don't know. He was gone, and then the next day he was back inside the fence. He had burrs and stick-tights all matted in his fur, so he'd been out roaming in the fields."

Lily frowned, puzzled. "That's strange."

Chaney turns to face Lily, drawing his knees up under his chin and bracing his back on a porch post.

"Lily, the pastor asked in his prayer that the sheriff would find the true murderer. Do you think we're in danger? I mean, we know you didn't kill her. And it wasn't Brother Meadows or my dad. Carothers might be guilty, but if he isn't, that means the killer could still be here in Cowherd."

"I can't say for sure we're not in danger, but I don't think Penelope's death was random. It seemed very personal. First poisoned, and a scarf wrapped around her neck like a garrote—those were acts with intention to kill. Her face pushed into the gravy and her hair cut off so dramatically; to me, that feels like something done to humiliate. The ketchup poured over her head, which could also be for humiliation's sake. Or, like we said before, it may be symbolic, an attempt to imitate her daughter's fiery red hair, whether by Bougie or someone trying to make it seem it was her."

"I still think it's Bougie," says Chaney. "But I'm thinking now our #2 person, Carothers, could've done it. He was around here at the time of the murder acting all crazy. Then he sneaks out of town, taking the church money with him. Maybe he was pushing back on what she was asking him to do, and he killed her. But that don't explain how he poisoned her or got his hands on the scarf or shears."

"That's true, but another thing I thought about when Pastor Meadows was talking is that Mrs. Rose and Tomás Cristo could also be fostering a long-held grudge against the Fitzgeralds. I think Tomás needs to be added to our board, and we need to look closer at Mrs. Rose. Two questions I have about her are: 1) After all the Fitzgeralds did to her family, why was she working for Penelope? and 2) why was she at the Fitzgerald house just a few days after the murder—the day you took her photo through the window. It was still a crime scene, so why was she allowed inside?"

"Good questions." Chaney nods. "*She* was the one who was doing the cooking. She could have put the poison in Mrs. Fitzgerald's food. Maybe she snuck back in to destroy evidence," says Chaney.

Lily has noticed Chaney has been referring to Penelope in a more respectful way since she mentioned it. He's a unique young man—willing to stand up for his father with the sheriff, refusing to fight kids younger than he, and not being uncomfortable hugging the pastor in broad daylight. On top of that, he's wicked smart. Despite Percy Bridges' recent trouble with alcohol, she can see he and his father have done an amazing job raising him. She's thankful that God has allowed her to be Chaney's friend. She just hopes she won't let him down. Marshal Kelly could still move her.

Even more reason to solve the mystery of who killed Penelope Fitzgerald. And fast.

"It's getting late, Chaney. I think we need to get ready for bed."

"All right. Let's update the murder board first, though." Chaney pops up and barrels into the kitchen. *The kid rarely does anything slowly*, thinks Lily with a smile, following him inside.

"Okay, Watson," he says, "We need to add Tomás Cristo. I think we can cross out Brother Meadows and my dad. And we can add the butcher's name now that we know it."

Lily takes the marker and follows his directives. She's not 100% sure they should remove those two names just on Chaney's trust in the men. *We can always add them back later if needed.*

1. Bougie Fitzgerald – daughter

2. Morris Carothers – current pastor

3. ~~Stanley Meadows – former pastor~~

4. Norma Jean Badger – beautician

5. Niles Gibbons – butcher

6. ~~Lily Jordan~~

7. Mary Rose – Fitzgerald cook and housekeeper

8. ~~Percy Bridges – Dad – innasent bystander~~

"Done. Okay, Sherlock, it's time…" Lily's eyes widen in panic. "I'm a terrible caretaker. I forgot to ask if you had any homework."

"Lily, relax. I was the very last kid to get picked up today," says Chaney with a huge grin. "I did it all while I was waitin' on you."

She Had It Coming

A WOLF IN PEARLS AND PUMPS

They say I was *called*. But it wasn't a call. It was a *selection*. A placement. Arranged like flowers on a table.

She told me Cowherd needed someone calm. Modest. Eager. She said I had the kind of voice that wouldn't upset people.

She edited my sermons like school essays, crossed out warnings. Softened conviction. *"People don't want to be judged. They want to be comforted."*

The old reverend? He spoke too freely. And look where that got him: pressured, slandered, accused, and pushed out.

She said if I did everything she asked, I'd lack for nothing. So, I've kept my head down. Smiled when I was told. But every time I compromised, it hollowed something out. And I've been hollowed more than I care to admit.

But she was a beguiling temptress. It wasn't long before I was skimming from the offering plate and giving her half. Heaven help me! *How did it come to that?*

When I told her I was done—done stealing, done letting her twist the Gospel—that's when she showed her true colors. And they're black. Black as sin. She told me the only gospel in this town was her columns, and that she could spin a story about me so convincing, so vile, the whole town would eagerly believe it. They always believed her.

They think I'm timid. Just the preacher who jumps at a church mouse. But even a timid man knows when the Devil's in the room.

I played the part she needed: quiet, compliant, unseen... until I didn't.

She had it coming. And maybe that's all the explanation anyone needs.

Reverand Morris Carothers

CHAPTER 17

November 7, 2024 – Thursday
Lexington, Kentucky

As a private investigator, Elton Jacks has spent years perfecting the skill of blending in. His goal is to always be indescribable. In order to avoid standing out, he opts for clothes that are neither flashy nor attention-grabbing, blending in with the others in the crowd. He studies the communities and people around him and adapts his behavior to match the flow of society, tries to look like he belongs, moves with a purpose, and varies his patterns. He's always prepared to change his appearance on the go: glasses, hats, or jackets that he can add or remove. He keeps social interactions to the bare minimum. And loud vehicles, in color or condition— backfires, rattles, and smoking, belching, or growling mufflers—are all taboo. He changes his place of residence after every job or every six months, whichever comes first.

Working as a private investigator, no day is the same as the one before. His work is strictly cash-only. He's worked for Fortune 500 companies rooting out hackers and thieves, found missing persons, tracked down witnesses, and recovered stolen funds. Throughout his career, he has conducted counterintelligence for rivaling organizations, negotiated hostage exchanges between warring gangs, completed domestic investigations, skip tracing, digital forensics, open-source and social media probes. He works only in the private sector, as working for law enforcement or governmental agencies would pose a significant conflict of interest. But he makes good money.

And if my personal relationships are nonexistent, well, that's just the way it has to be.

Currently, tracking down Elizabeth James is his one and only focus, and if he's successful, the reward of finding her alive will be of greater worth to him than anything he's ever known. She is desperately wanted, and failure will likely end him.

When the woman at the open house said she thought Elizabeth had died in a car wreck, he felt like someone had knocked the breath out of him. He's scoured the Internet and newspaper archives searching for a death notice or accident report and found no one matching her description. Upon delving into social media, he found that she, or *someone,* had deleted all traces of her previous accounts. The girl had disappeared.

I doubt she had the expertise to do something like that on her own, which means she had help. And the only help I know of that could accomplish something like that so quickly and completely is WITSEC.

෮෫෨

November 7, 2024 – Thursday
Cowherd, Mississippi

Thursday's school drop-off goes a little smoother; Lily gets Chaney there with two minutes to spare. On the way home, Lily passes the sheriff's office and sees a deputy setting up a podium and microphone out front. She parks and walks over to ask him about it, and she's told the sheriff is holding a press conference in 15 minutes to speak about developments in the murder of Penelope Fitzgerald.

Time enough to get a cappuccino at the little kiosk on the other side of the green.

On the way, she notices the butcher shop, The Cowherd Butchery. There's a large vinyl decal of a cow on the left side of the window and a pig on the other side with labels designating the various cuts of meat. Glancing inside, she can see a large glass counter with various packages of meat inside and a scale atop. Hanging from the ceiling is a large country ham. Though the shop looks open, there's no sign of Mr. Gibbons inside.

Returning with her coffee, she arrives to see Sheriff Timmons strut out of his office and waltz to the podium. She looks around for the media, but there's only the same deputy who had set up the podium taking out an iPhone, holding it out as if to record the "press conference." Nearby, two men play chess in the shade by the green, while a custodial worker picks up trash. Just before the sheriff begins, Bougie parades in, dressed in a fuchsia ruffled blouse with lime green slacks. She's still wearing stilettos, this time matching her blouse. Seeing Lily, she wrinkles her nose like she's just caught a whiff of an offensive odor and, making an obvious about-face, goes to stand in front of the sheriff. Lily sees Norma

Jean come to lean against the doorway of her salon, but she doesn't venture out. On the opposite side of the street, the door of the butcher shop opens. A short, middle-aged man with blondish hair and an apron covering his clothes comes to stand in the doorway.

That must be Niles Gibbons. So, he was there after all.

"Good morning, everyone," begins the Sheriff in an officious tone. "I've called you all together…" He pauses and makes a swipe of his hand, motioning to the deputy, who is recording the conference, to move over to the right. He bends down and whispers, "This here's my good side." Straightening, he starts over. "I've called you all here today to inform you of significant developments in the Fitzgerald murder case. Certain events have transpired that lead us to believe Penelope Fitzgerald's killer is…" another pause for dramatic effect.

Really, this man has missed his calling. He should have gone into show business. Lily holds her breath. *Please don't say Percy Bridges.*

"…none other than Reverend Morris Carothers."

Lily lets her breath out in a whoosh. *Thank you, Lord! Chaney's dad should be out by the time school is out.*

"We believe Mr. Carothers left in the wee hours of the morning on Wednesday, November 6th. A Bible study was to take place at 10:00 that morning, and a parishioner came to the church and found it locked. She next went to the parsonage, but the preacher didn't answer the door. She made several attempts but couldn't flush him out. Calling some men of the church, they arrived and began searching, and they discovered Carothers' car was gone from the garage, along with his clothing and personal items. It was later determined that he had scarpered with church funds. A witness has come forward stating they saw Reverend Carothers near the Fitzgerald house on the day of the murder about the time Mrs. Rose found the victim deceased."

Which witness is that? Lily wonders. *It wasn't me. Well, at least this means they'll release Percy.*

"We do not think Mr. Carothers acted alone, and therefore we will not be releasing our other suspect, Percy Bridges, at this time. That is all." And he turns to leave.

"Sheriff," Lily calls out, "That's not..."

"Iffin you're going to say," says Timmons, turning to face her, *"that's not fair,* I say, whoever told you life was going to be fair?"

"I was going to say," says Lily, rethinking her question because, in fact, she was going to say something very similar to that. "Can you please reiterate your reason for holding Mr. Bridges?"

"I just said why, if you were listening, but evidently you weren't. So, I'll spell it out for you. We think he and Carothers were in cahoots, and when the Reverend found out we were holding Bridges, he skedaddled for fear he was going to be implicated."

"And why do you think they were working together?"

"May I see your press pass, ma'am? This is a press conference, and only members of the press may ask questions. But seeing as all the Cowherd journos are either dead or in my jail, this briefing is over." At this, the sheriff pivots and stomps back into his office.

She would love to know just who told the sheriff about Reverend Carothers being in the area when the murder happened.

Whoever saw him could also be a suspect. *I wonder if Timmons has thought of that.*

Lily looks toward the butcher shop intending to snoop a little, but Mr. Gibbons has gone inside and flipped the "We're Here" sign around to one that reads "You're Too Late." Lily looks at her watch. *It's only 9:30. Surely, it's not normal for him to close so early in the morning.*

She walks to the storefront and peeks into the window, her breath fogging the glass as she leans closer. Someone had turned off all the lights; the space inside is dim, with only a faint glow from the morning sunlight streaming through the big front window. Trying the door, she finds it locked. *What would cause the butcher to close so early on a business day? Was it something the sheriff said?*

Instead, she decides to revisit her air rights investigation and makes her way to the Chamber of Commerce, which occupies a weathered Victorian directly opposite the butcher shop. A gentle breeze sends a few leaves spiraling to the ground, creating a colorful carpet that crunches underfoot. Sunlight filters through the branches, casting playful shadows on the sidewalk.

Upon entering, she's greeted by a young man in black horn-rimmed glasses who bounces on his way over. He's dressed in a blue and white seersucker suit and madras plaid bow tie with matching pocket square; not your typical Cowherdian, that's for sure.

"Hello, I'm Bradley Aubert. Can I help you with anything?" he asks, bowing toward her, his hands clasped in front of him in mock gallantry.

"Hello, Mr. Aubert. I'm Lily Jordan."

"Oh yes. The new girl in town. Don't worry. I never believe things I read in *A Penny for My Thoughts*. Well, not much anyway." He walks over to her, leans close and sniffs, causing Lily to take a step back. "You don't smell like a strumpet, nor look like a charlatan."

"Well, that's good to know," Lily replies with an awkward smile.

Aubert shakes his head in disbelief. "I don't know where that woman came up with the bizarre things she wrote. She didn't look like someone with that much imagination to me, but people can fool you."

"Yes, they can. Have you been here long, Mr...."

"Call me Bradley, please. I was born in Cowherd, and I've lived here most of my life. Shocking, I know. I went to New York for a bit but decided the big city wasn't for me. Hey, I was just going to make another latte. Would you like one?" He points toward a door at the back of the room.

The man has been talking like an audiobook set on triple speed and bouncing heel-to-toe the entire time I've been here. I'm not sure more caffeine is wise, and I don't want to be here when it kicks in.

"Oh, no, thank you. I appreciate the offer, though. I just came in to ask a question. Can you tell me if there has been anyone interested in acquiring air rights in Cowherd recently?"

"Now that's a question I never thought I'd hear in this town. Most folks around here wouldn't even know what you're talking about," he replies, a casual flick of his hand pushing aside his brown bangs.

"But you do?" asks Lily.

"I worked for a real estate firm while I was in Manhattan. I don't know much about air rights, but I have heard of them. What makes you ask?"

"My neighbor, Percy Bridges, was researching something about air rights for a series of articles, but his editor, Mrs. Fitzgerald, told him to trash the story. She fired him when he refused to give it up. This is all according to his son. I haven't been able to speak with him about it yet."

"You must mean Heir Rights. H-E-I-R," spells Bradley. "There was a documentary a year ago about Heir's Property or Heir's Rights. Seems many people in the South either don't have the money to make wills or don't trust lawyers and/or the legal system, or all of the above, especially older folks. So, lots die without a will, and their land becomes jointly owned by their descendants. As it passes through generations, the title to their land gets cloudy. One heir can't sell the land unless all heirs agree. If they don't agree or can't be located, the heir wanting to sell can take it to court, and the judge can order it sold at auction, most times way below market value."

"Wow. That does sound like it could be a problem," says Lily.

"Right. And another problem they run into is that most banks won't lend to people who don't have a clear title to their land," says Bradley, pushing his glasses up the bridge of his nose. "So, if farmers need to get a loan for crop production or what have you, they can't get one. Nor can they get energy conservation grants. Some can't even insure their homes without accurate deeds. When Katrina hit back in '05, many folks on the coast couldn't get FEMA assistance because FEMA relied on deeds to prove the land belonged to the disaster victims before it gave them any money."

Bradley couldn't have been older than five in 2005, so I'm amazed he picked all this up from his position here at the Chamber. Why would researching Heir Rights get Percy fired? There's got to be something there, though. If Penelope Fitzgerald didn't want people talking about it, then it's a safe bet she's into some shady dealings. There's a story here, and it might shed some answers on her murder.

"Thank you, Mr. Au... Bradley. That helps clarify things somewhat. Very nice meeting you," says Lily, turning to leave.

"Oh, honey, the pleasure is all mine," he says, giving her a wave and skipping into the back... literally skipping.

On the way out, Lily sees a table with brochures on it, highlighting many of the businesses in Cowherd and a brief introduction to their services. She flips through and sees it features both The Cowherd Butchery and Cristo Brothers Dairy. There's a photo of Niles Gibbons smiling at a ribbon cutting of his shop. There's also a photo of Tomás Cristo. Lily's eyes widen. *He's the man who was standing on the doorframe of the truck in front of the Fitzgerald house watching what was happening the day of the murder... the angry, buggy-eyed, grouchy camel guy.* She pockets a couple of brochures, thinking they can use these pictures for their murder board and spare them the pint-sized Polaroid paparazzi.

CHAPTER 18

November 7, 2024 – Thursday
Cowherd, Mississippi

Lily's halfway down the wide steps of the Chamber of Commerce when she hears shouting and squealing coming from across the green and looks over to see Bougie and Norma Jean in a knockdown drag-out. There's no other way to describe it. Not only are they yelling in the middle of the street, but they're also yanking each other's hair, pulling at each other's clothes, and screeching obscenities. The heel of one of Bougie's stilettos has broken off. It appears Bougie has torn out Norma Jean's hair clip, and any hair not clenched in Bougie's fist is flying everywhere.

Lily walks across the green, not wanting to get too close but hoping to find out what the ruckus is all about. Shoppers and store clerks peep out of windows and lean out of doors as the howls amplify.

"I already told you! I don't have it!" yells Norma Jean.

"You had it last Thursday night! It's there for the world to see on your Facebook page," retorts Bougie.

"Well, I don't have it now! Ow!"

"Then where is it, you jealous hag!"

"Who you callin' a hag, you hateful troll!"

Lily sees Sheriff Timmons lumbering down the steps of his office, breaking into an awkward jog to reach the women. He tries to insert himself between them, but this only earns him an elbow to his nose, causing his hat to fly off. He makes another go, and this time takes a finger to the eye. Grunting and panting, he takes a step back, landing on his hat. He pulls his walkie-talkie off his belt and screams, "Back-up! I need back-up on the green! Back-up stat, I tell ya'!"

Sheriff Timmons grabs an arm, but the brawling women spin him, and he's nearly thrown to the ground. "Stop it, you two heathens, or I'll toss you in for disorderly conduct," he yells.

Finally, two deputies arrive. They grab Bougie around the waist while the sheriff grabs Norma Jean. With significant effort, they separate the two, but the women are still hissing and cursing. They both have scratches on their faces. Bougie is breathing hard. Her face is fiery red, and her eyes are owlish and defiant, while Norma Jean, once she finished swatting her hair from her face, stands proud as a modern-day Joan of Arc.

"Now you two alley cats, calm down! I haven't had to break up a fight between y'all since you were in high school. Someone want to tell me what's going on?" asks the sheriff, wheezing out the words and gasping for breath.

At this, the caterwauling resumes with each talking over the other.

"One at a time! Norma Jean, you go first."

"Why does she get to go first?" screams Bougie, thrusting a sharp, red-nailed finger at Norma Jean.

"Cause I'm the law and I say so, so cut the cackle," he demands. "Norma Jean?"

"That cow accused me of stealing her scarf, which is a bald-faced lie! She left it in my shop, and I admit I wore it to the tap-house on Thursday night, but I didn't steal it. I expected she'd be there, so I was going to give it back to her."

"You wouldn't be talking about a Hermès scarf, would you?" asks Timmons.

"Yes, Sheriff, that's exactly what it was," screeches Bougie. "An expensive one, too. It cost more than she makes in a week."

"And where would said scarf be now?" asks the sheriff.

"She has it!" cries Norma Jean, pointing at Bougie. "It got hot in the taproom, so I took it off and put it on the table while I was dancing, and when I got back, it was gone. Niles said he saw her come in and take off with it."

"Niles Gibbons? Why, you man-stealing wench!" hisses Bougie.

"He ain't your man," yells Norma Jean, eyes narrowing like a viper, head wagging from side to side. "And we was just dancing, anyway. Not that it's any of your business. He said you grabbed it and ran off with it."

"Likely story! What'd you do with it? It was a gift from my mama," shrieks Bougie.

"It weren't no gift from your Mama," says Norma Jean, propping her hands on her hips. "You stole it from her; she said so right in her column."

"I thought you believed nothing she wrote in that rag," replies Bougie with a sneer. "She also said you made people's hair look like tumbleweeds."

"If people ask for tumbleweeds, I give them tumbleweeds," says Norma Jean with a smug smile.

Bougie gasps. "Why the nerve! Sheriff, I demand you arrest this harpy for theft and assault."

"I didn't steal nothin', and you were the one who pushed me first," screams Norma Jean, and, once again, they both lunge for the other with claws extended.

"Boys, cuff 'em both and bring them in. I've got lots of questions for these two, and they better hope to high heaven they have answers."

It takes all three of them to get the women into the sheriff's office, but they finally manage it despite the kicking, spitting, and ear-splitting wails. For the first time since she'd met him, Lily feels a little sorry for Sheriff Timmons.

☙❦☙

November 7, 2024 – Thursday
Cowherd, Mississippi

Returning home, Lily settles down to work on her actual job, which she's been neglecting. Even though she is part-time and can set her own hours, she's been feeling guilty for taking their money and giving meager time and effort in return this past week. Her latest assignment is to provide a synopsis and analysis of Edgar Allan Poe's *The Raven*. It's a poem she'd loved in college, and she once had every verse memorized. It's easy to understand *The Raven*'s appeal to a college student. The initial two stanzas beautifully capture the essence of melancholy, angst, and despair that permeates throughout:

> Once upon a midnight dreary, while I pondered, weak and weary,
> Over many a quaint and curious volume of forgotten lore—
> While I nodded, nearly napping, suddenly there came a tapping,
> As of some one gently rapping, rapping at my chamber door.
> "'Tis some visitor," I muttered, "tapping at my chamber door—
> Only this and nothing more."

The beauty and complexity of the ballad only expands and intensifies from these foreboding opening lines. All-consuming grief over the death of his Beloved leads the Bereaved into a journey from sanity to madness, from hopelessness to senseless and vain hope, a desperate resolve to ignore and forget the past wages battle with an inability to think of anything or anyone *except* the past and his dearest Lenore.

Ah, distinctly I remember it was in the bleak December;
And each separate dying ember wrought its ghost upon the floor.
Eagerly I wished the morrow;—vainly I had sought to borrow
From my books surcease of sorrow—sorrow for the lost Lenore—
For the rare and radiant maiden whom the angels name Lenore,
Nameless *here* forevermore.

Lily was well into her twenties before she understood why the poem bit so deep into her soul—the loss of her brother. And her mother as well. Though Poe was writing of a love interest, the undying devotion, intense grief, and temptation to pretend the Beloved are not lost forever were feelings that never left Lily—ever suppressed yet always simmering deep inside. Wounds that feel as if they will never heal yet wounds she will never relinquish even as she cries like Poe, "Take thy beak from out my heart."

Many times, like Paul's thorn in the flesh, Lily has begged God to make a way for her and Jackson to be reunited, even though she knows the reunion would only result in another sundering, more pain, more heartbreak. And she must keep her promise. So even as she prays for an end to their separation, she understands God knows they are half-hearted words. Words she must speak lest her heart burst…words to honor her devotion to, and love for, her brother. And gratitude too. She knows God understands her conflict and doesn't condemn her castle in the sky fantasies. The only "surcease of sorrow" for her heart is the assurance she and Jackson are both Believers and will both one day be home together with their God in a true castle in the sky. And most days it is enough.

CRES

Lily makes it to the school pickup queue a little earlier, and Chaney's not the *very* last to get picked up today. She spends the time in line trying to figure out how to tell him everything that happened that morning. The press conference had officially named Carothers as the murderer and Percy as his accomplice. Gibbons had taken off right after it ended. Then there was her visit to the Chamber of Commerce, where she learned that Tomás Cristo was the angry man she'd seen on the day of the murder. And of course, there was the brawl between Bougie and Norma Jean in the middle of the street.

As she expected, Chaney doesn't take it well, the part about Percy at any rate. Lily had expected at least a comment about how cool the cat fight was or that he wished he'd have seen it, but even the thought of that spectacle didn't lighten his heavy heart. At home, he goes to the murder board and adds the photos of Gibbons and Cristo from the brochure. Then he turns to Lily with a face of flint.

"Okay, Lily, let's go over the suspects, their motives, and what we've found out about them in the past few days."

Lily grabs the marker and a large piece of newsprint, waiting for Chaney's direction.

"All right," he begins. "The sheriff might think it's Carothers, but my number one pick as murderer: Bougie Fitzgerald, daughter of the victim. Belittled by PF all her life, PF cut off allowance. She's in debt, and she told Norma Jean she was going to come into money soon. She went for a haircut the day before the murder, even though she didn't need one. According to Norma Jean, Bougie left the scarf in her shop after her haircut. Bougie claims Norma Jean stole it, but Norma Jean claims Bougie retrieved the scarf at the taphouse according to Niles Gibbons. If Bougie is telling the truth, is someone framing her, or is she making these claims to throw suspicion off herself onto someone else? Maybe Norma Jean? Did Bougie steal the shears?"

Lily smiles at Chaney's concise, professional verbiage as she transcribes his summation using abbreviations and bullet points to keep up with his quick mind.

"Suspect Number 2 and the sheriff's favorite—along with my father, of course—Pastor Morris Carothers. He left in the middle of the night, and he was stealing from the church. Was PF in on it, or did she just find out about it, and he knocked her off?

"Suspect Number 3—Norma Jean Badger, beautician. PF slandered Norma Jean and nearly ruined her business. Norma Jean has some fierce bitterness toward PF and husband. She was once best friends with Bougie; now it seems they're all out enemies. Did the shears used at the murder belong to her? Is she trying to cast blame on Bougie, or is she lying? If she's lying, is it because she's actually the killer, or is she covering for someone else?

"Suspect Number 4—Niles Gibbons, butcher. PF insulted his business. I didn't see him as the killer until today, when he locked up his shop in the middle of the workday and left right after the press conference. Plus, he lied to *someone* about the scarf. That has suspicious written all over it. He's got ties with both Bougie and

Norma Jean. So, you think they're *romantic* ties? Could he have kept the scarf himself? But what about the poison and the shears? How did he get into the house? If he is involved, I'd say he has an accomplice—but NOT my dad.

"Suspect number 5—Mary Cristo Rose, Fitzgerald cook and housekeeper. PF and husband basically stole her family's land and house with their stuff inside. Of all the suspects, it would be easiest for her to put poison in PF's food, *and* she had keys to the house. She sneaked back into the Fitzgerald home after the murder, while it was still a crime scene. Was she trying to hide or destroy evidence?

"Suspect number 6—Tomás Cristo. PF and husband stole his family's land. Did he blame PF and/or her husband for father's death (arson) or brother's (hit and run)? But PF seemed to like him. She was talking up his business and using his products. Why was he so angry at the crime scene? Was it because he was sorry she was dead? That doesn't seem right to me, considering what she'd done to his family. If it's him, how did he get the scarf? Like Gibbons, he'd need an accomplice to gain access to the house. And what about the poison? Where would he have gotten it, and how did he give it to PF? Could he and his aunt, Mary Rose, be working together? Any other ideas, Lily?"

"That's a very thorough summation; I'm not sure what I can add, but I think it might be helpful if I could speak to Mrs. Rose. One thing I'm still trying to piece together, though, is why Penelope got so upset when your dad was researching Heir's Rights? I think there's more to that than we yet know. And what were she and Percy arguing about at the bank? Did he say anything to you about that?"

"No, but I'd say it had something to do with money. Pop's pension doesn't go very far, and Dad's not bringing in any money right now. I can see Dad gets tense whenever he pays bills. Maybe he wanted a loan, and she tried to block it. I think she was put on the Board in place of her husband."

"Sounds plausible. The only other question I have is…who let the dog out?"

She Had It Coming

QUIET DON'T MEAN STUPID

My family's name was once respected in this town—not for money or politics, but for the way we treated people. We just helped when we saw a need, we brought food, showed kindness, didn't ask for anything back. Folks said we were the kind of people who didn't judge, didn't boast, just worked the land and did what was right.

It was the kind of legacy you'd think would matter. But not to people like the Fitzgeralds.

People say you can't steal land if there's a signature and money exchanged. That just means they've never been on the losing side of a deal. A signature makes it legal. Doesn't make it right.

The lawyers say my grandmother signed willingly. Maybe she did. But no one talks about what leads a woman to give up the land her children were raised on. What grief does to judgment.

The truth is, the Fitzgeralds saw an opportunity. They dressed it up in legalese, wrapped it in kindness, called it a favor and a mercy—a chance for our family to "get back on our feet." But it wasn't charity. It was greed, plain and simple.

And if you made too big of a fuss... the Fitzgeralds had a way of silencing it.

Ask my brother, Luís. Someone opens the farm gate, and the cows get out. One minute he's herding 'em back across the road, and the next he's being dragged under a car. The sheriff said hit-and-run. No witnesses. Case cold in a week. Just because something can't be proven doesn't mean it's not the truth. But even if they could prove it, in Cowherd truth doesn't matter.

They took my father's good name. My brother's life. My family's land.

They think I'm quiet. Just the man who brings the milk.

That's fine.

Let them.

Tomás Cristo

156

CHAPTER 19

November 8, 2024 – Friday
Cowherd, Mississippi

Lily wakes a couple of minutes before the alarm is set to go off. She stretches, thinking about what she has to do today. Breakfast and getting Chaney to school on time are at the top of the schedule. *So far, he hasn't been technically late. If the bell is still ringing, it's just like when your car starts through a stoplight on a yellow light and it turns red in the middle of the intersection. You haven't run the light, right? Or is it left up to the discretion of any officer who may see you? Well, if that officer were Sheriff Timmons, a person might not only get a ticket, but he may haul them in for questioning, or worse. You gotta' love small-town America. Or not.*

It's Friday—one week after the murder. Will the toxicology results come today? Will they finally know what killed Penelope Fitzgerald? No newspaper today, since, as Sheriff Timmons so tactfully put it, all Cowherd journos are either dead or in jail. But hopefully, he'll release Percy tomorrow as the 96 hours will be up. I wonder if the sheriff kept Bougie and Norma Jean overnight.

Lily turns her alarm off and tosses off the covers. *I think I'll take a trip to visit the Cristo Dairy after I drop Chaney off. The bro-*

chure didn't say they allow tours, but it couldn't hurt to stop by and meet the man. Still, the thought fills Lily with a little frisson of unease. *Maybe I'll just drive by and scope out the place first.*

They arrive at school with five minutes to spare. It may not seem like much for seasoned parents, but for Lily, it's a huge win. Chaney is still downcast from yesterday's revelation that the sheriff has decided Percy is an accomplice to the murder. He slips out of the car whispering, "Bye, Lily," and shuffles across the pavement into the school. It breaks Lily's heart. *I will prove Percy's innocence if it's the last thing I do.*

CR&O

Lily programs the address for the Cristo farm into her GPS. Although it is directly behind her house, one must go around the town to access Raven Ridge Rd. If she were brave enough, she would just walk through the back gate, but it's clear she's not.

The day is pleasant, and Lily lowers the windows to enjoy the scents and sounds of nature. In Kentucky, they call unseasonably warm temperatures in autumn an Indian Summer, but she's been told some people call it Saint Martin's Summer. She remembers reading a legend about Martin of Tours. The story goes that on a rainy, cold day in November, Martin, a soldier and Christian, was traveling through Amiens, France, and came across a naked beggar. The sight moved him to pity and, taking his sword, he removed his own cloak and cut it in half, giving the other half to the beggar. At that very moment, the rain and clouds disappeared, and the sun appeared. Whether any of it's true, it's a beautiful lesson of humility and mercy, and it stuck with Lily.

Lily turns onto Raven Ridge, where a long stretch of pavement lies ahead, flanked by trees whose branches intertwine overhead, creating a canopy that fills her with a sense of wonder. The sun filters through the leaves, creating a sparkling tunnel of color. The road makes a 90-degree turn to run alongside a calm lake that reflects the sun and blue sky on its mirrored stillness. Peaceful and lovely.

Up ahead, a flock of birds is clustered around and circling over a brown mass on the lake shore, likely a deer considering its size. Vultures. A wake of vultures, to be exact—the taxonomical term used when they are feeding on a corpse. They slightly resemble professional wailers at a wake watching over and mourning for the dead. Except for the whole pecking the blood-soaked body to pieces and feasting on the carcass. Not for the first time, Lily wonders why it's not a murder of vultures instead of a murder of crows. During one sleepless night, she went down a Google rabbit hole in search of these unique names, with her favorite being the term "grumble" used to describe a group of pugs. So appropriate.

As she gets closer, the putrid smell of something dead wafts into the car, and she moves her hand over to the switch to raise the windows, only to grab the steering wheel again in a hard grip. She slams on the brakes and comes to an abrupt, jarring stop. Her body rocks forward, causing her seatbelt to pin her in place. The noise and commotion send some vultures flapping into the air, leaving only a few brave birds to guard their meal, which isn't a deer as she supposed. It's a man. Or what's left of him. Lily inches the car closer and sees fixed, glassy eyes staring into the heavens. And above the eyes, red hair once again standing on end like a legionnaire's plume. The dead man is Reverend Morris Carothers.

CR§∞

Two 911 calls—Lily dropped her phone, clumsily disconnecting the first after being dive bombed by a vulture—one dead man and about ten emergency vehicles later, it seems this is the most excitement this county has had since… well, since last week. But this time they showed up in hordes: law enforcement, forensic crime scene unit, emergency search and rescue, ambulance, coroner, fire department. They're all here. Sheriff Timmons is holding court, pointing, gesturing, blowing his whistle, and issuing commands, looking more like a school crossing guard than an officer of the law.

Lily has retreated into her car but still has a ringside seat to the proceedings. The sheriff had ordered her to "stay put," stating he would be with her "momentarily" and then they're "going to have a good long talk." Lily is sure the "good" will not be good at all and is hoping the "long" was a slip of the tongue.

A few locals have gathered to watch the action. This portion of the lake forms a half-moon inlet, with the opposite shores being only about 30 yards apart. Woods grow up close to the lake on the far side, and Lily notices a lone figure standing among the trees. It takes a moment, but she soon realizes it's Tomás Cristo staring stone-faced across the lake. Following his gaze, she sees Niles Gibbons standing on the other bank, glaring back with clenched fists and his face full of menace and rage. After a few minutes, Gibbons turns on his heel and walks to a car parked on the grass beside the road about 50 feet behind Lily. He doesn't look to the right or left as he goes and either doesn't see her or doesn't care to acknowledge her. She looks back across the lake, and Cristo has disappeared.

Lily sees Sheriff Timmons making his way toward her, and her heart sinks. She slinks down in the seat a bit but catches herself and jumps out of the car for fear Timmons might want to use it as an interview room. Being in a closed car with Sheriff Timmons is the absolute last place she wants to find herself.

"Well, Miss Jordan," he begins, "fancy meeting you here—at another murder scene. Two in one week. That don't feel like a coincidence to me."

"How do you know it's murder?" Lily asks.

"See that man right there in the white bubble suit?" He turns to point toward a man on the lake shore. "That's the coroner. He hasn't done a full exam yet, but he's seen wounds like that before. It's from a shotgun. It's definitely murder."

"Just what are you saying, Sheriff? You can't think I have anything to do with this death?"

"And why wouldn't I think that?" he asks, taking a menacing step toward Lily.

"You're free to search my car." Lily throws up her hands in surrender and takes a step back. "You'll not find a shotgun. Plus, I'm no expert, but he looks like he's been in the water for a while."

"And what causes you to say that?" asks the sheriff, glancing toward the lake.

"Well, for one, the body is bloated, and second, the smell."

"I didn't say you just now killed the man. You could be returning to the scene of the crime."

"Sheriff, do you treat every person who calls 911 for an injury or death as if they're a criminal? I can't see how that would win you many votes," says Lily. *Although why a town would elect this man is a mystery to me.*

"Don't change the subject." His voice turns gruff as he leans forward, piercing eyes fixed on her. "Just tell me what circumstances caused you to discover the body."

"I'm getting acquainted with the community, as you yourself suggested. It's a beautiful day, and I thought a pleasant ride in the country would be relaxing. When I turned the corner, I could see the vultures devouring something. I first thought it was a deer, but as I came closer, I could see it was Mr. Carothers."

"And how did you identify him?" he asks, putting his hands in his slacks pockets and rocking back on his heels.

"I've seen no one else in town with hair quite like his, and I had heard at the press conference he was missing. I just put two and two together."

"He has distinctive hair, I'll give you that," mumbles Timmons, glancing over to where the coroner is zipping the body bag.

"Sheriff, you don't have a smidgeon of evidence that I am responsible for this murder. Not even circumstantial evidence. You have insisted I sit here for hours, and I need to get back to town to pick up Chaney from school. Am I free to go?"

"You can go, but I will tell you what I told you before: don't leave town. I'll know if you do. I have eyes and ears everywhere."

Clearly, not everywhere, otherwise he would have cracked the case before it cost someone else their life.

ॐ

The delay at the lake caused Lily to be the caboose of the pick-up line again. She's been musing over just what the episode between Niles Gibbons and Tomás Cristo at the lake could be about. She reaches into her purse and pulls out the extra brochure she had picked up at the Chamber of Commerce. Something about the picture of the ribbon cutting at the butcher's shop has been niggling about in her mind. In the center is Niles Gibbons, the look on his face the polar opposite of what she witnessed today at the lake. The phrase "smiling from ear to ear" could have had its genesis in this man's joy. To his left are people she doesn't know, but the man on his right with his hand on Gibbon's shoulder is Tomás Cristo. He is also smiling like a fool, which is why she didn't recognize him at first. The touch of his hand, leaning forward toward Gibbons, the smile of delight. Something has happened to these men between the time they posed for this photo and the malevolence evident today on the shore. It's obvious they were once friends. The photo reminds Lily of a Poe quote: "*Years of love have been forgot, in the hatred of a minute.*"

Lily is still a few cars away from the front and can see Chaney shoving books and papers in an already overflowing backpack. He must have been doing his homework again. He pops up and runs to the car as soon as she approaches. As he hops in, she can see his mood has improved. Some people just have a buoyant spirit and good humor that can't stay crushed for long. One more thing to admire in this young man.

"Lily, I heard all kinds of sirens this morning. Do you know what's up?"

"As a matter of fact, I do, as I was the one who summoned them." She can't suppress a grimace as she says this.

"Really? Spill!" says Chaney, turning sideways in his seat.

She tells him about her plans for the morning, the vultures, the body and its identity, her conversation with Sheriff Timmons, accompanied by "Whoa!" "For real?" and "Dang!" from Chaney.

"The sheriff will have to let my dad out now," Chaney declares, his voice jubilant. "He couldn't have killed the guy if he was in jail."

Lily hopes this is true. She doesn't know much about the science of decomposition, but the poor man looked like he had been in the water for at least a few days, which may or may not take Percy out of the frame. But knowing the sheriff's methods up to now, she finds herself unsettled about the situation. Timmons is prone to jumping to conclusions and throwing caution to the wind. But she doesn't share these fears with Chaney. She can't bear to see him regress into despondency and despair.

"Can we drive out and see what's happening now?" Chaney asks.

Lily would love to see how things are progressing, and so it doesn't take much to convince her. When they arrive at the lake, they see divers on the bank and a tow truck backed up to the shoreline. Its driver has extended the truck's boom and stretched a heavy steel cable into the water, the winch turning to retract the line. Foaming water erupts with a whoosh and hiss, and the rear of a car becomes visible. The winch continues to rotate, and brown lake water spews from broken windows and around the chassis of the vehicle. Inch by inch, the cable reveals the car, looking like a prehistoric behemoth being dragged ashore, spouting and spuming its displeasure at being disturbed.

A deputy looks at the bumper and enters the plate number into an iPad and nods to the sheriff. Timmons looks around and notices Lily and Chaney and other bystanders gawking at the operation.

"Move along now, ya' hear? This is a crime scene, not a tourist attraction," he yells, waving his arms in a shooing motion.

The onlookers sidle off one by one. Lily and Chaney make a U-turn and do the same. Chaney is talking a blue streak, and Lily lets him talk as she ponders over the events of the past couple of days. The marshals had cautioned her to keep a low profile. That's a little difficult when accusations, fights, and murders are becoming an everyday occurrence—not to mention being looked at as a murder suspect herself. She just hopes Marshal Kelly doesn't call for an update. It may seem that she lies for a living now, but lying to him isn't something she's willing to do.

CRBO

November 8, 2024 - Friday
Lexington, Kentucky

Lying has become a way of life for Elton Jacks. Since he began his private eye career over a decade ago, he's told hundreds, possibly thousands, of lies. He tries to keep to the truth as much as possible, but his job demands a certain level of dishonesty. Each morning, he wakes and wonders if that day will be the day his deceptions catch up to him. Will it be the day all hope of a future where his actions once again align with the man he wishes to be—the man he once was—is lost forever?

Will the time ever come when he can put this life behind him? He has relentlessly wrestled with that question but cannot find an acceptable answer—an answer that doesn't betray promises made. Still, for now, he knows he can't escape it. He owes too much to people who matter.

The search for Elizabeth James has stretched his skills, and he has thrown himself into the search, excluding everything else. He's had to rely on every bit of his training in trying to outsmart WITSEC and the U.S. Marshals to locate her. It will take more than just trying to think like them; he *must* find a thread to grasp onto and follow.

The woman at the open house had said movers had put Elizabeth's furniture into storage the first or second week of May. He's scoured the police reports for that time frame, as well as death notices. There has to be something there that he's missing. But he won't quit. He can't.

If the government has placed her in WITSEC, she could be anywhere. And likely, the only way he'll find her is to find the one who put her there.

CHAPTER 20

November 9, 2024 – Saturday
Cowherd, Mississippi

When Lily was growing up, Jackson would make pancakes and bacon on Saturday mornings and then spend the day watching cartoons with her, even though he swore he was too old for them. That didn't stop him from belly laughing at *TaleSpin* and *Darkwing Duck*. So today, she gets up early to cook breakfast for Chaney, who's still snoring on the couch like a typical pre-teen.

Gathering the ingredients, Lily realizes she's never actually *made* pancakes. *But how hard can it be? Right?* She remembers seeing a cookbook on the shelf above the stove, and she tiptoes to reach it, hoping to find an easy recipe. Fumbling it on the way down, she grabs at it, and a piece of paper flutters down. She sets the book on the counter and picks up an old black-and-white photo of two small children, a boy and a girl. Turning it over, she sees the names Mattias and Maria written on the back.

A streak of light from outside the window grabs her attention, and she looks out to see blue lights flashing over at the Bridges' house. She slides the photo in her back pocket and, careful not to wake Chaney, slips out the back door. She searches for the opening in the shrubbery that Chaney had forged earlier. Unable to locate it, she forces and flounders her way through, emerging on the opposite side with scratches and leaves clinging to her hair and clothes. She heads to the Bridges' front door, brushing and swiping and smoothing—hoping she doesn't look like a demented birdwatcher.

The deputies have set up a crime tape around the perimeter of the yard, and she isn't able to reach the porch. Seeing a lone deputy stationed at the drive, she makes her way over to him, hoping he will explain what's happening. But evidently, the sheriff had warned him against speaking to the public, or maybe just to her, and he stands stoic as a guard at Buckingham Palace.

Lily looks toward the door, and Sheriff Timmons is heading her way. Had the man put a tracker on her? He seems to always know when she shows up.

"This is an official police investigation, Miss Jordan. Individuals with a proclivity for prying are unwelcome. *Once again,* I must ask you to disperse," says Timmons.

"I am simply looking after my neighbor's property, Sheriff."

"You are simply snooping and nosing into official matters. Please return to your house before I slap you with a citation for obstructing the course of justice. I plan to hold a press conference today at noon where I will inform you of any developments, just like every other town resident." He puts his hands on his belt, rocks back on his heels, and proceeds to stare her down. Seeing she has no other choice, she returns home, praying Sheriff Timmons concludes his search before Chaney wakes up.

CR80

Lily and Chaney walk downtown for the "press conference". News has gotten around, and the square is full of townspeople. Lily looks for Bougie and Norma Jean but cannot locate them, nor does she see Niles Gibbons or Tomás Cristo.

At noon, Sheriff Timmons walks out of the station to the microphone set up at the front of the group. Clearing his throat, he calls for attention.

"As most of you are already aware, we received a 911 call yesterday reporting the discovery of a deceased individual on the shores of Raven Lake. Upon arrival, we found the body of the Reverend Morris Carothers. We later retrieved his car from the lake. An autopsy revealed a shotgun wound inflicted at close range. The perpetrator then pushed the body, along with his car, into the lake from a high altitude, most likely Roost Ridge. The coroner estimates he has been dead for four to five days. Given this time-table, our assumption that he left his house in the early hours of Wednesday, November 6th, is in doubt. It's possible that he may have been as early as Sunday afternoon. Indeed, evidence found in his car points to a date prior to Tuesday, November 5th."

Hearing this, Chaney whispers, "November 5th. That's the afternoon the sheriff took my dad to jail." He moves a little closer to Lily and slips his hand into hers. She can feel a slight tremor in his fingers. His face is taut with tension, and his Adam's apple is quivering. She knows his mind is racing, making connections, and weighing the implications of Timmons' words.

"Inside the car we found…" he pauses, cutting his eyes toward Chaney. Clearing his throat, he continues. "Inside Carothers' car we found a watch with an engraving on the back stating, *To PB from PF for twenty years of service to the Cowherd Register.*"

Chaney now has Lily's hand in a death grip, and she thinks this may be the only thing keeping him on his feet. He knows what's coming.

"Given this finding, we conducted an additional search this morning of Percy Bridges' home, this time extending the scope of the search to include his car, which was not searched in the first examination of his property. Inside, we found strands of hair belonging to Penelope Fitzgerald, our first murder victim. Based on this evidence, I have charged Percy Bridges with two counts of first-degree murder."

At this announcement, many in the crowd gasp. Lily hears exclamations of "No!" and "Ah, come on, Sheriff!" Through the clamor, a gruff voice rises above the others. "You've got the wrong man!" Lily searches the crowd but cannot see who spoke, yet it seems the consensus of the community. It's obvious the locals hold Percy in high regard. Lily looks at Chaney and can tell he's barely holding himself together.

"Calm down, calm down!" The sheriff raises a hand, signaling for quiet. "We have a witness who has testified that on the morning of the murder, Mrs. Fitzgerald was visited by the now deceased reverend. The visit was brief, and we believe that he either unlocked the rear French door or exited through it, thus allowing access for the murderer to enter. According to Mrs. Rose, the cook and housekeeper, Mrs. Fitzgerald was still alive when the reverend left.

"As to the scarf and shears found at the scene, we believe that as an accomplice to the killer, Carothers stole these items to throw suspicion elsewhere and either planted them at the scene or gave them to the murderer. This is an educated guess based on and supported by the knowledge that he is a known thief. The toxicology lab has not yet determined the type of poison, which was the actual cause of death. But they have determined that it was ingested. We expect to have the results no later than Monday.

"It is a known fact that Mr. Bridges and the deceased have had a long-standing feud. He's an educated man and capable of procuring said poison. At this time, we are holding no other persons in connection with the murders. That is all." He then spins and hastens back into his office.

People from the audience crowd around Chaney, patting his shoulders, and saying they don't believe a word of it and not to worry, while many seek to encourage him by insulting the sheriff and his entire staff. Lily jumps when she feels someone touch her shoulder. She turns to find Pastor Meadows beside her. He reaches for Chaney's other hand and, taking it, leads them through the throng to his car parked down the block. A beautiful lady with silver-gray hair in an elegant French twist is sitting in the passenger seat. Pastor Meadows opens the back door, and Lily and Chaney slide in. The woman reaches her arm over the seat to introduce herself to Lily.

"Hi Lily, I'm Serena Meadows. It's so nice to meet you."

Serena is the perfect name for her, Lily thinks. *Her whole countenance emits peace and calm. Her smile is like sunshine bursting through stormy clouds.*

"Very nice to meet you, too. Thank you both for the rescue."

"It's our pleasure. I'm just happy we were here," says Pastor Meadows. "We'll just take you two on home now."

Relief washes over Lily, but then she hears Chaney beside her, sobbing as one stricken with an age-old grief. Heartbroken, she puts her arm around him, and he weeps into her chest. Crowds of townspeople still fill the streets, and it takes thirty minutes to maneuver around everyone to reach Lily's cottage. By then, Chaney's tears had worn him out, and he's cried himself to sleep.

Pastor Meadows lifts Chaney from the car and carries him inside, laying him on the couch. The adults then escape to the kitchen, where Mrs. Meadows sees the murder board and the suspect/motives list.

"I'm relieved to see you've ruled my husband out as a suspect." She chuckles, walking closer to inspect the board.

"Chaney didn't want to put him on there in the first place," admits Lily. "It was at my insistence, considering all Penelope had said about you both. To be fair, I hadn't met you then. I can see now it was off base."

"In truth, it should have been my name up there instead of my husband's," Serena says, turning toward Lily. "I was doubly angry—angry at what she said about me but mostly angry at how it hurt Stanley and cast a shadow over his ministry. We both hated to leave this church, but we fought the accusations until we were mentally and emotionally exhausted. I believe Stanley may have been the first and only person to have ever stood up to Mrs. Fitzgerald. In their hearts, I think the congregation wanted to support him, but dread of the Fitzgeralds is too ingrained into the fabric of the community. It's a fear passed down through generations."

"A generational fear… that's tragically heart-rending." Lily grabs a chair and motions for them to sit. "How does a family or a community get past an incessant cycle of fear?"

"Well, one way is to find the source and kill it. Which it seems someone has done," answers Pastor Meadows, pulling a chair out for his wife before sitting himself.

"I know of at least one person in town that would agree with that conclusion," says Lily. "I went for a manicure with Norma Jean Badger. She told me the murderer was 'no different from an assassin taking out a ruthless dictator.' She also had some pretty strong words to say about Frank Fitzgerald, saying anyone who crossed him lived to regret it or they could no longer regret anything."

"Oh, there were whispers of bullying and worse. Much worse. Nothing could ever stick to Frank Fitzgerald, one reason being his lifetime best friend, Timmy Timmons," says Brother Meadows.

"Timmy Timmons? Are you serious? The sheriff's first name is Timmy?" Lily's face glows with barely suppressed bemusement.

"His full name is Wilbur Timothy Timmons." Meadows nodded his head as he spoke. "Timmons' father, Wilbur, was Fitzgerald senior's right-hand man, not unlike a Mafia enforcer. There's a long history of intimidation and regret in Cowherd, going back even further than Frank's father, and it seems each generation of Fitzgeralds brings a new level of evil and abuse. There's a slew of stories, and they all have money and power behind them all."

"I haven't seen Timmons as all that corrupt. He seems more like an immature, bumbling oaf," Lily says, shaking her head slightly.

"That's what he wants everyone to see, but don't let it fool you. He's a dangerous man. Even more so since Frank died," Serena says, her expression serious.

"When did he die?" Lily asks, curiosity evident in her voice.

"It was in 2010, wasn't it, Stanley?" Serena glances at her husband for confirmation.

"That it was," agrees Pastor Meadows.

"The same year someone ran over and killed Luís Cristo?" Lily's eyes widen.

"The very same. Just a few weeks afterward, in fact," Serena adds, her voice thoughtful as she watches Lily process the information.

"How did Mr. Fitzgerald die?" Lily asks, leaning in, eager to understand more.

"He died of carbon monoxide poisoning," Meadows says. "Frank had issues beyond his insatiable greed for wealth and power—alcohol and women were two of them. He often visited his women, got drunk, and drove home, thinking he wouldn't get a DUI, which was true. My guess is that he came home late that night, drunk as usual, and instead of facing Penelope's wrath, he decided to sleep it off in the garage. But when they found him that morning, the car was still running, and the door was closed."

"Is it possible it was suicide?" Lily asks, her brow furrowed with concern.

"It's possible, I suppose. It would have been contrary to his character, but sometimes people can surprise you," says Meadows. "The sheriff ruled it an accident. I've always suspected it was murder."

"Murder? Do you think it could have been Tomás Cristo or Mrs. Rose? They may have thought Fitzgerald was involved in Luís' death. If so, that'd be a motive," says Lily.

"Sheriff Timmons checked that out before ruling it an accident. Tomás was in the hospital with a ruptured appendix. There's no way it could have been him."

"What about his aunt, Mary Rose?" asks Lily.

"I don't think he seriously looked at her. There were rumors Penelope wanted to get a quick insurance payout, so she pressured Timmons to go forward with the accident theory."

"Who do you think it was, Stanley?" Serena leans forward, her hands clasped together on the table.

"I think it was a family member," he replies, tapping his fingers thoughtfully against the tabletop.

"As in Bougie or Penelope?" Lily interjects, her gaze shifting between them, curiosity flickering in her eyes.

"It could have been either, in my mind. Odds would be on Penelope, spurned wife and all. But in my gut, I always felt it might have been Bougie. She was recovering from grief over the death of her boyfriend, Luís Cristo."

"What? She was dating Luís Cristo?" Lily's jaw dropped in astonishment.

"Indeed. And you know, I've always felt there were a lot more horrors going on in that house than anyone outside of it knew."

"Secrets," murmurs Lily. "Every house has secrets." And as Lily knows too well…

There are some secrets which do not permit themselves to be told.

CHAPTER 21

November 10, 2024 – Sunday a.m.
Cowherd, Mississippi

Lily and Chaney attend Brother Meadows' church in Seaton on Sunday morning. Titled "Trusting Through Tough Times," the message centers on the passage from Habakkuk 3:17-19.

> ¹⁷ Though the fig tree does not bud
> and there are no grapes on the vines,
> though the olive crop fails
> and the fields produce no food,
> though there are no sheep in the pen
> and no cattle in the stalls,
> ¹⁸ yet I will rejoice in the LORD,
> I will be joyful in God, my Savior.

> ¹⁹ The Sovereign LORD is my strength;
> he makes my feet like the feet of a deer,
> he enables me to tread on the heights.

"We can come through difficult times with our faith strengthened and refined instead of shattered. How? We must come to the point in our lives where we long for God more than we desire *anything* else—relationships, personal comfort, wellness, prosperity, earthly security, and freedom from hardship. God may not take us out of hard or hurtful or seemingly hopeless situations in the way or in the time we want. If He doesn't, we not only need to trust He *will* bring us through but trust His goodness *while we're still walking in them.* Remember the confession of the three Hebrews boys—Shadrach, Meshach, and Abednego in Daniel 3. As the soldiers were throwing them into the blazing furnace, they professed, 'the *God* whom we serve is able to save us… but even if he doesn't…'"

In his conclusion, he gives a challenge to ponder: "What if things don't change in your present circumstances? What if it never gets better on this earth? What if you must wait for heaven to receive full healing and restoration?"

Sobering thoughts. Lily bows her head. *Lord, help me to always profess that I know You are able, but even if You choose not to change my circumstances, I will praise You. I will trust You. You are Sovereign, and You are good.*

CR&SO

Chaney's Pops calls him not long after he gets home from church. Through many tears, he explains the updates to the case and that Sheriff Timmons had charged his dad with two counts of murder. His grandfather tells him he'll be back the next day. And he'll insist on seeing Percy then and try to get the sheriff to allow Chaney to visit, too.

Lily had been thinking about her statement that every house had secrets. Then the thought struck her: *What about my cottage?*

What secret is it keeping? She thinks about the upstairs with all the abandoned and forgotten Cristo history. It seems the Fitzgeralds caused a lot of grief to the Cristo family in the past. Could there be something up there that might help the case? She hates to go through someone's personal papers, but finding anything that might help Percy would be a blessing. Plus, it might keep Chaney busy and keep him from dwelling on his father's situation.

"Hey Chaney, want to go on a treasure hunt?" Lily asks when Chaney hangs up the call with his Pops.

"Treasure hunt? Whatcha' mean, Lily?"

"Let's check out the second floor. There's lots of stuff left from the Cristos up there. Maybe we can find some information related to the case."

"I thought you said it was haunted?" says Chaney, giving her the side-eye.

"I didn't say haunted; I said it was spooky." Lily's eyes dance with mischief, hoping to ignite his curiosity.

"Same thing." He scrunches his nose and puts his hands on his hips.

"Not quite. It was a cloudy day when I was there before. It's sunny today, and we can open the windows. Plus, there's a light hanging from the ceiling. I tried the switch before, but it didn't work. It might just need a new bulb."

"Well, alright," says Chaney, still looking at her like she's crazy.

Lily retrieves a new bulb, and with the help of Chaney holding her cell phone's flashlight, she's able to replace the old one. A flick of the switch and light floods the room. It doesn't do much to squelch the spooky factor, but she puts on a brave face and opens the sooty, dust-covered windows, bringing in some fresh air and relieving some of the mustiness.

Lily looks around the room and, now that there's more light, she can see a bed, nightstand, dresser with a cracked mirror, desk, and chair. On the right wall, there are four filing cabinets with nearly empty drawers. Papers and file folders cover the floor in dozens of haphazard stacks. Knee walls, rising three feet high before angling up to the ceiling, have peeling wallpaper hanging in strips. And cobwebs. Lots of cobwebs.

Surveying the place, Chaney exclaims, "Whoa! I never seen anything like this before. Look how thick that dust is. When did Pastor Meadows say the Roses had to leave this house?"

"It was after Luís died, so around 2010."

"So, maybe fourteen years since someone was up here. Longer than I've been alive."

Fourteen years doesn't seem all that long ago but also like a lifetime. A lot can happen in that time…like a person could be going on their third identity…

"Maybe," says Lily. "But it looks like someone was searching for something. See how the filing cabinets are nearly empty, with files and papers scattered across the floor?

Chaney nods. "Whoever decided it was a good idea to put wallpaper on the ceiling?" He wonders aloud, his eyes making a track from the wall up to the ceiling.

"That was popular back in the day," Lily replies, staring at the peeling paper.

"Looks plumb stupid to me." Chaney wrinkles his nose skeptically, his gaze darting between the wallpaper and Lily.

Lily studies the knee wall and angled ceiling up to the apex in the center of the room.

"Sometimes there's a door in knee walls leading to an attic," she says. "But with this wallpaper being a single swath from the floor to the ceiling, if there is one, it's hidden."

"A hidden door?" Chaney's eyes widen. "Really? Like leading to a secret room?"

"Well, not a finished room, just an attic." Lily surveys the space, wondering what secrets might lie hidden in the wall's recesses.

"Think there's one here?" Chaney asks, his expression eager as he inspects the walls for any sign of a concealed door.

"Only one way to find out." Lily goes to a knee wall and runs her fingers over the wallpaper, feeling for ridges. Chaney tears into the wallpaper like it's the best job he's ever had. At first, she thinks she should stop him but then decides it doesn't matter.

"Here!" exclaims Chaney, stripping more paper to expose a door about three feet high and slightly less wide. He squeezes his fingers into the crack between the door and the wall and gives several hard tugs. The door drags open with a slow scrape and a screech, just like a real haunted house.

Taking out her phone, she clicks the flashlight app. Both she and Chaney kneel to look in. The attic is hot and stuffy and smells like mothballs and somewhat of smoke. She sees ancient, degrading insulation between the joists. *Probably asbestos insulation.*

"Chaney, don't touch the insulation," she warns.

"Look, Lily. Over there! It looks like a metal box." He points across to a dented and scarred blue metal box on a board laid over the joists. It looks like a lunch box with a domed lid. She puts a knee on the joist closest to her and stretches across to it.

"Open it up!" exclaims Chaney.

"Let's take it over by the window," Lily suggests.

Once there, Lily depresses the push button latch mechanism and opens the box. The first document on top is the missing life insurance policy for Mattias Cristo and, underneath, the Cristo home insurance documents.

"I guess Mattias didn't tell his wife where he had stored the insurance papers," Lily murmurs.

"Why would he keep them there, though?" asks Chaney. "Seems weird to me."

"Me too. What else is in here?"

"Here's a marriage license for Mattias and Miss Camilla in February 1978," says Chaney.

Lily removes a faded photo that appears to be from the '70s, based on the clothing. Six teenagers look out of the picture. She turns it over and reads aloud the names listed there: "Frank, Andrea, Jeanie, Timmy, Penelope, and Mattias. And look, underneath the names someone has written, 'The Mockingbirds—May 3rd, 1976.'"

"Wait—they were all friends?" Chaney raises his eyebrows in surprise.

"Maybe," says Lily. "The two guys on the ends don't appear to like each other much based on their body language and expressions."

Chaney grasps a corner of the photo and leans in. "There's Frank Fitzgerald, Penelope Fitzgerald, Timmy Timmons. Is this Mattias Cristo?" he asks, pointing to one boy on the end. "So, who are Jeanie and Andrea?"

"I don't know, but Jeanie looks somewhat like Norma Jean Badger." Lily puts the photo aside as she notices some yellowed newspaper clippings. She reads the articles one after the other, her mind filling with astonishment and suspicion. *How could we have been so wrong?*

1976

CHAPTER 22

April 30, 1976 - Friday
Cowherd, Mississippi

Penelope Lloyd studied her reflection in her locker mirror and applied another swipe of mascara. Her mother didn't allow the *devil's wand* in her house, so Penelope kept it at school, along with hairspray, lipstick, blush, and perfume. She also kept a sewing kit in case she needed to take her skirt hem up a few inches. Her mom had a strict "no more than one inch above the knee" rule. It was puritanical and priggish in Penelope's mind. She refused to look like a Victorian spinster. Her mother had her heart set on Penelope snagging Frank Fitzgerald, and there's no way he would ever look twice at a goody-goody, plain-faced prude.

Grabbing her hair spray, she coated her hair for the third time. The kids on either side of her locker are used to her primping, and they ducked and ran just in time. Penelope had doused them too many times. She painted her lips blood-red, blew herself a kiss, grabbed her binder and English book, and slammed the locker door with an echoing boom.

English was her favorite class, not only because it was the last class of the day, but also because the teacher, Mr. Keith, said she had a future in journalism. He had put her in charge of the *Daily Life at Cowherd High* column in the school newspaper, of which he was the editor. Her articles seemed to bring him a lot of pleasure considering all the chortles, snorts, and sniggers he made while reviewing them. But then he took out the best parts, saying he valued his job.

But really? What in the world was wrong with telling the truth? I mean, Miss Love IS short on love, and she and everybody else would be better off if she'd find herself a man. And I DID see Mary Cristo and Sam Rose coming out from under the bleachers after Homecoming looking guilty to the max. I need to tell it like it is if I'm going to be a hard-hitting journalist like Diane Sawyer: beautiful, smart, and invincible.

Penelope walked into class and saw Frank sitting in the back row against the wall. In front of him, his shadow, Timmy Timmons, sat backward atop his desk, facing Frank. *I wish Frank had a more respectable best friend. Timmy is a putz who thinks he's Casanova. He's always saying things like, "Hey foxy mama, you are slammin today!" or "My man, my man! What it is?" Frank says Timmy's just going through a phase and calls him a wanna-be jive-talker. Jive-turkey is more like it. If I'm going to marry Frank Fitzgerald, Timmy-boy will need to take a chill pill.*

On the back row, on the opposite side of the room by the windows, sat Mattias Cristo. *Frank Fitzgerald is handsome, though not as handsome as he thinks he is. But Mattias Cristo is drop dead, out-of-sight gorgeous, like the pictures my mom has of James Dean. Total dreamboat. I just wish he had as much money as Frank. 'Not in your league,' my mom would say. What she'd really be saying is, 'he's not able to keep you (meaning us) in a style to which you (we) aspire'. My dad would just say, 'He's Eye-Tal-Yun'. End of story. We sure would give them some pretty grandchildren, though. Of course, Mattias' mother has those buggy eyes. It'd be a real shame if any of our future kids were to inherit those.*

Momma said Frank and Mattias have been rivals since they were in diapers. They're neighbors and got into dozens of fistfights in the fields around their homes before they even started first grade. They're still crazy competitive, playing every school sport. Cowherd High doesn't have a wrestling team—otherwise they'd have joined just for the chance to 'legally' try to squeeze the life out of each other.

Penelope slid into the front middle desk next to her best friend, Jeanie Badger, just as Mr. Keith came bustling in carrying a stack of books with papers tumbling out at every angle. He's known for his disorganization and personal disorderliness and is easily the most eccentric teacher at Cowherd High. At only 4'11", he was almost as round as he was tall. His bushy beard and wild, curly salt-and-pepper hair only added to his eccentricities. His frequent outrageous comments meant he was habitually in trouble with the principal, which also made him the most popular teacher at Cowherd High.

"Okay, hush, you Philistines! I'm assuming Big Brother knows which delinquents are missing, so I will forgo the onerous and banal roll call." Mr. Keith dumped his bundle on his desk.

"Nobody could ever accuse you of being onerous or banal, that's for sure!" someone in the back heckled. Penelope craned her neck around and saw it was Frank. He was sitting, slunk down in his seat, vainly running his fingers through his jet-black hair. His crooked smile looked like trouble. *Yeah, he's cute, but so pompous and egotistical. Still, he's richer than Fort Knox… well, his dad is, anyway. He would know how to keep a girl in style.*

"Mr. Fitzgerald, I doubt you know the definition of either of those words." Mr. Keith folded his arms across his chest, smirking as the class erupted with laughter. Frank laughed too, but Penelope could see his face had stiffened like hard plastic, his electric blue eyes boring into Mr. Keith. He didn't like to be laughed at, but he knew he'd look more the fool if he didn't join in.

"All right, I've got fun news for you geniuses. The guys sitting up there in their ivory tower have decided that the last week of school we're going to have a Literature Showcase and Science Fair. So, each of you will submit an entry into this inspired extravaganza. The fun part? This will be a group activity—think bosom buddies," Mr. Keith said with a snicker. "The project will count for 10% of your grade, and the group that vanquishes all others will receive 5 points added to their final grade. I expect this will take up each class period until the showcase on May 14th, as well as additional after-school convos and confabs, since you only have two weeks to finish the project.

"Each group will pick a book we've read this year. The assignment is to create a literary review centered on the chosen book. There will be two parts to the project, which you will combine into a publication, such as a newspaper or folio. Here are the requirements:

"Character Interview: Each group member will choose a character to represent. I expect this aspect alone might cause internal feuds, but you'll just need to employ your highly developed negotiation skills to get it sorted. Through a series of interviews, each character will gain insight into the desires, motivations, and thought processes of their counterparts. You will then draft an account of the interviews. For some of you," he paused, looking squarely at Timmy, "this may require re-reading the book, which you will need to do in your own time.

"Book Review: Each member will draft a book review using their own impressions of the book, as well as information they've gleaned from the character interviews. You need to discuss plot, conflict, character arc, etc. Additionally, you are to explore any metaphors, symbolism, and overall message of the work.

"Your group will spend today choosing the book you wish to use for the assignment. There will be NO yelling, hitting, or mauling on penalty of death. Or banishment to the principal's office, whichever I feel is most appropriate. The groups will be:

"Group 1—Jeanie Badger, Mattias Cristo, Frank Fitzgerald, Penelope Lloyd, and Timmy Timmons…"

Mr. Keith continued to assign groups, but Penelope had tuned him out. Mattias and Frank in the same group—one she was in as well? *This could be fun.*

ᙎᘓᙇᘔ

Frank Fitzgerald pulled his desk into a circle with his project mates, being sure to be positioned between the two girls and as far away from Mattias as possible.

Timmy scooted his desk to the other side of Penelope and put his arm around her shoulders. "Hey, pretty lady. I hope you know CPR, because you take my breath away."

Penelope groaned and gave him an elbow to the ribs; still, he looked as happy as a pig in the sunshine.

"Hey now! Teach just said there was to be none of that," said Timmy, rubbing his side.

"He also said 'no mauling,' which can mean several things, one of which is 'cruel or harmful treatment or abuse.' I consider *you* touching *me* to be exactly that. You better watch yourself… I'll sic a hunky beefcake on you." Penelope's flirtatious smile danced between Frank and Mattias as she spoke.

Timmy threw up his hands. "Chill, Jill! And you can stop giving me the hairy-eyeball. I's just razzin' with ya'. Some people just can't take a joke."

"Some people have better things to do than put up with a clown like you," said Penelope, tossing her hair over her shoulder.

"Agreed. Okay, what book do you all think we should do? Let's make a list of the books we covered. There was *Jane Eyre*…"

"Too girly." Frank's lips twisted into a mock grimace.

"There was *The Count of Monte Cristo.*" Penelope winked at Mattias, a mischievous glint in her eyes.

"Too long." Timmy dropped his head onto his desk with a thud.

"We don't have to read it again; we can just go from our notes," said Jeanie.

"What notes?" Timmy jolted upright, mischief dancing in his eyes. "Plus, I'm going to confess to y'all right here: I did the Cliff Notes translation for every book we read except *Animal Farm.* That one was far out! Comrades unite! No clothes for anybody!"

"That's not exactly how it went." Mattias crossed his arms, shaking his head.

"Close enough. Don't ya' think it's a great motto, though?" Timmy opened his arms wide, as if welcoming them to embrace his vision.

"No!" Penelope and Jeanie chorused, their synchronized denial echoing through the room.

"We read *Emma.*" Penelope twirled a strand of hair around her finger.

"Too stupid," Frank said, rolling his eyes as he slouched back in his chair.

"And *Emma* was last year. What about *Anna Karenina*?" Jeanie asked.

"Too depressing!" said Frank and Mattis in unison, then proceeded to give each other the hairy-eyeball.

"Well, we've got to pick something," Penelope said, glancing around the room. "What else did we read?"

"*Middlemarch*," said Jeanie, which brought blank stares around the circle.

"I didn't understand half of that brick," Penelope admitted with a rueful shake of her head.

"What about *To Kill a Mockingbird?*" suggested Mattias. "It wasn't all that long. Not girly, stupid, depressing, or confusing."

"Only if I get to be the cat," said Timmy.

"What cat?" they asked in unison, turning to look at Timmy.

"The one that kills the mockingbird, of course," he said to their astounded faces. "I'm just joshing ya'," he said, laughing. "But I want to be Dill."

"Done," said Penelope. "I'll be Scout."

"I'll be Calpurnia," said Jeanie.

"Well, we know who needs to be Tom Robinson, the rapist." Frank looked pointedly at Mattias.

"Glad you volunteered," said Mattias. "In that case, I'll be Atticus."

"I didn't volunteer, you jerk. I was going to be Atticus." Frank's face twisted into a sulky pout, his expression falling flat of the condescending sneer he envisioned it to be.

"And Tom Robinson wasn't a rapist; he was an honorable man," said Mattias.

"Yeah, whatever." Frank rolled his eyes.

"Mattias said Atticus first, Frank. You can be Jem… or Boo, but we really need a Jem," said Penelope.

"I'll be Boo for the interview portion only," offered Mr. Keith, who had been eavesdropping. "He's the hero, after all."

"Great! That's all settled," said Penelope. "Let's all go home tonight and review our notes—or in Timmy's case, start reading the actual book. We can exchange telephone numbers to arrange times for the interviews outside of class."

"I think we should do the interviews in class." Frank looked at Mattias with contempt. "There's a few of y'all I don't care to see any more than I have to."

"Well, we can start them in class, but we need to budget our time so we get everything done. I'll write up a timeline of our objectives to keep us on track. We can approve it tomorrow." Penelope insisted.

"Listen to our girl, Frank. Timelines, objectives, budget. She's downright Polly Professional," said Timmy.

The classroom door swung open, and Andrea Gibbons, the new preacher's daughter, walked into the classroom, capturing everyone's attention. Her family had moved to Cowherd during Christmas break. This caused a significant disruption of the hierarchy among the female students. Penelope and her posse typically dictated whether a newcomer would be accepted or shunned using an ever-evolving criterion known only to Penelope. The rest of the class would follow suit, whether consciously or subconsciously.

Penelope had given Andrea a thumbs down, evidenced by a smirk and snort. Likely because Andrea was blond, fit, and an excellent gymnast. The rejection, however, didn't stick to Andrea, and most of the class, both girls and boys, welcomed her to Cowherd with open arms. She had been a cheerleader at her old school, and when Andrea asked to join the squad mid-year, the coach had eagerly agreed. This may have been because she could execute back handsprings and aerial cartwheels almost the entire length of the gymnasium, beating Penelope's record by 20 feet.

"Oh yes, Miss Gibbons," said Mr. Keith. "I forgot you were going to be late today. We're starting a group project for the end-of-year Literature Showcase. You can join this group. Miss Lloyd will fill you in on the assignment," he said, pointing to Penelope.

Frank pulled his desk aside so Andrea could pull hers into the group next to him, and Timmy got up and tugged and scraped his desk over to her other side. It wasn't difficult to see how Penelope felt about this development when she sniffed and scooted her own desk back a few feet, as if afraid of contagion. But either Andrea was oblivious to her censure or couldn't care less. Andrea was confident in herself, and her warm personality usually won over any faultfinders. She hadn't been in Cowherd long enough to realize Penelope's icy heart was impervious to most charms.

"I'm sorry I'm late," Andrea said. "Can y'all fill me in?"

Frank and Timmy were happy to cozy up and catch her up.

"So, who should I be?" she asked.

"Well, I think it's obvious the only other female main character is Mayella Ewell. I think you'll make a smashing Mayella," said Penelope, with thinly veiled disdain.

"No way," said Frank. "There're other girls. There's Aunt Stephanie, Mrs. Dubose, or Miss Maudie."

"I think she best suits Miss Maudie," said Mr. Keith.

"Hey, we should call ourselves 'The Mockingbirds,'" says Andrea. "I love mockingbirds."

Just then, the bell rang. "Yay! They're kicking us out early!" said Timmy, springing from his seat.

"It's a pep rally, you dork." Frank stood.

"Yay, a pep rally!" said Timmy.

They gathered up their things in a rush to get out of class; the boys needed to change into their basketball uniforms and Penelope, Jeanie, and Andrea into their cheerleading outfits. Frank saw Penelope turn to Mattias and whisper something in his ear, causing him to put his hand on her back and laugh.

"That dude better watch himself," Frank said to Timmy as they left the classroom.

"Don't worry about losing out on Penelope, Frankie," replied Timmy. "She's too high maintenance for that cat. He's all hat and no cattle. Why, give him two nickels for a dime, and he'd think he's rich."

CHAPTER 23

April 30, 1976 - Friday
Cowherd, Mississippi

The gym was loud and hot and smelled like varnish and sweat. The custodian had recently re-coated the gym floor, and it shone like glass. Teachers had opened windows at the top of the bleachers and propped open the exterior doors to let air circulate.

Frank peeked out of the dressing room and saw the band filing in, hitting each other with their instruments as they navigated the bleachers' steps. Some horns began warming up, sounding like elephants on parade. Around the gym, banners with pictures of the seven graduating athletes announced Senior Recognition Day.

Once the band had settled and situated, the director raised his arms for them to stand, and the underclassmen cheerleaders raced onto the floor with three rolled banners. The principal stepped into the announcer's box and welcomed the students to the last pep rally of the year, and rowdy applause erupted.

"Today and at tonight's game, we are honoring our graduating seniors, and here to introduce them is Cowherd's very own 'Howard Cosell'—Skip Matthews!"

The band struck up the school fight song while two cheerleaders rushed to the front of the locker room door, unrolling the first banner, which said, "We're Big!" painted in large letters.

"Welcome, Cowherd Bulls!" Skip screamed into the microphone, accompanied by a roar of applause and shrill whoops and whistles. Hundreds of feet stomped and stamped, reverberating through the gym like thunder. Skip extended his arms and motioned, with his palms down, hoping to lower the din enough to be heard, and the band director constricted the motion of his baton to signal de-crescendo.

"First the Senior boys!" announced Skip. "Welcome our co-captains: Mattias Dante Cristo and Franklin Norman Fitzgerald!"

The fight song again blared through the gymnasium as the two boys battered down the banner. The coach had told them to give each other high fives once they were on the floor. Instead, they pushed each other and moved to stand as far away from the other as the coach would allow.

The crowd loved it, and their volume amped up.

Two more cheerleaders sprinted over and unfurled a second banner reading, "We're Bad!"

"Next, we have Samuel Collins Rose and Wilbur Timothy Timmons!" continued Skip.

The two boys punched through the banner, and Timmy dropped to the floor to execute several somersaults, springing back to his feet with raised arms and bowed to the crowd. The student body shrieked and guffawed, pointing and punching the air in shared revelry.

A third set of cheerleaders unfurled a banner proclaiming, "We're Boss!"

"Finally, welcome the femme fatales of Cowherd High Cheerleading: Jeanie Badger, Andrea Gibbons, and Penelope Lloyd!"

The three girls burst through the banner, flipping and twirling through the air. The already frenzied crowd broke out in wolf whistles, howls, and catcalls. Penelope and Jeanie stopped tumbling mid court, and Andrea pulled up, as well.

The boys ran to the bench, grabbed basketballs, and began their warm-up drills. The cheerleaders gathered in the center of the gym to pump up the crowd. As if it needed it. As it was, the windows were vibrating, and several teachers had covered their ears. Mr. Keith sat on the sidelines in a webbed lawn chair with his arms folded across his chest and earmuffs perched atop his bushy hair.

The staff had arranged for some of the younger teachers to play against the boys' team, and for the next 45 minutes, the gym rang with raucous laughter, punctuated by playful boos and taunts. Finally, the last bell of the day rang out, and the students poured out of the bleachers like ants. Frank reached out to pull Andrea close and leaned toward her.

"Hey, would you like to go to prom with me?" he asked loudly, cutting an eye at Penelope.

"Well, I'll need to ask my dad. But if he's okay with it, I'd love to go with you," Andrea answered.

"Cool! You can let me know at the game tonight." He winked, his swagger on full display.

"Sure," she said with a smile, and turned to bounce off to the locker room. Frank cocked his head and stared at Penelope with raised eyebrows and a crooked grin. She stared back—knives were in those eyes—then she flipped her hair, turned, and flounced off the floor.

CRSO

The Cowherd Bulls lost to the Seaton Saints 79-80. Just when they felt victory was in their grasp, Frank decided he was going to make the last shot, regardless of how many other players were open. He threw an air ball just as the buzzer screeched.

"Serves him right for being so catty to me," Penelope told Jeanie as they gathered the pom-poms after the game.

"Can boys be catty?" asked Jeanie with a wry smile.

"Of course they can!" said Penelope. "Someone who's catty is spiteful and cruel; they have claws that pierce and slice and tear. Frank is the embodiment of catty."

She watched as Andrea ran to grab her father on the sidelines and pulled him over to meet Frank. They had a brief conversation emphasized by grins and nods, but Frank's smile didn't quite reach his eyes, and he struggled to mask the tension in his shoulders. But Andrea was all smiles.

"Did her dad make Frank ask permission to take his daughter out?" asked Penelope, astounded. "How Victorian. Will he go with them to the prom as well?"

"I think it's kind of sweet," said Jeanie, watching them with a winsome smile.

"You would!" retorted Penelope, picking up the pom bags and flinging them at the foot of the ball rack for the team manager to take care of. Swinging their cheer bags on their shoulders, she and Jeanie headed for the locker room.

"I'm supposed to be going to prom with Frank," Penelope whined. "I've got to get him back."

"I don't know why y'all broke up in the first place," said Jeanie. "I mean, you two had the longest running off-and-on romance in the school—since 8th grade. Tell me again why you broke up?"

"Because he's controlling, predictable, and boring. Frank plans on taking over his dad's construction company after high school. He doesn't want to go to college or see the world. I want to get out of this hick town and backpack across Europe. He laughed at me when I suggested it. He's got no imagination or sense of adventure whatsoever."

"Yeah, but he's rich as Croesus and has those blazing blue eyes and wavy black hair," Jeanie sighed. "You've got to admit he's the most handsome guy in school."

"Maybe if he didn't frown so much. Honestly, I think Mattias is tons cuter and way nicer. He's polite and chivalrous and kind. He talks to me like I'm a lady."

"Why don't you date *him,* then?" asked Jeanie, throwing open the locker room door.

"He's poor and bourgeois according to my mother. She'd never allow it."

"What's bourgeois mean exactly?" Jeanie's nose wrinkled, as if the word held an unpleasant aroma.

"You know, common, middle class. Mother calls them pretentious, grasping, covetous, wannabe elites." Penelope dropped her cheer bag onto the bench.

"Your mother is such a snob." Jeanie shook her head. "And that doesn't sound like Mattias."

"Daddy calls him a foreigner and an immigrant and other vile things. They may be Italian, but it's not like they just landed at Ellis Island. They're just as American as we are."

"And your dad's a racist bigot," said Jeanie, putting a foot onto the bench to unlace her cheer shoe.

"You have no idea," said Penelope.

CREO

Frank hated to lose. His dad hated it when he lost. He told Frank before he left for the game tonight that if Frank didn't beat those Seaton rednecks, he'd beat him black and blue.

Beat the rednecks or be beaten like a redneck. Some people might call that an ironic dichotomy—more like demonic. I thought I could make that last-minute shot and win the game. I'd be the hero. But heroes aren't losers. I might even have to head over to the Cristo farm tomorrow and pick a fight with that jerk, Mattias, like when I was a kid so people wouldn't know Dad had put bruises on me. Get more bruises to hide others.

Since middle school, his dad had gotten more creative in his "discipline" so as not to leave marks where people would notice. Sometimes it was a wooden paddle with holes bored in it. He wouldn't be able to sit without pain for days. Sometimes he would make him sleep in the damp basement or make him sit naked in a tub of ice. Sometimes he wouldn't let him eat for days. One summer at the lake, his dad pushed him out of their boat and left him.

It took me two hours to swim back to shore. That was the summer Mom left. Left Dad and left me. I was nine.

Sneaking in his window, he thought he was home free—until he saw his dad sitting in his room in the dark. Waiting. He tried to go back through the window, but his dad grabbed him by his hair and dragged him back inside. Frank knew he could fight back. Arthur Fitzgerald was a big man, yet Frank was as big as his dad now. But experience had conditioned him that fighting back was a poor idea. An extremely poor idea. "Try to hurt me, and I'll hurt something you love," his dad had told him. A toy, a pet...mom. He threatened once to hurt one of his friends. Timmy...Penelope. *No, it's better to just stand here and take it like a man.*

CRBU

Penelope had intended to start the project timeline when she got home. She needed a good grade on this. She had flubbed the Middlemarch exam.

Seriously, what was that book even about? A million pages of people making the worst life choices imaginable. Everyone was either miserable, manipulating someone, or stuck in some kind of Victorian midlife crisis. And politics galore. Totally incomprehensible! Plus, I'm sure Mr. Keith never mentioned George was actually a woman. I think I would have remembered that. Honestly, I deserved extra credit just for surviving it.

Staring at her paper, Penelope's thoughts wandered to Frank and Andrea. *Does he really like that prim little church mouse? Or did he ask her to the prom to get back at me? I only flirted with Mattias to make Frank jealous. Could he be pulling the same bluff on me?*

Okay, back to the project. We should start the interviews on Monday. We are to examine the desires, motivations, and thought processes of the characters. Let's get the worst over first... I'll pair Frank and Mattias, me and Preacher's girl, and Jeanie and Timmy.

What could go wrong?

ॐ૮ॐ

May 3, 1976 - Monday
Cowherd, Mississippi

On Monday afternoon, the school photographer visited Mr. Keith's room to take photos of the groups for the upcoming edition of the newspaper. The Mockingbird team lined up with Frank and Mattias standing on opposite ends. Penelope walked toward Frank, but he pulled Andrea over to stand next to him, so Penelope strode over to stand by Mattias as if that's what she'd wanted all along. Jeanie and Timmy filled in the center.

Afterward, the students again gathered their desks together. In the Mockingbird circle, Penelope took the lead, as was typical for her.

"Okay, today we're going to start the interviews, remembering to examine the desires, motivations, and thought processes of each character. I've made a schedule for the interviews," said Penelope as she passed around the list with the order of the interviewees. Groans issued from both Frank and Mattias upon reading it.

Frank pulled out a piece of paper from his binder and folded it into an airplane, saying as he folded, "Knowing this was going to happen eventually, I have come prepared. I've got no desire to sit close enough to that plodder to interview him, so I've written out a list of questions. He can write his answers and give them back to me," said Frank, launching the airplane in Mattias' direction. Mattias snagged it, opened it, and read it aloud:

1. "What are your motivations for defending a scummy, despicable rapist?

2. What thought process led you to decide to defend a scummy, despicable rapist?

3. What is your desire in your defense of a scummy, despicable rapist?

"Did you not read the book, dipstick?" asked Mattias. "Like I told you on Friday, Tom Robinson wasn't a rapist. He was an honorable man. More honorable than you and your dad, that's for sure." He wadded the plane into a ball and hurled it at Frank, catching him square in the face.

Frank was up in a flash, propelling the desk away from him, causing it to overturn and crash to the floor as he headed for Mattias. Mattias was half a second behind him, springing up and jumping over his desk to meet him. They got face to face, chest pushing against chest in challenge. Frank's face was set in an ugly, tooth-baring scowl. Mattias' face looked chiseled out of stone. Both had clenched fists, eyes fixed and unblinking. No words were spoken, but none were needed. Their body language spoke plenty.

Mr. Keith bolted over and tried to insert himself between the two boys. Of course, that was impossible, so he stood on his tiptoes and put his face as close to theirs as he was able and said, "If you boys want to graduate, you'll get your sorry butts down to the principal's office right now. In fact, I'll accompany you!" Turning to the class, he shouted, "Everyone else, carry on!"

The rest of the week passed the same, minus the head-to-head confrontation, though hostile looks, insults, grousing, and a general churlishness persisted, mostly from Frank. Penelope decided she had waited long enough for Frank to admit his mistake in asking Andrea to the prom, and so she asked Mattias. He took a while giving her an answer, which surprised and irritated her. Likely, he suspected he was being used as a pawn in the Frank-Penelope tug-of-war. But in the end, he agreed, for Penelope's charms and gift of persuasion are unrelenting and border on sorcery. As he would soon find out.

CHAPTER 24

May 7, 1976 - Friday
Cowherd, Mississippi

Penelope Fitzgerald was living a nightmare. On Thursday, Frank and Andrea officially declared they were going steady, and she was now wearing his class ring, filling Penelope with mortification and bitterness, which spread like venom in her veins. How dare she? How dare *he*? Thoughts of vengeance endlessly swirled in her mind. She was determined to hurt Frank as he had hurt her, while somehow convincing him of his love for her. She didn't stop to think how contradictory these desires were. A red madness had filled her soul, and she resolved to do whatever it took to be reconciled with Frank. Not from love for him, but from love of herself, though she would never admit that. She didn't even acknowledge it to herself. Throughout the week she had theorized and skulked, nourishing and feeding her outrage, until at last she had a plan, and tonight, prom night, she would put it into place. She would make Frank Fitzgerald pay.

CR80

The banner above the gymnasium door read, "Welcome Cowherd Bulls! Let's Get Our Groove On!" Colorful streamers enveloped the gym, while a spinning disco ball suspended from the ceiling cast a mesmerizing and starry light show. The DJ had turned up the bass, the songs indistinguishable between themselves, but the students couldn't care less. They were deliriously jumping and bopping and gyrating to the beat.

Timmy had asked Jeanie to go with him at the last minute. She said yes so she would have a ride to the dance and for no other reason. Timmy didn't care. He wasn't a one-woman man anyhow, and he planned to boogie with every smokin' hot girl at the dance. He was in his element, cavorting and grooving under the disco ball in a circle of girls—the Bump, the Funky Chicken, the Robot. Timmy had all the moves.

As fate would have it, Frank and Andrea and Penelope and Mattias arrived at the dance at the same time. Andrea, oblivious to the awkwardness of the moment, was bubbling over with joy and going on about how "fab" everything was. Penelope had rolled her eyes and jerked Mattias into the gym.

Penelope and Mattias walked past the DJ, and she slipped him a handwritten note—a song request. The DJ, bobbing his head to the driving rhythm of *Born To Run*, gave her a quick thumbs-up. Soon, the ringing guitar and crashing drums gave way to soft piano, airy vocals, and the quiet trill of birdsong in *Lovin' You*. The mood shifted from electric to tender in an instant. Penelope smiled, took

Mattias by the hand, and led him onto the dance floor. Frank also took Andrea's hand and stepped into the dancing crowd, careful to keep a few couples between them and Penelope and Mattias. Still, he craned his neck to keep his eye on them when Andrea wasn't looking.

Frank could see Penelope whispering into Mattias' ear. It seemed she had a lot to say. Occasionally he saw Mattias shaking his head "no," and each time he did, Penelope tilted her head back and gave him an impish smile. Several slow songs followed until the other students complained. Andrea said she was thirsty, so Frank led her to a table and went to get a cup of punch. Earlier he'd seen Timmy tipping something into it, so he filled her cup to the brim. He turned to see Mattias in his path, also seeking some punch. Frank continued walking, but their eyes never strayed from the other.

The night continued much the same. Frank tracked the two, but Penelope never once looked his way. She continued her discourse, and Frank wondered what she was trying to talk Mattias into. He'd been on the other side of those imploring eyes before, and he knew she was trying to bewitch Mattias into doing her bidding. The lips, the eyes, stroking his arms and hair—it was classic Penelope on the make. The guy was toast.

Andrea excused herself to go to the restroom, and Frank did the same. Inside the boy's bathroom there was a guy selling something, and considering the crowd around him, he was doing a booming business. Curious, Frank peered around some boys to see what was up.

"Want some?" the seller asked, eyebrows wagging up and down.

"What is it?" asked Frank.

"Disco biscuits," the guy replied with a lewd grin.

"I'll take one," said Frank, thinking tonight was about to get a lot more fun.

ॐ

May 8, 1976—Saturday, early a.m.
Cowherd, Mississippi

Mattias was a much harder sell than Penelope ever imagined. She'd found he had, in her mind, a misplaced sense of moral integrity and high-minded principles. What red-blooded boy would turn down what she was offering? She had tempted him; she could see that. With each "no" uttered, his resistance seemed to waver and fade a bit more.

Still, it's clear he doesn't fully believe in the ideals of virtue and honor; otherwise he'd have told me to find my own way home.

When they left the prom, she still hadn't completely succeeded. But she wasn't ready to give up. Not yet. She had a secret weapon, and she knew there was no way he would refuse a damsel in distress… especially when she convinced him that his mortal enemy was the one who'd caused the distress and was about to bring about her ruination.

CR80

May 8, 1976—Saturday, early a.m.
Cowherd, Mississippi

Sheriff Wilbur Timmons crouched down to get a closer look at the body. Dead. Definitely dead.

He looked across at the boys fidgeting by the wall. His boy, Timmy, had called him an hour earlier.

"Dad, you gotta' come. Right now!"

"Calm down, son. What're you going on about?"

"It'd be better to explain in person," Timmy had said, gasping for air. "Please. Just come to the barn at the back of the Cristo's farm. It's back in a clearing past the woods." His voice was thick, sounding as if he were choking back tears.

"Where're you calling from?" He'd asked Timmy patiently, hoping to calm his boy. But inside, he was anything *but* tranquil. He could tell this was serious. His happy-go-lucky son was frantic. And frightened.

"I'm at the Fitzgerald house now, but I've got to go back. Please, just meet me there," he'd begged.

And so that was what brought him to this barn at three in the morning. He still hadn't heard that explanation. To be honest, he's afraid of what he's going to hear. He sniffed and looked around. The place smelled of hay and manure, alcohol, and vomit, among other things.

"All right," he said, looking at Timmy and Frank, "one of you needs to tell me what happened."

Timmy sidled away from Frank, glancing in his direction but not looking him in the eye. Frank's Adam's apple was convulsing. He was sweating even though he had discarded his tux jacket. The collar of his starched shirt shook, as though he might go into shock at any moment. The sheriff took off his windbreaker and threw it to Timmy.

"Put this on him," he said, pointing to Frank.

Timmy obeyed, but just then they heard a footstep from outside the barn, and they turned to see a man standing in the doorway. It was Arthur Fitzgerald. He stepped inside and looked around, taking in the sheriff, the dead body, and his son, who looked at him in terror.

"What's happened here?" he asked in a voice made even more frightening by its softness. "Who's responsible for this?" He pointed to the person lying in the hay.

Silence.

"Tell me what's happened here! NOW!" he roared, taking a step toward the boys.

"Dad, it's... it was an accident. I didn't mean to. It just happened... I just..."

Before anyone realized what was happening, Arthur had bolted across the room and grabbed his son by the throat, lifting him so his feet were off the floor. Timmy tried to push the man off his friend, but Arthur used his other hand to backhand Timmy across the face, knocking him to the ground.

Quick as a flash of lightning, Wilbur was on Arthur. Grabbing him, he pinned him against the barn wall and put his gun under Arthur's chin.

"If you ever touch my boy again, you're a dead man," he said through clenched teeth.

"You would never. You've got too much to lose. I'll tell everyone of your involvement with the White Chapter," squeaked out Arthur, making an attempt at bravado, yet his eyes were wide with fear.

"Maybe so, but you'd bring yourself down too. Plus, it wouldn't change a thing. You'd still be a dead man. And besides, there's the not-so-insignificant matter of what happened that summer in '68. You didn't think I'd forget about something like that, now did ya'?" said the sheriff. "Yes, indeed, I've got plenty of ammunition, both literal and figurative. So, I'm going to holster my gun now, and you're going to keep your stinking, bloodthirsty hands off both of these boys."

Timmons slowly backed away from Arthur, holstered his gun, and turned back to Frank and Timmy. "Sit down," he ordered them, pointing to the floor.

The boys slid down the wall, none too soon, as Frank's legs were giving out.

"Now, which one of you is going to tell me why the new preacher's daughter is lying dead in this here barn?"

ଓଃଣ

May 8, 1976—Saturday, early a.m.
Cowherd, Mississippi

Penelope lay back on the bed with a smirk. Mattias lay beside her, passed out drunk. He had somehow stayed conscious throughout the ceremony, although she doubted he would recall it in the morning. But regardless of whether he remembered, she had the marriage certificate to prove it. They were legally married. Who knew she'd have to go to such lengths to progress in her scheme?

He likely wouldn't remember what happened after the ceremony either, but I'll gladly remind him.

She knew her trump card would take the trick and win the game. All she had to do was play on his chivalrous sense of honor. She was quite creative and convincing in her tale of woe. *She had been violently and selfishly used, then rejected and forgotten.* Mattias was all too eager to hear that Frank was the scoundrel he'd always thought him to be, and worse. It took a while for Penelope to realize that trying to seduce a righteous man was an exercise in folly and frustration; building up his ego was fruitless. But when he heard she was expecting a child, fiction known solely to herself, he was ready to rush in on his white stallion and save the princess. Living in sin or fornicating was an abomination to him and all he stood for, although he didn't use such lofty words. He would rescue her, but only by marrying her.

They were both eighteen, so they didn't need parental permission. Finding a Justice of the Peace at nearly midnight on a Friday night proved challenging, but Penelope had prevailed. It took a little liquid courage for Mattias to follow through. But she was now Mrs. Mattias Cristo. Penelope Cristo. And though her first choice had always been to be Mrs. Frank Fitzgerald, this consolation man, while not bliss, was bliss adjacent. Plus, it came with the delicious joy of backstabbing the backstabber. And as her drama teacher had often quoted:

> Heav'n hath no Rage, like Love to Hatred turn'd,
> Nor Hell a Fury, like a Woman scorn'd.

Of course, she doesn't mean to *stay* married to him. She's sure her parents will shell out for a quickie divorce, especially since their new son-in-law was so unsuitable for their little girl. Then she will repeat the deception with Frank, and all her dreams will come true. She *will be* Penelope Fitzgerald, the richest woman in Cowherd.

ᏅᏺᏛ

May 8, 1976—Saturday, early a.m.
Cowherd, Mississippi

Frank ran his hand through his hair and fixed his eyes on a divot on the floor.

"At prom, this guy was selling ludes. I just wanted to have a good time, and I slipped one into Andrea's drink. She got real relaxed, but she could still walk if I supported her. I'd seen Mattias earlier this week building a fence; I hid in the trees and watched him. When he left, I came in to check the place out. I already had it in my mind that I'd bring her back here for…" he paused, swallowing as if trying to remove a demon from his throat that seemed determined to crush his vocal cords and silence his confession, "… for some fun. I had some whiskey and convinced her to drink a bit, but it made her sick, and she threw up. Then she just started groaning and laid down on the hay and then went still, like she was sleeping. I tried to wake her but couldn't, and I realized she was dead," Frank said. "I didn't know what to do, so I ran back to the house and called Timmy. And when he saw… saw her, he called you."

"Okay, thanks for the overview, but now tell me the rest of the story," said Timmons.

"What?" asked Frank, raising his eyes to the sheriff but refusing to look in his father's direction. "That's it."

"Do you think I just fell off the turnip wagon? That dog just won't hunt. If that's *all*, can you explain to me why her long dress is hiked up to her thighs? Where did you get those fresh-looking scratches on your cheek? I guess the ludes were wearing off a bit by the time you got her here. She wasn't as helpless as you'd hoped. Here's how I see it: you were determined to get what you came here for, but she fought you. And you raped her. Isn't that right? In fact, if you look here, you'll see bruising on her throat and around her eyes. You choked the life out of that girl."

Timmy gasped and whipped his head around to look at his friend. It's clear this had taken him by surprise. He pushed up from the floor and, giving Frank a disgusted look, moved to sit on the other side of the barn. Frank remained silent, yet his face betrayed him, revealing the truth of his guilt. He buried his head in his hands and began sobbing and pulling at his hair. A raw wail burst from him, as if a piercing grief had forced it from deep inside.

The sheriff had learned that, in *some* instances, remorse and regret are the fruits of a truly repentant heart, but in other cases, they are simply the adornments and trappings of hypocrites and liars and tricksters disguising the guilty as penitent. He knew this boy's father was all the latter, as well as angry and depraved and wicked. And most times, anger and depravity beget the same.

Did this boy ever have a chance?

CHAPTER 25

May 8, 1976—Saturday, Early a.m.
Cowherd, Mississippi

The sheriff once again kneeled and studied the body. He was quiet for so long, everyone in the barn was getting twitchy. Timmy cleared his throat to remind his dad they were all still there.

"Quiet. I'm thinking," the sheriff replied.

A few minutes later, Arthur interrupted, "Wilbur…"

"Shut your trap! Like I said, I'm thinking."

What may have seemed to others to be a cut and dried decision for the lawman was far from it. Although Timmons had enough dirt on Arthur Fitzgerald to put him away for a long time. Arthur was right in that he also had enough information to bring himself down with him.

Ten minutes later, he stood. "Okay, so here's what we're going to do. You boys take off your t-shirts and wipe down any surfaces you touched."

While the boys did that, Timmons put on gloves and took a hand scythe from the wall. He walked over and took some of Andrea's hair and sawed it off.

"What the…," began Arthur, and both boys stared with open mouths and wide, worried eyes.

"I told you to shut up. If you want me to keep your boy out of prison, you just stay back and let me do what needs to be done," said Timmons.

He threw the scythe onto the ground and grabbed a string discarded from a hay bale, wrapped it around the hank of hair and tied it, like farmers tie up dried tobacco leaves. When the boys had finished their task, the sheriff tried handing Frank the hair. Frank put out trembling hands, but in the end, he couldn't do it, so Timmy grabbed the bundle and wrapped it in his T-shirt. He had replaced his tux jacket, and he stuffed the shirt and hair in his jacket pocket.

"Alright, now you two are going to go to my cruiser and get some gloves from the trunk. I guess I don't need to tell you to be quiet, do I?" the Sheriff asked, and both boys shook their heads. "Then you're going to sneak up to the Cristo house. There weren't no cars when I came through, but that might have changed. I heard the parents and Mary were visiting her sister in Seaton this weekend. They might be back by now, but I doubt it. If it's still dark and appears vacant, you need to sneak into the house. I bet they keep a key under a rock or mat or something. Get in and find Mattias' room. Hide that mess of hair somewhere that's not too obvious. Then grab a T–shirt or drawers or socks—anything the Cristo boy could have worn to prom. When you've got it, get out and replace the key and get back here with the piece of clothing as fast as you can."

"What if there's no key? What if someone's there?" asked Timmy.

"Then you hightail it back here, and we'll figure out a Plan B."

Frank and Timmy ran toward the sheriff's car. They didn't talk or even look at each other as they retrieved the gloves from the trunk. When they reached the Cristo house, it was just as the sheriff had said—dark and vacant, and a key was, indeed, under the back doormat. Once inside, they found Mattias' room, and Frank grabbed a T-shirt from the hamper. They made it back to the door, but Timmy stopped.

"I forgot to hide the hair," he said and scurried back into Mattias' room. He returned just as fast, and they took off across the field.

Arriving back at the barn, they noticed Arthur hunched over in the weeds taking deep breaths, holding his fist to his mouth as if trying to keep from vomiting. When they entered the barn, they saw why. The sheriff had taken the posthole digger and bashed a hole in Andrea's skull. Then he placed the blood splattered digger beside the body.

"Why'd you do that?" Frank asked, shocked and sickened.

"Fingerprints. You said Mattias had been building fences earlier this week. I'm assuming he wasn't digging them with his hands?" the sheriff asked, not waiting for a reply. "So now this here digger has the girl's blood *and* the boy's fingerprints on it. Cold, hard evidence."

Frank gagged and flung the T-shirt onto the ground. He turned to run outside, but Timmons caught him by his arm.

"Don't you do it. Swallow it if you gotta', but if you leave any evidence indicating you were anywhere around this barn, you're done for."

Timmy could see Frank was struggling to keep the sick in. He grabbed a bucket from the floor and thrust it toward Frank, who grabbed it like a lifeline. He put his head into it and vomited, groaning and spewing and retching.

ဢ၆

May 8, 1976—Saturday, Early a.m.
Cowherd, Mississippi

One of the best things about small towns is that everyone knows each other. One of the worst things about small towns is that everyone knows each other... and has friends or relatives in adjacent towns. Which is why there was a pounding at Penelope and Mattias' motel door at 5:00 a.m. Saturday morning. Penelope knew who it was even before she heard the bellowing.

"Open up! I know you're there, and I know you've got my little girl in there with you!"

Mattias roused, grabbing his head as he tried to sit up but put his face back into the pillow, moaning. Penelope went to the door, and with the chain on, peeked out.

At least he's alone. Oops, no. There's Mom scrambling out of the car and barreling over, as well.

"Daddy, I can explain. It's not what…"

But she didn't have time to say what it did or didn't look like. She saw her dad raise his leg, and she jumped back just in time to avoid the door crashing in on her. This caused Mattias to jump up from the bed despite his pounding head. Penelope thought it only fair to protect the boy and rushed over to stand between him and her father.

Her father stampeded in, looking like a rabid bull. His face was red, and he was perspiring. His breath came in gasping heaves. The veins in his neck and forehead were bulging, and his eyes looked ready to pop from their sockets. Were this a cartoon, there would be steam coming from his ears. But this wasn't a cartoon, and no one was laughing. In fact, when Jefferson Lloyd clutched his chest and staggered over to plop down onto the bed, it was obvious he was having a heart attack.

"Daddy!" said Penelope, rushing over to him.

"Jefferson!" screamed her mother, coming to kneel beside the bed, frantic and saying, "No, no, no" like a scratched record.

Mattias grabbed the telephone on the bedside table, cradling it between his shoulder and ear. He grabbed his pants to get at least partially dressed. Finally reaching the front desk, he told them to send an ambulance right away. Then he went over and loosened the top button on Mr. Lloyd's shirt, ignoring the man's ineffectual attempts to slap his hands away. When the man lost consciousness and his body went limp, Mattias rolled him onto the floor and began

CPR. It had peeved Penelope last night that Mattias acted like such a Boy Scout. This morning, she couldn't be more thankful for it. He continued the chest compressions until the ambulance arrived to take the man to the hospital. Penelope and her mother rushed after, leaving Mattias looking after them, exhausted and confused.

ᘓᘓᘏᘌ

May 8, 1976—Saturday, Early a.m.
Cowherd, Mississippi

Back at the Fitzgerald home, Sheriff Timmons told Frank to go pack a bag and said he was going home with them. Timmy opened his mouth to complain, but his dad shut him down with a stern look. Frank noticed Arthur didn't protest.

Just as well. The sheriff's probably afraid Dad's going to kill me. I doubt he'll kill me, but he'll make me wish I were dead.

"All right, now we wait until I get a call from Pastor Gibbons, telling me his daughter is missing," said Timmons.

Just then, his walkie-talkie squawked and a deputy on the other handset said, "Sheriff? Come in, Sheriff."

"Sheriff here. What's the problem, deputy?"

"You're needed at the station. We got a missing girl."

"Roger that. On my way."

He ushered the boys into the squad car.

Timmy sat in front with his dad. Frank was squirming in the back, working up the courage to ask the sheriff to explain what he'd said to his dad at the barn. Whatever it meant, it had scared his father. He doesn't remember ever seeing his dad afraid.

"Sheriff, what's the White Chapter?" Frank finally asked.

Timmons cut his eyes to the rear-view mirror and looked at him. Frank didn't think he was going to answer, but eventually the sheriff looked back at the road and said, "It's just a fraternal organization… like an exclusive social club."

"What did you mean about not forgetting what had happened in the summer of '67?"

This time, the sheriff took even longer to answer. "Son, that's something I can't tell you. I promise you, you'd be best to forget that was ever said."

"What you're saying is, it's something I don't want to know?"

"Exactly."

But he did want to know. The summer of '67 was when his mother left. Was there more to it than he believed? Did his dad force her to leave? Did his dad make her leave? As in leave him, leave Cowherd, leave Mississippi, leave this world?

As soon as I graduate, I'll be the one leaving. I never want to see my dad again.

ᘓᘓᘓ

May 8, 1976—Saturday
Cowherd, Mississippi

With great urgency, a search party set off, hoping to locate Andrea Gibbons. After a few hours, Sheriff Timmons and some deputies found her body at the Cristo barn. Forensics gathered evidence, and the authorities wasted no time in issuing a warrant for Mattias' arrest.

A police presence met Mattias when he returned home from the motel, still dressed in his prom tux. A deputy read him his rights, put handcuffs on him, and put him in a cruiser while Frank and Timmy watched from Sheriff Timmons' squad car. Mattias passionately declared his innocence, but the deputy ignored him. He had his orders from the sheriff. As the deputy pulled out of the Cristo's driveway, he passed the sheriff's car, and Frank's eyes met and held Mattias'.

ᘓᘓᘓ

May 10, 1976—Monday
Cowherd, Mississippi

On Monday, Frank visited the hospital where Penelope's dad was recovering. He pulled Penelope out into the hall and told her if she'd marry him, she'd never want for a thing. He'd treat her like a princess—in exchange for one thing. She must swear she was with him on prom night—all night—not Mattias. Penelope's mother had already had the marriage annulled. How she managed that, Frank would never know, since they weren't Catholic. Penelope agreed under the condition that they go away for a bit after her dad was better—9-10 months at least. She didn't care where Frank had been or why he was asking so desperately, as long as she got his ring on her finger. Frank immediately began making plans for their departure.

The Mockingbirds never finished their literature project. Four of the six never graduated. On graduation day, Mattias was in jail. Frank and Penelope had already run away. And Andrea... Andrea was dead.

CHAPTER 26

Cowherd Register

Monday, May 10, 1976

SPECIAL EDITION

LOCAL PASTOR'S DAUGHTER FOUND MURDERED

By: Hank Bridges

In the early hours of Saturday morning, Reverend Nathan Gibbons reported his daughter, seventeen-year-old Andrea Gibbons, missing. Sheriff Wilbur Timmons immediately formed a search detail. Several neighboring police departments assisted. Law enforcement found the body of Miss Gibbons at 10:15 a.m. in a barn belonging to Carlos Cristo. She had been murdered. The coroner at the scene noted she had been strangled and struck on the head by a sharp object. A blood-splattered post hole digger was lying beside the body. On a curious note, the murderer had cut off some of Miss Gibbons' hair. The authorities have found no trace of the hair as of the writing of this column.

The sheriff and his deputies found a bloody T-shirt at the scene of the crime belonging to Mattias Cristo, son of Carlos Cristo. Forensics determined that the fingerprints on the posthole digger also belonged to Mattias Cristo. At the time of this printing, authorities have taken Mr. Cristo in for questioning.

According to the sheriff, Andrea Gibbons attended prom the night before with Frank Fitzgerald. Mr. Fitzgerald told authorities he had dropped Miss Gibbons off at her front door around midnight. He then returned home, where he received a call from another student and friend, Miss Penelope Lloyd, asking him to meet her at a motel in Jaimeson, just outside of Seaton. According to Miss Lloyd, Mattias Cristo, her prom date, had taken her to the motel after the prom against her will. Mr. Fitzgerald stated that when he arrived at the motel, he found Mr. Cristo insensate from alcohol. As it was extremely late, he and Miss Fitzgerald got a room at a neighboring motel where they stayed the rest of the night.

The sheriff would not allow this reporter access to Mr. Cristo for an interview, and as yet his parents have offered no comment except for declaring their son innocent of all charges.

The *Cowherd Register* will keep the community informed as fresh developments come to light.

Cowherd Register

Tuesday, May 11, 1976

CAUSE OF DEATH REVEALED
ANDREA GIBBONS' CASE

By: Hank Bridges

A coroner's examination has revealed the cause of death of Andrea Gibbons as strangulation. The coroner also reported that the object responsible for the head wound *was* the posthole digger found next to the body; however, this wound was made post-mortem. Additionally, the coroner has determined Miss Gibbons had been sexually assaulted. The sheriff expects the toxicology results will be available in 3-4 days.

The Cowherd Sheriff's Office has officially charged Mattias Cristo with rape, murder, and tampering with a corpse. The Cristos continue to disavow the charges against their son. They have agreed to meet with this reporter in the coming days to make his side of the story known.

Cowherd Register

Thursday, May 13, 1976

MEMBERS OF THE WHITE GUARD THREATEN LOCAL FAMILY

By: Hank Bridges

Members of the White Guard burned a cross at the home of Carlos and Elena Cristo last night. The Cristos made a call to the sheriff's office. However, they were told by a deputy that the department was currently short staffed, as the sheriff and many deputies were out of town at a crime scene. No physical harm came to the Cristos, and eventually the White Guard dispersed. Members of this covert group have historically avoided identification and arrest. This reporter has always believed that law enforcement in our county protects, abets, and/or supports the White Guard. Sheriff Timmons has once again declined to comment.

The *Cowherd Register* does not sanction the actions of this secret society, and we go on record to declare we bitterly oppose bullying, discrimination, and acts of violence against any individual. Because of this incident, the Cristos have withdrawn their consent to an interview regarding the arrest of their son.

Cowherd Register

Saturday, May 15, 1976

SPECIAL EDITION

MAJOR DEVELOPMENTS IN THE ANDREA GIBBONS CASE

By: Hank Bridges

There have been considerable developments in the death investigation of Miss Andrea Gibbons. The toxicology results revealed that Miss Gibbons had Quaaludes and alcohol in her system. A student has come forward stating he observed Mr. Frank Fitzgerald in the boys' restroom buying a "disco biscuit." This reporter has confirmed this is a street name for Quaaludes. Mr. Fitzgerald has denied this accusation. The sheriff has commented that this is "one person's word against another." He has cited his knowledge of Mr. Fitzgerald's character as a deciding factor in his decision not to pursue this allegation. Mr. Fitzgerald's father, Arthur Fitzgerald, has threatened to bring a libel suit against the student informant should he repeat the claim.

As previously reported, Miss Penelope Lloyd declared Mattias Cristo took her to a motel against her wishes. She stated she went to a pay phone to call Mr. Fitzgerald to "rescue" her, which he did. Fitzgerald further stated that they were together the rest of the night at a different motel until approximately 9:30 a.m. when Mr. Fitzgerald took her home. It is the law enforcement's opinion that after Penelope left, Mr. Cristo left the motel and met up with Miss Gibbons, taking her to his barn where he raped and murdered her.

However, this reporter visited the two motels named in the statements by Mr. Fitzgerald and Miss Lloyd. An employee at The Jaimeson Inn stated that on May 8th, Miss Lloyd and Mr. Cristo arrived at approximately 1:00 a.m. He related it was Miss Lloyd who signed the couple in after producing a marriage license stating the two were legally married. A Justice of the Peace in Clifford County had signed the license, which was dated May 7, 1976. Further, the employee reported that Mr. Cristo's car was parked directly outside the lobby window, and it remained there until 6:30 a.m. that morning.

The motel clerk was an acquaintance of Penelope's dad's law partner, and soon after they checked in, he called this person to inform him about the marriage. According to authorities, this coworker then reached out to Mr. Lloyd, and sometime around 5:00 a.m. Mr. and Mrs. Lloyd arrived at the motel looking for their daughter. The clerk gave Penelope's parents the room number. Shortly thereafter, a call from Mr. Cristo came into the main desk from this room, requesting an ambulance, as it appeared Mr. Lloyd was having a heart attack. The clerk observed the ambulance's arrival and departure with Mr. Lloyd, with his wife and Penelope following in the Lloyd's car. The clerk noticed Mr.

Cristo in the room, looking bewildered. At 6:30 a.m. Mr. Cristo settled the bill for the room and left in his vehicle.

Because of the statement and corroborating word of the ambulance attendants, the sheriff's office has released Mattias Cristo and has exonerated him of all charges. Sheriff Wilbur Timmons held a press conference confirming this information. This reporter asked the sheriff if he would be charging Mr. Fitzgerald and Miss Lloyd with lying to a police officer and whether he planned to investigate either regarding their involvement in the murder of Miss Gibbons. The sheriff's response was that Miss Lloyd was embarrassed about her elopement. Afterward, she was distraught because of her father's heart attack and was, therefore, not thinking clearly when she made her statement. Mr. Fitzgerald said he lied to protect the reputation of Miss Lloyd, which, in Sheriff Timmons' words, "was an honorable action."

The sheriff went on record to say he believed both Mr. Fitzgerald and Miss Lloyd were innocent in the murder, noting there has been an additional fingerprint found on the latch to the barn. This print has been matched to a drifter his office had taken into custody the week before for theft but released for lack of evidence. It is the sheriff's opinion that this person is the murderer, and he has issued an APB for his arrest. The sheriff offered no opinion on how this drifter met up with Andrea, his motive, or how she arrived at the barn.

This reporter would like to state that it is our opinion that the sheriff's office has handled this investigation with extreme

prejudice and police incompetence. We no
longer have any faith in our elected law enforcement and encourage all patrons to consider the mishandling of this case when the
spring elections come around. At the very
least, question and challenge the incoming
administration and make clear and informed
judgements.

2024

CHAPTER 27

November 11, 2024 - Monday
Cowherd, Mississippi

Lily re-reads the articles several times, and it causes more questions than answers. She can't help noting two similarities in the murders: both women were strangled—although Penelope was post-mortem. Both women had their hair shorn. Andrea was bashed in the head post-mortem.

Instead of mimicking Bougie's hair, could the killer have poured ketchup on Penelope's head to mirror the blood on Andrea's head wound? Are the two murders somehow connected, either committed by the same person or an act of retributive justice? Or was Penelope's murder just simply revenge? Could it be a copycat murder? Or am I just reading too much into it?

The life and death of Andrea Gibbons troubles her spirit. Lily's heart breaks over the girl killed in such a violent manner.

Who mourned this child? For she was still a child at death. Her parents would have been beyond grief, beyond misery. What parent could bear up under such innocence viciously ripped away? But what about her friends and classmates? The students noted in the articles seem to only be concerned with shifting blame and whitewashing their own actions. Is Andrea Gibbons related to the butcher, Niles Gibbons? The name seems too unusual to be a coincidence. If so, this would significantly raise Niles in the standings.

Was Andrea's killer ever brought to justice? Mattias had been ruled out, but could it be one of the other teenagers in the photo who killed Andrea? One of The Mockingbirds? Why were they called The Mockingbirds? Is it from the book To Kill a Mockingbird?

Lily thinks back to her literature classes. Admittedly, she's stronger in 18th and 19th century literature, but she well remembers reading the book and how it made her uncomfortable but also challenged her. Thinking back to the meaning of the title, she remembers Atticus saying it was a sin for someone to kill a mockingbird; killing one would be unjustifiable and cruel since they live to bring us joy with their songs.

Did Andrea's life bring joy to others? Her death was senseless and brutal; innocence destroyed by evil.

One thing is clear: while generational fear is prevalent in Cowherd, so is generational police malpractice. Is it incompetence or corruption? Or both? Sadly, the long arm of the law seems to embrace only select individuals in Cowherd, Mississippi. In fact, it seems a law unto itself—functioning as a landlocked, sovereign entity independent from any other jurisdiction; an absolute monarchy in which the legislative, executive, and judicial powers rest with one individual, like the Vatican. So, the question is… who's the Pope?

Lily makes copies of the newspaper articles, marriage license, and insurance policies and snaps a picture of the photograph, then places everything back in the box. She never made it to the Cristo farm on Friday, and she now has a legitimate reason: she'll return the box to Tomás Cristo.

The drive to the farm isn't as magical this time. Lily's remembrance of the body by the lake has tainted the once serene atmosphere. That's not a vision that's easy to banish from your mind. It reminds Lily of a Sherlock Holmes quote:

> "It is my belief, Watson, founded upon my experience, that the lowest and vilest alleys in London do not present a more dreadful record of sin than does the smiling and beautiful countryside."

White plank fencing flanks the farm entrance. A winding dirt road leads to a modest farmhouse and several large barns with silos and outbuildings. A beat-up 4 x 4 truck sits near the house. She sees a herd of cows in the distance. *Does the barn where Andrea was murdered still stand?*

Lily goes to the front door and knocks, but there's no answer. She walks over to the largest barn and peers inside, breathing in the sweet, earthy scent of hay mingling with the rich odor of damp earth and the sharp tang of manure. The barn has several stalls flanking a wide dirt floor. Some barn cats prance up to Lily and rub themselves against her legs.

"Nice kitties," Lily says. "Where's your owner?"

As she moves around the barn, she catches a whiff of fresh straw from the nearby calf pens. "Hello?" she calls. "Mr. Cristo, are you here?"

She turns around, and the man is standing close behind her, his protruding eyes boring into hers. She jumps in surprise and takes a couple of steps back. He's still got the angry camel expression, and she wishes he would smile like in the brochure photo with Niles Gibbons.

"Can I help you?" he asks. His voice doesn't sound as gruff as she'd expect given his countenance.

"Mr. Cristo, I'm Lily Jordan. I'm sort of your neighbor. I live across the field," she says, pointing in what she hopes is the direction of her house.

"I know who you are and where you live," he responds. "What do you want?"

"Pastor Meadows told me a little about your family history. How my house once belonged to your family. I was on the second floor recently, in the attic, and I found a box with some documents and various papers inside. I wanted to return it to you," she says, holding out the metal box. He grabs it and secures it under his right arm.

"Thank you. Now, if there ain't anything else, I've got work to do," he says, pivoting on his heel to go.

"Well, there's one thing I'm curious about. I saw a brochure at the Chamber of Commerce, and it had a photo of you and Niles Gibbons. From your expressions, you seemed to be good friends. But when I saw you both on Friday at the lake…"

"That's none of your business," he said, turning and quickly closing the few feet distance between them. "I think if it were me, I'd keep my nose out of things that don't concern you. Understand?"

Lily did understand. Something has happened to this man. The person standing before her bears no trace of the smiling man in the photo.

"I'm sorry. I didn't mean to pry. I'll just be leaving now."

She runs back to the car and locks it, hands trembling. So much for that. She does a three-point turn and heads back down the lane. When she arrives home, she's pleased to see a large motorcycle parked in the Bridges' drive. Coming across the yard is a burly, older man who can only be Chaney's grandfather.

He walks over and extends his hand. "You must be Lily. I'm so pleased to meet you at last. I'm James Bridges, but you can call me Pops. Thank you for taking care of Chaney."

"You're very welcome." She smiles warmly and gestures toward the door. "Would you like to come in for some iced tea?"

He meets her gaze with a kind smile. "That sounds terrific. Thank you."

Once inside, Mr. Bridges' eyebrows rise at the sight of the murder board.

"My, my, that's quite the list."

1. Bougie Fitzgerald - daughter

2. ~~Morris Carothers—current pastor~~

3. ~~Stanley Meadows—former pastor~~

4. Norma Jean Badger—beautician—slandered by PF

5. Niles Gibbons—butcher—slandered by PF

6. ~~Lily Jordan~~

7. Mary Rose—Fitzgerald cook and housekeeper, family wronged by the Fitzgeralds

8. ~~Percy Bridges—Dad - innasent bystander~~

9. Tomás Cristo—dairy farmer, family wronged by the Fitzgeralds"

"We're trying to prove Percy's innocence by finding the true killer," says Lily.

"One relationship you're missing that might be pertinent. Norma Jean Badger *may be* the daughter of Frank Fitzgerald and Jeanie Badger. Frank's full name is Franklin Norman Fitzgerald. It's common knowledge that Frank and Jeanie had a long-standing affair starting in the late '70s until he died in 2010. Jeanie never married, but Frank provided well for her. He sent her to beauty school and set her up in that beauty shop that Norma Jean inherited. It had a different name then, Jeanie's Touch, I think it was," says Mr. Bridges. "Most people think it's true—that Norma Jean is actually Frank's daughter. It makes sense. His middle name is Norman. Plus, the resemblance is strong with the blue eyes and inky-black hair."

"Really? Does the sheriff know about this possible paternity?" asks Lily, shocked.

"Oh, yes. He and Frank have been best friends since they were kids."

Lily takes a marker and writes "Possibly Frank Fitzgerald's daughter" next to Norma Jean's name.

So, Bougie and Norma Jean could be half-sisters? Do they know?

"Is Jeanie Badger still living?" asks Lily.

"Jeanie died a few months after Frank in a car accident that wasn't really an accident," replies Pops, shaking his head. "Someone cut her brakes. But the authorities never charged anyone, and to my knowledge, there wasn't much of an investigation."

"Seems like that's a common thing in Cowherd," says Lily. "Chaney and I found a metal box in the attic. Among other things, we found newspaper articles about the death of Andrea Gibbons and the unlawful arrest of Mattias Cristo. Hank Bridges wrote them. Chaney said he's your father."

"That's right," replies Pops, nodding his head and walking over to look out the kitchen window. "In fact, he was the one responsible for proving Mattias Cristo innocent."

"I've been thinking there may be a connection between Andrea and Penelope's deaths. I found this photo in the attic," Lily says, pulling up the photo on her phone and handing it to Mr. Bridges. "It was taken in 1976, just before Andrea's murder: Frank, Andrea, Timmy, Jeanie, Penelope, and Mattias. They were in the same class and, if not friends, were at least classmates. Don't you find it interesting that two people in that photo were murdered and three died under suspicious circumstances? Timmy Timmons, aka Sheriff Timmons, is the last man standing, so to speak. Timmons Senior investigated the murder of Andrea, and now his son is investigating the murder of Penelope Fitzgerald. I'm wondering if we should add Sheriff Timmons to the murder board."

"It's a fair point," says Pops, turning again to study the murder board. "It's not unthinkable that he could have killed Andrea and now killed Penelope to be sure that the secret remained untold. But why now? Something to ponder for sure."

"The board is Chaney's brainchild, by the way," Lily adds.

"That doesn't surprise me," says Pops with a chuckle. "He's got a very logical mind."

"*And* he's kind and polite. You've raised him well."

"Thank you. It's been a joint effort, that's for sure. Percy's alcohol problems are recent."

"When Mrs. Fitzgerald fired him from the newspaper?" asks Lily.

"That's right. Work and providing for his family makes up a lot of a man's identity, even for a Christian man. Plus, everyone needs a reason to get up in the morning. Percy feels like a failure. He's a good man, though. I'm proud he's my son."

"Do you know why Mrs. Fitzgerald fired him? Chaney thinks it had to do with his researching Heir's Rights. A young man at the Chamber of Commerce explained it's a big problem in Mississippi," says Lily.

"Yes, it is. I just don't know why that put a bee in her bonnet. Percy found information on her desk about how to file an affidavit of heirship, as well as a letter from an attorney explaining Heirs' Rights. Percy asked her about it, and she told him it wasn't important, but he felt she was lying. So, he did a little digging. When she found out he hadn't dropped it, that was it. She fired him but told folks he was retiring. She even got him a cheap watch and had the back engraved. 'Thanks for twenty years of service' or something like that."

"Actually, according to the sheriff, it reads 'To PB from PF for twenty years of service to the *Cowherd Register*'. He found the watch in Carothers' car when they dragged it out of the lake, and he's using it as evidence against Percy," says Lily.

"No way. Percy never wore that watch. He hated it. It was always in his dresser drawer."

"How do you think the sheriff got it then?" asks Lily.

"Likely he took it when he searched the place," says Pops.

"I just don't understand what the sheriff would gain from insisting Percy is the murderer or involved in the murder," says Lily.

"The sheriff's always held a grudge against my family. My father's reporting of the Gibbons' case exposed incompetence and negligence in the sheriff's office. My dad denounced the sheriff and urged the newspapers' readers to consider the mishandling of the case when the elections came around. Timmons barely won the next year, and even then, my dad thought someone rigged the election—Fitzgerald influence."

"From all I've learned about the Fitzgerald family, their money and control, I don't doubt it. Another thing the sheriff keeps going on about is the dog. He says no one except a Bridges could let the dog out without it attacking them."

"Well, that's not true. There's one other person in Cowherd who Gabe loves. Niles Gibbons gives him scraps from his shop. Some days, Niles would walk to the Cristo house through the field. He took a liking to the dog despite his barking and brought him meat from his shop. Gabe would eat right out of his hands."

She Had It Coming

A RECKONING WAS ALWAYS COMING

Penelope Fitzgerald liked to have ruined me. That woman's words could cut deeper than any knife in my butcher's block. Her column wasn't just gossip. It was a weapon. A weapon that sliced through my business and my reputation. I lost customers. Friends stopped speaking. But that wasn't the worst of her sins.

Long before she set her sights on me, my aunt, Andrea, was murdered. And I know in my gut that Penelope was part of it.

That was back in '76. A girl with her whole life ahead, but the town just shrugged and forgot about her. No justice. No answers. It left a hole in our family and a grief that never went away.

Penelope and Andrea were classmates, maybe friends. I found a photo after my old man died: six kids smiling, full of dreams. They called themselves *the Mockingbirds*. Five of them grew up; Andrea didn't even make it to graduation. Someone, Dad, I think, had circled two of the faces, Penelope and Frank. One word scrawled over each: *"Liar."*

Somebody knows what happened that night. And someone needs to pay.

That's why I came to Cowherd five years ago, to find the truth buried for decades. I came to confront her. But first, I sent letters. Mean, accusing letters. Threats wrapped in scripture and promises: "You'll get yours one day." "An eye for an eye." I quoted the good book just to remind her what justice looks like. I wanted her to be scared, to know the past wasn't buried like she thought. But words only go so far.

Still, I didn't rush it. The perfect moment for revenge would present itself when the time was right.

And when it did, well—she'd had plenty of warnings.

The reckoning was always coming for her. That much I knew.

And, yeah, she had it coming.

Niles Gibbons

CHAPTER 28

November 11, 2024 – Monday a.m.
Washington, D.C.

It had not been Eamonn's intention to re-open the case of Judge Garrett Elliott. Not at the beginning. It all started with the postcards. The postcards strongly supported the assumption that Jackson Elliott was still alive as of Lily's birthday in 2023; he can find no other explanation. He has sat and squinted and studied and scowled at his art project—the board with the cards, locations, and dates—for weeks, willing some new information to burst out like a Jack-in-the-box. But Jack remains hidden away and locked down tight. The whole thing is a quandary. Not only the cards, but the mystery surrounding the Judge's death.

I'm sure there are secrets here to uncover. But when they're brought to light, will they help Lily, or hurt her? Still, I have to look. It's my job. I can decide what to do with what I uncover later. Och! I can't believe I'm wanderin' down such paths of thought. Sure, and she's scramblin' my head proper.

Still, he can't help but recall the look on Lily's face when, on the plane, he said he thought she'd be safer once they discovered who killed her father. He hadn't meant to upset her, only to offer some sense of direction. But the moment stayed with him. It comes back now, uninvited, as he tries to focus on the next step. He repeats the words in his head, wondering if they meant something different to her than they did to him.

So, this morning he's taken out the case files on the murder, and as he reads, he sees anomalies that, if the marshals had investigated them, they failed to record.

Why, for instance, were the *only* fingerprints on the garage workbench and the hammer Jackson Elliott's? Possible, yes, but probable? Unlikely. Forensics had found Jackson's DNA, most notably in drops of blood on the floor leading out of the garage into the driveway before disappearing, but no other DNA except for the Judge's.

The files noted Grace was so distraught she had to be sedated by the family doctor. Was she questioned later when she had somewhat recovered? If so, it's not in the case notes. They didn't even record the doctor's name. And where is the interview with the judge's cook?

The lead marshal on the case was Kenneth Galloway, a man known for his unshakable integrity. Galloway had led a team of two junior field agents in the investigation of the Judge's murder. One of those agents is no longer with the Marshal Service, but the other, Ted Stith, is still serving and now works at Headquarters in Arlington.

Eamonn picks up his phone and places a call to Stith. It goes to voicemail.

"Hi, Ted. Eamonn Kelly here. Not sure if you remember me. We met on a training course a few years ago. Could you call at your convenience, please? I have a few questions regarding the Garrett Elliott case."

He disconnects and turns his attention again to the file.

I wonder if the cook, Bernice Childers, or Miles Fairchild are still living. I need to locate the name of the family doctor as well. There's more to learn here. The agents don't seem to have questioned Fairchild's statement or further investigated, and there's no statement for Mrs. Childers or the doctor at all. Why is that? Twelve years… well past the five-year statute of limitations for federal obstruction of justice… but not for murder.

He emails his assistant and asks him to locate contact information for Childers and Fairchild.

CR&O

By lunchtime, his assistant has already located the information on the cook, Bernice Childers, and Miles Fairchild. Miles has done well for himself. From working as the judge's assistant, he advanced to mayor of Briny, the county seat of McCoy County, Kentucky. From there, he was elected to the Kentucky Senate. Eamonn receives no answer on Fairchild's cell or office, so he leaves a message, briefly explaining the reason for his call.

He tries the marshal, Ted Stith, again, and this time receives an answer.

"Ted Stith."

"Hello, Ted, Eamonn Kelly here."

"Hi Eamonn. It's been a long time! I got your message. You're not reopening the case of Judge Garrett Elliott, are you?" Ted asks.

"Not officially. I've come across a related matter. I pulled the case notes for the judge's murder. It's surprisingly thin."

"Yes, I expect it is. That was my first case. I was as green as grass and as ignorant as dirt. I was excited to be working with Kenneth Galloway, but to be honest, I never met the man more than twice."

"Why's that? I thought he headed up the investigation," asks Eamonn.

"Officially, yes, but he was going through treatment for cancer at the time; he didn't want the big bosses to know, as he only had a year and a half before retirement. So, the other agent, who was senior to me, Tony Church, was the one who ran things."

"HR says he's not in the service any longer. Do you know where he moved?" asks Eamonn.

"He just sort of dropped out of sight a few years after the Elliott investigation, but I heard a rumor he's been doing PI work," answers Ted.

"Ted, there are quite a few irregularities in the file," says Eamonn.

"I don't doubt it. To be honest, Eamonn, I was as lost as a sailor on a starless night without a compass. I'm not proud of it, but it's the truth."

"Do you think we could meet for coffee sometime soon? I'd love to hear more about the case," says Eamonn.

"Sure. Just text me the time and place. Trust me, if any case deserves to be reopened, it's the Garrett Elliott case."

CRULD

Mrs. Bernice Childers' last known address was in Manassas, Virginia, less than an hour away from WITSEC Headquarters. Eamonn dials the number, which must be a landline, as he waits through eight rings before a woman answers.

"Hello?"

"Hello, is this the Childers' residence?"

"May I ask who is calling?"

"Hello, ma'am. My name is Eamonn Kelly with the U.S. Marshal's service. I am looking into the death of Garrett Elliott. I need to speak with Mrs. Bernice Childers. Do I have the correct number?" Eamonn asks.

After a few seconds' pause, she answers, "This is Mrs. Childers' daughter, Tammy Underhill. I'm afraid my mother passed away a few years ago."

"My condolences on your mother's death. Could you tell me if she ever said anything about the murder of Judge Elliott? Or the whereabouts of his son, Jackson?"

The silence that followed was much longer than before. Eamonn is afraid she has quietly hung up, and asks, "Mrs. Underhill?"

"Judge Elliott's death? That was quite a long time ago, Marshal Kelly," she pauses again. When she resumes, Eamonn can hear a tremor in her voice. "I apologize, Marshal Kelly... I'm sorry. I can't help you," she says. "Now if you will excuse me..."

"Mrs. Underhill," Eamonn interrupts before she can hang up the phone. "Please..."

But the line goes dead.

His brows draw together as he looks at the silent phone. Slowly, he sets it on his desk. A knot settling in his stomach. Whatever she knew—whatever she was afraid to say—was now locked behind fear, pride, or something worse.

CR&O

November 11, 2024 - Monday
Cowherd, Mississippi

On the way to the school pickup line, Lily drops Mr. Bridges off at the jail to visit Percy, praying the Sheriff will let him in. She thinks about what she'd just learned about Norma Jean, Niles Gibbons, the watch, and the dog. She also thinks of what she's heard about Frank Fitzgerald over the past few days. The similarity between him and her father is impossible to miss.

Thoughts of her father trigger a wave of heartache, reminding her of the torment he had unleashed on the town, her family... herself. The pain he inflicted, the lives he shattered, are all etched into her memory. The weight of his wickedness fills her chest, constricting her breath and threatening to smother her. Lily's mind betrays her as it replays memories of her father's cruelty and now intertwining them with the stories she's heard about Frank Fitzgerald.

Mrs. Meadows had said that the fear and dread of the Fitzgeralds had been ingrained in the community for generations. That description mirrors my family and the people back home perfectly. Briny and its citizens were victims of Garrett Elliott's tyrannical mandates and control much longer than I've been alive. I'd asked the Meadows how a family or community gets past an incessant cycle of fear, although I already knew the answer. It was the same answer as Pastor Meadows': to find the source and kill it.

Chaney jumps in the car, mercifully interrupting her musings. Composing herself, she tells him about his Pops' return.

"I knew it! I heard his motorcycle drive past the school earlier. He's the only person in Cowherd with a motorcycle that sounds like that. Where is he? I can't wait to see him!"

"He's over at the jail trying to visit your dad. We can go to the ice cream shop and wait for him if you'd like." Of course, Chaney doesn't turn down ice cream.

As before, they go outside to eat their treat. She hears her name called and turns to see Bradley Aubert skipping over from the Chamber of Commerce. Today he's dressed in orange and yellow plaid slacks, a military green shirt, and khaki canvas sneakers. Lily's a little disappointed he's missing the bow tie. It suited him.

"Miss Jordan, I'm glad I caught you. I've been thinking about our conversation the other day about heir's rights. It jogged my memory on something," says Bradley. "About three months back, two men came in asking for a Chamber Directory. I struck up a conversation with them, and they said they were from Southern Fields Oil and Gas. One of them let slip they were in town to meet with Penelope Fitzgerald about mineral and timber rights. The other guy gave his colleague the *shut zee heck up look*, and they left. Not the same as air rights, I know, but maybe related."

"Thanks, Bradley. That might be relevant." Lily bites her lower lip, her mind racing with possibilities.

"My pleasure." He looks at his watch. "Gotta' run! I'll not make it the rest of the day without an espresso."

Chaney sees his grandfather emerging from the sheriff's office and bolts across the green, his legs a blur of motion. Pops scoops him up in a bear hug, and Chaney's face lights up with pure joy. Just then, a sharp, metallic click pierces the air, followed by an intense orange flash and deafening boom that shakes the ground. The explosion tears through the tranquility of the town square, its shockwave rippling across the bystanders, who clutch their ears and recoil into a protective posture. Some instinctively drop to their knees and cover their heads. Others stagger and sprawl onto the grass or are thrown roughly onto the sidewalk.

Pops and Chaney fall to the ground, and Mr. Bridges shields his grandson with his body. The blast knocks Lily off her feet, and she hits the ground hard. When she lifts her head, she chokes on heavy, acrid smoke that billows over the green, obscuring visibility. The stench of burning gasoline invades her senses, scorching her eyes and nostrils, clinging to the back of her throat. Her ears ring with a relentless high-pitched whine; the world around her reduced to a muffled, disorienting haze. As the smoke clears, Lily sees shards of glass covering the sidewalk outside The Butchery, and the green is littered with debris.

As Lily struggles to stand, a man staggering out of the shop catches her attention. Flames consume Nile Gibbons' clothing, his body like a living torch. His screams testify to his agony and terror. Pops runs to him and yells, "Roll, man! Roll!" When Niles drops to the ground, Pops takes off his jacket and places it over the burning man. Lily grabs her cell and calls 911.

The ambulance station is just around the corner, and they arrive within minutes, followed by the fire department. Looking around, Lily sees that the surrounding storefronts appear to have survived relatively unharmed, save for some broken glass. Once the EMTs arrive, Pops grabs Chaney by the hand, and they run over to Lily.

"Is he alive?" Lily asks. "Are you two okay?"

"We're both fine. He's alive, but his burns are serious. He lost consciousness, which is good, as the pain will be unbearable," replies Mr. Bridges, trying to regain his breath.

"Man, that's terrible," says Chaney. Lily sees he's close to tears. "I hope he's going to be okay."

Lily hopes so, too. She also hopes the niggling feeling in her gut is wrong and that the explosion has nothing to do with Niles Gibbons' ex-best friend, Tomás Cristo.

CREO

Once they've returned to Lily's cottage, Chaney is eager to hear news about his dad.

"He's doing just fine, son. He looks good. His spirits are a little low, but he still has hope."

"Did the sheriff say if I can visit him?" asks Chaney.

"I'm sorry, but he won't allow it. He was adamant, but I'll keep asking. I told the sheriff about Niles and the dog. I told him that Percy never wore that watch, suggesting the killer planted it to implicate Percy. He said he'd take that into consideration, but until he knows more about the poison, he would not be releasing your dad."

Just then, Chaney notices the updates on the murder board.

"Whoa! Norma Jean and Bougie might be half-sisters? And now I remember Mr. Gibbons would feed Gabe sometimes. He got along with him as well as we did," says Chaney.

"I've been wondering," says Lily, turning to Mr. Bridges, "do you know if any of Andrea Gibbons' family still live in Cowherd?"

"I believe someone told me they moved away after Andrea's death. The way I heard it, Mr. Gibbons had a breakdown and had to be institutionalized, which isn't surprising. I can't imagine what I'd do if I lost Percy or Chaney like that."

"Did he have other children?" asks Lily.

"Yes, he had an older son who was away at college at the time of Andrea's murder."

"I feel certain Niles Gibbons must be a relative. Gibbons isn't a common name. But he's too young to be her brother," says Lily.

"It's possible they're related. Niles has only been in Cowherd for about five years. He's never said where he was from," says Pops.

"If they *are* related, that lends more credence to the possibility that he's involved in Mrs. Fitzgerald's murder."

"But if he is, what's up with the explosion?" asks Chaney.

"That's an excellent question," says Mr. Bridges. "I heard the sheriff telling a deputy that the toxicology report was due in any minute, and he's planning to have a press conference tomorrow at noon to speak about it. Maybe he'll comment on the explosion as well."

"I just hope he tells the truth this time," says Chaney. "I've had about enough of his lies."

"Chaney, your dad knows he's innocent. We know he's innocent. I have faith the sheriff will release him soon," says Pops.

"But we both know that *being innocent* isn't always enough, especially in this town. It doesn't always mean *being found innocent*," says Chaney.

Lily looks up sharply as the weight of that statement crashes into her heart, clawing its way inside and demanding to be heard, demanding someone listen. Demanding justice.

Chaney's right. I've only experienced this to a minute degree, but he's lived it, breathed it, bathed in it, and slept with it. In a world where the scales of justice can sometimes tip unevenly, and are many times weighted to favor certain individuals, the sickening reality is that innocence alone doesn't always guarantee freedom.

CHAPTER 29

November 12, 2024 – Tuesday a.m.
Cowherd, Mississippi

Chaney had moved his things back to his house when his grandfather returned home. Lily realizes she's going to miss him. Before he left, he had begged his Pops to let him stay home from school for the press conference. But Mr. Bridges said he'd prefer Chaney didn't miss school and that he'd be sure to fill him in when school's out. Chaney had looked at Lily for an allied front, but she'd agreed with his Pops. She told him she'd record the press conference for him. Mr. Bridges wanted to visit Percy again before the conference, so Lily offered to take Chaney to school and drop Pops off at the police station.

Dressing in the morning, Lily sees the photo she found in the cookbook sitting on her dresser where she had placed it when getting ready for bed Saturday night. Mattias and Maria—now Mary, she assumes—were beautiful children who appear to have once been joyous and carefree. That was before Penelope Lloyd stole Mattias' integrity and innocence... before Frank Fitzgerald nearly perjured Mattias' freedom away. And before someone decided they'd had enough of Mattias' second chance and set his home and life ablaze.

Considering all of this, why would Mrs. Rose have worked for Penelope Fitzgerald? And why was Mary at the Fitzgerald house the day after the murder? She slips the photo into her back pocket. *Pastor Meadows had said the Roses had a farm on the outskirts of Cowherd going toward Seaton. I think I'll return the picture to Mrs. Rose and hopefully find some answers to these puzzles.*

After dropping Chaney off at school and letting Mr. Bridges out at the square, Lily sees Bougie galloping out of Dye! Dye! Dye! looking like she'd just sat on a nest of fire ants. She's followed by Norma Jean, who's whipping a towel at Bougie's back like a lion tamer. Norma Jean is screaming something indecipherable, and Bougie is yelling similarly unintelligible words. Lily rolls her window down and slows to a stop, hoping to hear what's caused such a fracas.

Her mouth drops open when she sees Bougie pick up a rock and hurl it at Norma Jean, causing the beautician to bolt back inside her shop, lock the door, and put out the closed sign. Bougie turns and sees Lily watching her and gives her a look that puts starch to the phrase "if looks could kill" before spinning and shimmying over to the sheriff's office.

Lily inhales deeply, grateful for the safety of her car and its automatic locks, as she redirects her attention to finding Seaton and the Rose farm. She travels down a winding country road, flanked by expansive harvested soybean fields, once green, now only cropped, brown stubble. Ahead is a wide gravel drive, and she slows to see a sign bearing the name Rose Farms.

Driving up the gravel lane, rocks spit against the car's chassis, and dust wafts from behind. A white farmhouse comes into view, bordered by fields on two sides. Behind the house are several barns, grain storage bins, and large combine harvesters in open-sided machinery garages.

Stopping near the farmhouse, Lily can see Mary hanging wash on the line. Mary looks up as Lily gets out and shuts her car door. Walking over, Lily sees a woman she can only describe as "fluffy." Mary Rose appears to be the quintessential grandmother, with gray, short curling hair and a ruffled apron over her housedress. She walks out to greet Lily, smiling as she comes.

"Hello, dear. Can I help you?" Mrs. Rose asks.

Lily introduces herself, but like her nephew, Mary Rose informs her she knows who she is, albeit with kinder words and a softer tone.

"You're the girl living in our old cottage. Tomás said you'd called on him yesterday. I must apologize for my nephew. I'm sure he wasn't very kind. He rarely is of late. He's not always been like he is now. I just wish I knew why," she says, tutting and shaking her head. "I've made some fresh lemonade. Would you like to sit a bit and have some with me?"

"That would be nice, Mrs. Rose," answers Lily.

"Oh, you must call me Mary," she asserts, leading her to a pair of old-fashioned metal chairs and a small table positioned under a shade tree. Once there, Mary lifts a cloth off a pitcher filled with ice and lemonade, pours, and offers a glass to Lily. Taking a quick sip, Lily is unprepared for its sweetness. It's a pleasant surprise, as she had expected it to be sour, not unlike what she had expected in her companion. Considering her visit with Tomás, she'd been fearful that rudeness and ill-temper might run in the family.

Cranky, snappish, crotchety, waspish… yes, he was all of that, but that doesn't mean he's dangerous. Looks can deceive, and I should give him the benefit of the doubt. But then the man did kind of threaten me, and there seemed to be a dark craziness behind those angry eyes, so maybe not.

"Mary, I found something in the cottage that I'd love to return to you," Lily says, handing her the photo.

Mrs. Rose's eyes fill with tears as she studies the picture, rubbing her fingers across the surface like a caress.

"This is my brother and me. We were best friends when we were little. He said he was my protector, but I let him know I could protect myself, and I could also protect him. But I was wrong…" She fades off, lost in memory. "Anyway, thank you for bringing this. I don't have many family photos."

"Is that because of Frank Fitzgerld?" Lily risks asking.

Mary's head pops up. "What do you know about Frank Fitzgerald?" she snaps.

"Not much, but Pastor Meadows told me a little about how Mr. Fitzgerald treated your family. Everything I've heard of him points to his being domineering and spiteful."

"Oh, he was that and so much more," she says. "Frank Fitzgerald was a con artist, a victimizer, a tyrannizer—vile and evil—I'm not sure I can even find the words that would portray the type of person he was."

Yes, just like my dad.

"He and Penelope nearly ruined my brother, and only the grace of God, working through a dogged, smart, kind, decent man, saved him."

"I've read Hank Bridges' articles," Lily says.

"Well, then you know the gist of it, then. That was just the beginning, but it's in the past and that's where I need to keep it. It's the only way I can keep the hatred tamped down and the bitterness from festering." She stops and sighs. "But it's still there. I'd like to deny it, but I can't. It's like a toxic sludge that still burns and boils deep inside me. I wish it were different…wish I were different… but it is what it is, and I am who I am."

Okay, so maybe she's not so unlike her nephew. She sounds like a volcano on the verge of exploding. Or has the eruption already happened?

"Mrs. Rose, there's something I've been wondering about. With all that the Fitzgeralds had done to your family, why would you work for Penelope?"

"It was because of what you found in the box you gave my nephew—the life and home insurance policies. I knew Mattias wouldn't have left his family penniless. I thought that after Frank Fitzgerald forced us to leave our house, he might have moved the paperwork from the second floor to his home. I searched their house, but I never found the policies."

"It must have been quite a shock to find Mrs. Fitzgerald dead that morning," says Lily.

"Oh, yes. I still have nightmares," asserts Mrs. Rose.

"The sheriff said that she was still alive when Pastor Carothers left. How long was it between when he left and when you found her?" asks Lily.

"Oh, it was about twenty minutes. See, she had sent me back to the kitchen because she didn't like the first batch of eggs I had served her. There was nothing wrong with those eggs at all! She just liked to find fault, as you know. I might have gotten them back in earlier except for the Bridges boy coming to the door asking about his dog."

"Yes, he came by to ask me about the dog, too. According to the sheriff, they believe the killer entered through the rear French doors. Were you able to see that door from the kitchen?"

"Oh, no. The kitchen is in the east wing of the house. It's not too far from the dining room, but there's a thick hedge blocking the view from the kitchen window to the back patio, which is directly outside the French doors. If the window had been open, I might have been able to hear something if I hadn't been talking with Chaney."

"I see," says Lily. "There's one more question I'd like to ask you, Mrs. Rose. Why were you at the Fitzgerald home the day after the murder?"

She's quiet for a solid minute before she answers. "I went because I was afraid."

That wasn't what Lily was expecting. "Afraid of what?"

"All that searching didn't turn up the insurance policies, but I did find some letters that Penelope had hidden away. Threatening letters going back nearly five years."

"Really? What did they say?"

"They were harsh letters. Most were just one sentence, but they were unquestionably threats. They said things like 'You'll get yours one day,' 'I know what you did,' 'You reap what you sow,' 'My parents taught me to believe in an eye for an eye.'"

"Scripture...," murmurs Lily.

"Yes, there were many that quoted Scripture. 'The Lord hates haughty eyes, a lying tongue, hands that shed innocent blood, and a heart that devises wicked plans,' and 'you shall purge evil from your midst.'"

"Mercy. Do you know who they were from?" asks Lily.

"There was no signature, but they were postmarked from Cowherd. And I could tell a left-handed person had written them—backward slant and smudged ink and all. I wanted to get them out of there before the sheriff found them and jumped to the wrong conclusion and blamed the wrong person. You don't know how he is."

Oh yes, I am well aware of the sheriff's thought processes. They swing hard to the abstract, associative, and creative spectrum rather than concrete, critical, and analytical.

Lily watches as Mary pours herself some more lemonade using her right hand. Mary likely isn't left-handed. But a memory surfaces... it was something Lily hardly noticed at the time... Tomás Cristo grabbing the blue box from her hand and shoving it under his arm. His right arm.

"Do you know any left-handed people, Mary?" Lily asks, caution in her voice.

"What? If I did, that would signify nothing whatsoever. There are lots of people in town who are left-handed," she replies, setting her glass down forcefully, causing her lemonade to slosh onto the table. Then, closing her eyes, she sighs again, smooths her hair and apron, and continues, "Miss Jordan, I have a lot to finish up before Sam comes in for his lunch. Thank you for bringing the photo. You are a dear." And just like that, the grandmother reappears with a kind face, soft voice, and warm smile, leaving Lily to wonder if she's witnessed a wolf transforming into sheep's clothing or just the opposite.

Like I said, appearances can be deceiving.

She Had It Coming

THE EGGS WERE FINE

The Fitzgeralds always said they paid good money for my family's land. My mother didn't want to sell, but she was drowning in debt, and they showed up with papers and promises. They said it would help us. They said it was fair. It was far from it. But at least she got to keep the house.

After Mama passed, Sam and I moved into her house only to find out she was behind on the mortgage. Once again, Frank and Penelope rushed in to *help*. They paid us a tenth of what it was worth. They said it was just business. Funny how *business* always worked out in their favor.

She never apologized. Never even looked uncomfortable. Just went on like nothing had happened. That's how she was. Never got her hands dirty; just made sure everyone else ended up in the mud.

That morning, she sent the eggs back, calling them everything but good. I went to the kitchen, thinking about how easy it'd be to change that recipe in a way she'd never expect, to see if she'd taste a little of the bitterness she served everyone else. I'd stood at that stove countless times, thinking how simple it would be: a little something in her tea, a pinch of this or that.

I guess you're wondering, after all the Fitzgeralds had done to my family, why I kept working for her? I showed up every day, cooked her meals, and cleaned up her messes. Why?

That's not really your concern. Maybe I was waiting for something. Maybe I needed the money. Maybe I wanted to look her in the eye every day and remind her I was still standing.

You want to know if I did it? I'll say this: if I did, she had it coming.

Some debts can't be settled with money.

And that's all I've got to say.

Mary Rose

CHAPTER 30

November 12, 2024 – Tuesday
Cowherd, Mississippi

Still turning over her conversation with Mary Rose, Lily leaves the house and drives to the church. With time before the press conference, she walks up the hill behind it, scanning the graveyard for Andrea's tombstone.

A plucky November sun flickers through the trees, slicing at the shadows in a frenzied attempt to prove it hasn't already got one foot in the grave.

Strolling through the rows of monuments, Lily sees familiar names: Fitzgerald, Timmons, Lloyd, Badger, and Cristo. Just beyond, she finds Andrea. It's a single headstone in the shape of an angel. The stone reads, "Andrea Renec Gibbons, October 10, 1959 - May 8, 1976—Beautiful daughter and devoted sister. Taken much too soon." Moss had partially covered an engraving on the top. Lily takes her Swiss Army knife out of her jeans pocket and scrapes it clean. It's a mockingbird.

Lily looks at the monument to the left of Andrea's. There are her parents. Her mother died in 1970 and her father in 1978— under their names it reads "Loving Parents of Andrea and Phillip."

The names on the stone on the other side of her parents read Phillip and Lola Gibbons—loved by their only son, Niles. *So, Niles would have been Andrea's nephew.*

Mrs. Gibbons died prior to Andrea's murder, her brother was away at school, and a doctor had admitted her father to an institution sometime after the murder. Then, around five years ago, Niles moved back to Cowherd according to Mr. Bridges. Why? He had no remaining family here. Could it have been to avenge his aunt's death? Mrs. Rose had also said the threatening letters Penelope had received went back five years. The timing seems too in sync to be coincidental.

To the right of Andrea's grave is a koi pond surrounded with ferns and stones and a well-worn bench flanking it.

Does anyone come here to mourn for the innocent girl who had her joy and song taken from her so senselessly?

Lily moves to sit on the weathered bench, seeking peace and serenity to calm her burdened spirit. Her eyes fix on the tranquil water and vibrant colors of the koi swimming gracefully beneath the surface, a sharp contrast to the disquiet swirling through her mind. Lost in thought, she hears a slight rustle behind her, causing a quickening of her senses. But before she can fully process her feeling of unease, a sudden impact against the back of her head sends a jolt of pain radiating through her skull. The force of the blow causes her vision to swim in a dizzying haze as she topples off the bench and crumples to the ground, confused and shaken.

As her senses slowly return, she hears fading, hurried footsteps behind her. Panic mingles with relief as she realizes her attacker is fleeing. Struggling to steady herself, she digs her fingers into the ground. Her heart pounds in her chest and throbs in her ears. Gritting her teeth, she fights against disorientation and nausea and, with a groan, pushes to her elbows and rises to her knees. As her mind grapples to regain its bearings, she staggers to her feet.

Putting her hand to the back of her head, Lily recoils at the sharp pain radiating from the knot already swelling on her scalp, and she tries to focus and slow her racing heart. Questions scramble through her mind, chasing answers to what had just happened, and who could have lashed out at her with such violence. Lily surveys the graveyard for any hint as to the identity of her attacker. But there is nothing. No scrap of fabric, no distinguishable footprint, no trace of the weapon.

Lily makes her way back to her car and slips into the driver's seat, locking the doors, and with deep breaths wills herself to relax. She thanks God for protecting her, for surely this attack could have been much worse. He *or she* could have killed her if they wanted. There would have been no witnesses. So, were they trying to scare her or just lashing out in anger? She thinks of Bougie's face in town superimposed with Mary Rose's recent metamorphosis at the farm. Could either have been her attacker? It's doubtful this was a random attack, so someone must think she's a danger to them. Is she getting close to exposing sins and secrets of the past? Close to uncovering the truth? One thing is certain: this once peaceful town is becoming more dangerous by the day. Lily can't help but feel a chill run down her spine whilst the sun retreats behind the clouds, giving up the ghost as it surrenders to the gloom.

ଓଃଓ

November 12, 2024 – Tuesday
Cowherd, Mississippi

Driving from the church, Lily keeps an eye out for her attacker. She touches the goose egg on her head… the left side. *So, likely the person who attacked me is left-handed.* She thinks back to what Mrs. Rose had said about the threatening letters—that they were written by a left-handed person. Did the person who wrote those letters also kill Penelope Fitzgerald?

Lily reviews the suspect list in her mind…

Bougie Fitzgerald… when I saw her coming out of the tanning salon on Monday. She had shopping bags hanging from the crook of her right arm, and she was holding her cell phone in her left hand, which she used to take a selfie. Also earlier today, she threw a rock at Norma Jean. She used her left hand for that as well. So, almost definitely a lefty.

Morris Corothers… had he done anything when he was on my stoop to show he was left-handed? He ran his hands through his hair with his left hand, but that doesn't necessarily mean he's left-handed. And he couldn't be my attacker; but that doesn't exclude him from being the murderer.

Next on the list is Norma Jean. When I was at the salon, she used her left hand to file my nails, so she's probably left-handed.

I've no idea whether Niles Gibbons is left-handed.

Mary Rose didn't appear to be a lefty.

Tomás Cristo… he grabbed the metal box with his left hand before shoving it under his right arm. Still, that's not conclusive evidence that he's left-handed.

There's another person who's left-handed in town that's not on the list: Sheriff Timmons. He wears his gun on his left hip.

Is this entire town left-hand dominant? Maybe there's something in the water. Still, just because someone wrote threatening letters to the victim doesn't mean they're the killer. It's at best circumstantial. Thoreau had said, 'Some circumstantial evidence is very strong, as when you find a trout in the milk,' meaning some insignificant details may be indicative of larger issues. So, what's in the milk in Cowherd?

What's in the water… what's in the milk… maybe that hit on the head is worse than I first thought.

CHAPTER 31

November 12, 2024 – Tuesday
Cowherd, Mississippi

When Lily arrives at the press conference, the green is full of townsfolk standing in groups talking or sitting on the lawn enjoying the sunshine. She sees Mr. Bridges standing in front of the boarded-up butchery and goes to meet him. The smell of charred wood still hangs in the air. *With so many people around who may overhear, I think I'll wait until later to tell him about the attack.*

"Hey, Lily. I was just checking out the shop," he says. "I'm no incendiary expert, but it almost looks like there was a flare-up here by the door. See where it's darker? It's astonishing that the fire didn't spread beyond the one shop. Some others smell of smoke, but that's all."

"You're right. Why weren't the other shops affected? The flash and boom were intense," she says.

"Indeed, they were," he replies. "It seems like whoever did it was very intentional."

They hear microphone feedback and turn to see that the sheriff has come to the dais. He clears his throat and puts his mouth up to the mic. "Check one-two." Feedback again fills the air. A deputy runs and pulls the loudspeaker further away from the mic, and to the relief of the audience, the screeching stops. Lily takes out her cell phone to record the conference, as she had promised Chaney.

"Attention everyone. I know y'all have gathered to hear about the latest developments on the spree of carnage that has befallen our quiet town. First off, I'd like to report that Niles Gibbons is in stable condition. However, he remains unconscious as the doctors have placed him in an induced coma due to the onset of seizures upon arrival at the hospital," says the sheriff, referring to his notes. "He has deep partial-thickness second-degree burns on his chest and arms and superficial second-degree burns on his neck and face. The doctor said his prognosis is good, but recovery will take a while.

"The fire inspector has completed his investigation into what caused the explosion. They have determined the cause was two half-filled punctured gas containers concealed in a gym bag on the shop stoop. The perpetrator rigged the containers with a pull-start igniter tied to the outside door, which sparked when Mr. Gibbons opened the door from the inside, causing the explosion.

"Also, the toxicology results have come back in the Fitzgerald case." He looks again at his notes. "The poison was an herbicide called Paraquat, administered in her breakfast drink. Farmers who produce commercial crops use this poison for weed and grass control on farms where large crops are grown, such as soybeans and corn. The EPA has classified Paraquat as a restricted-use substance. Only licensed applicators can legally use it, as it is extremely poisonous. The EPA treats Paraquat sold in the U.S. with a blue dye and an added emetic to induce vomiting. The Paraquat that was used in the murder of Penelope Fitzgerald did not have any such safeguards.

"When a person ingests Paraquat, they will experience immediate pain in the mouth, followed by nausea, vomiting, and abdominal pain...um... among other unpleasant things. Ingestion can lead to heart, kidney, and liver failure, muscle weakness, coma, seizures, or respiratory failure. The poison paralyzed Mrs. Fitzgerald's heart muscle. She was taking the medication, Amiodarone, to slow her heartbeat to treat tachycardia—a heart rhythm disorder where the heart beats faster than usual, and this exacerbated the effects of the toxicant.

"As I said, there were no EPA preventative additives identified in the toxicology results; therefore, the killer had to have bought the Paraquat used to kill Mrs. Fitzgerld out of the country, most likely in Mexico. This office plans to bring in any commercial farmers in the area for questioning. I will provide more updates as they develop. That is all."

Lily and Mr. Bridges look at each other with open-mouthed astonishment. "What about Percy?" they say at the same time.

They both take off toward the sheriff's office, undoubtedly looking like insurgents headed to storm the Bastille. They barrel their way through the door, and Sheriff Timmons turns to them in annoyance.

"Now, what're y'all thinking you're doing?" He asks with hands on hips.

"Why haven't you released Percy?" Mr. Bridges asks. "He'd have no use for a powerful herbicide like Paraquat, and he was in jail at the time of the explosion."

"That doesn't rule him out as an accomplice to the murder," says the sheriff.

"In what way?" asks Lily.

"Well…," says the sheriff, taking his time. "There's the dog…"

"Enough about the dog! I told you Niles Gibbons could feed that dog out of his hand," yells Pops.

"Are you insinuating that I should bring in a poor man nearly burned to death here for questioning?" asks Timmons.

"I never said that…"

"Plus, Gibbons definitely didn't set the explosion. There's no way he would intentionally burn himself up like that or risk his shop and livelihood."

"Just because someone else set the explosion doesn't mean Niles wasn't an accomplice to Mrs. Fitzgerald's murder," says Lily. "The murderer could have set the explosion to get Niles out of the way in case he tries to implicate him… *or her.*"

"Seems Niles has been friendly with both Bougie and Norma Jean of late," says Pops.

But would either be smart enough or have the resources to set off that explosion?

"Sheriff, I'd like to know why you insist my son is guilty of this atrocity?" asks Pops. "You keep prevaricating and inventing scenarios intent on incriminating Percy. What I'd like to know is, does it have anything to do with the color of his skin? It appears racially motivated from where I'm standing. I'm sure many of your electorate might agree."

The sheriff's gaze hardens, and a vein throbs at his temple. "Are you calling me a bigot and a liar?" he growls, coming around the desk to stand in front of Pops.

"I just might be. I have the constitutional right of free speech, even in Cowherd. That's the First Amendment. Have you ever read the Constitution, Sheriff?" asks Mr. Bridges, taking his own step toward Timmons. "There's also the Fifth Amendment that guarantees due process, equal and fair treatment by the justice system. The Sixth Amendment guarantees the right to a lawyer. Percy said it's been days since his lawyer has been to see him, so I'm going to go to Natchez first thing in the morning to get him a new lawyer."

"His lawyer not being here is hardly my fault," says the sheriff. "And I do know the Constitution. I just may interpret it a little different than you."

"Sheriff," interrupts Lily, hoping to avoid an exchange of blows—the testosterone in the room is suffocating. "Was Andrea Gibbons' murderer ever convicted? Have you noticed similarities between the Gibbons' murder in 1976 and the Fitzgerald murder? Because I have."

That shut the sheriff up. In fact, he looks like he just swallowed his tongue.

"What do you know...," he chokes out, but just then two deputies burst through the doors, dragging Sam and Mary Rose in with them. Both are in handcuffs.

"You sure were right about them resisting arrest, sheriff," says one deputy. "They've hollered and squawked the whole way from the farm."

"Timmy Timmons, I'd like to know what the meaning of all this is!" bellows Mary.

"Well, it's like this, Mary. We found out what killed Penelope. An herbicide. A dangerous one called Paraquat. You see, only commercial farmers licensed to use it can purchase it. Your husband is a licensed applicator according to the EPA database," says Timmons.

"Well, I didn't poison the old bat," begins Sam, "and if I had tried it, she wouldn't take but a midge of a sip 'cause it stinks to high heaven, and they put blue dye..."

"I know, I know. Blue due and stuff to make a person vomit," says Timmons. "But Paraquat bought out of the country—say from Mexico—doesn't have all those safety measures. And I happen to know you just came from Mexico a few weeks back. You went looking to buy cheap land down there to move your farm operation, now that fewer migrant workers are coming to the U.S. legally."

"What! Sam, is that true? I'm telling you right now, I'm NOT moving to Mexico," says Mary, wagging her head.

"Mary, can we talk about that some other time? Sheriff, I can tell you in absolute honesty—hand-on-Bible—I didn't kill Miz Fitz, though I guess I can see why you might suspect me. But why have you hauled Mary down here like a common trollop?" asks Sam.

"Really, Sam, couldn't you have thought of a different metaphor?" asks Mary, rolling her eyes.

"Hush, woman! I'm trying to help you here," says Sam.

"I've brought Mary here because I believe, while you provided the means," he points a stubby finger at Sam, "she provided the method," he continues, jerking his finger toward Mary. "She's the one who had unhindered access to Penelope and her breakfast, specifically her milk, which was the method of delivery according to the lab. We all know how the Cristos hate the Fitzgeralds, and so there's your motive. Means, method, and motive—figuring those out is what solves cases like this."

"When have you or any of your kith or kin ever solved a case like this?" asks Mary, surging toward the sheriff, dragging a deputy in her wake. "Your daddy incarcerated my brother for days, and him an angel. And no one ever solved that poor girl's murder. All your daddy had was conjecture and imagination."

Well, that at least answered that question, thinks Lily.

"Now, Mary," say both Timmons and Sam, but Lily can see the sheriff is a little afraid of Mary's fury.

"Boys, put them in a holding cell. Better put them in different cells, for Sam's sake," says the sheriff, scurrying back behind his desk.

Mary struggles and calls down all sorts of curses on the sheriff and his kin. In the end, they have to call in reinforcements to get her into the cell. Lily feels sorry for the deputies at the mercy of the sheriff's lack of spine.

"Sheriff…" says Lily.

"Are you two still here? I have nothing else to say to you," he says, leaning over his desk and slapping his hands on top.

"Do you think there is a connection between these two murders, sheriff?" asks Lily.

"I can tell you for *positive*, the person who killed Andrea Gibbons *cannot be* the same person who killed Penelope."

"But what about a revenge killing?" asks Mr. Bridges. "You know, she would have been Niles Gibbon's aunt had she lived."

"There you go again," says Timmons, straightening up and throwing his arms in the air, "blaming a man who's fighting for his life, or at least for his skin, right now."

"Why would both women have their hair shorn?" Lily continues, determined not to be put off. "Why would someone put ketchup on Penelope's head? Was it to imitate the blood from Andrea's wound? And there was an attempt to strangle Penelope. Andrea *was* strangled. Doesn't that seem like the Penelope's murderer was trying to replicate Andrea's murder, at least symbolically?"

"Okay, so someone tried to strangle Penelope with the scarf, even though she was already dead. Andrea was choked by hand, causing fingertip bruising to her throat. Two different modus operandi. Now, unless either of you is here to confess to any of the multitude of murders or attempted murders in Cowherd in the past

50 years, I want you out of my station," orders Timmons, pointing toward the door.

"Fine, but I'll be back tomorrow afternoon with a new lawyer for Percy," says Mr. Bridges.

"Fine," says the sheriff, settling himself in his chair and propping his feet on the desk. "We'll all be here sitting on our duffs just as Mrs. Mary Rose implied. They might as well hang me for sheep as for a lamb."

She Had It Coming

FIFTY YEARS IS A LONG TIME TO HOLD YOUR BREATH

You'd think a secret kept for fifty years would be long dead and buried. But some secrets don't stay buried. Not really. They claw their way back to the surface, no matter how deep you try to sink them. Like a shadow you can't outrun.

I've tried to forget that night. But Penelope wasn't about to let me. You ever had someone hold your past over your head like a guillotine? That's what it felt like *after*.

When I was young—*before* that night—I swore I'd be a better man than the one who raised me. But that night showed me just how naïve that dream was. Because once you've tied yourself to the Fitzgeralds, that rope only pulls tighter. I covered for Frank Fitzgerald, same way my father covered for Frank's father. Tell one lie, and you're stuck telling another to cover it. One after another, the lies build up, steady as stone, holding back the truth like a dam holds back the flood.

And Penelope had a talent for stepping just close enough to the floodgate to make you sweat. I told her not to stir it up—to leave it buried. She just smiled like she already had the headline written.

The last time we talked, she brought it up—that night. Just floated it out there like it was an old inside joke, like it was harmless. But then she looked at me, really looked, and said, *"Timmy, you know there's no statute of limitations on the truth."*

That's when I knew. She wasn't bluffing anymore.

You start poking holes in a dam, don't be surprised when it breaks. And if you're standing too close when it does...well, accidents happen.

She thought she was untouchable.

Looks like she got that one wrong.

And now, I'm the only person alive who knows the truth.

Sheriff Timothy Timmons

CHAPTER 32

November 12, 2024 - Tuesday.
Cowherd, Mississippi

Lily sits in the backyard reflecting on what the sheriff had said earlier. *Penelope's killer attempted to strangle her with the scarf, even though she was already dead. Andrea was choked by hand, causing bruising to her throat. He also said he could say positively that 'the person who killed Andrea Gibbons could not be the same person who killed Penelope.' He could be lying. But if he's telling the truth, that can only mean one thing: he knows who killed Andrea.*

The articles didn't mention that whoever killed Andrea had choked her by wrapping a hand around her neck. Timmons Senior may have told him, but it could mean something else entirely—it could mean Timmy Timmons killed Andrea himself or was there when she died, or shortly thereafter. If it wasn't him, then he knows who killed her. And that person was never charged. So likely it was a close friend. Mr. Bridges said the sheriff and Frank Fitzgerald had been best friends since they were kids. Frank was Andrea's prom date. Frank later lied, saying he had been with Penelope at the time of Andrea's death. A student said he saw Frank buying Quaaludes in the restroom at prom.

Toxicology reports showed Andrea had Quaaludes and alcohol in her system.

Penelope provided a false alibi for Frank, who should have been the number one suspect. She also lied about Mattias, who then became the top suspect instead of Frank. And the authorities never considered Penelope or Frank as suspects.

There's only one logical conclusion: Frank Fitzgerald was the one who had killed Andrea. And the sheriff either took part in the murder or was an accessory after the fact.

And now the sheriff knows I'm making connections and asking questions about the two murders. Both Pastor Meadows' wife and Mr. Bridges have warned me that Sheriff Timmons is a dangerous man despite the bumbling good-ole'-boy image he tries to portray.

Lily picks up her cell and dials, reaching a voicemail service. She relays to Marshal Kelly all she's learned about the two murders and the sheriff. She doesn't tell him about the attack at the cemetery, afraid he might just send in Army Delta Force to extricate her. When she ends the call, she goes to the murder board and writes: "10. Sheriff Timmy Timmons."

☙❧

November 13, 2024 – Wednesday a.m.
Cowherd, Mississippi

Since Mr. Bridges planned to leave early for Natchez the next morning, he had arranged for Lily to take Chaney to school.

Chaney said he'd come over when he was ready. School starts at 8:45, and when Chaney hadn't arrived at 8:30, Lily began to worry. Still, he could just be running late. At 8:45 she thinks he either overslept or something is wrong. That's when she hears the dog.

Hurrying next door, she knocks loudly and persistently, but there's no answer. Going to the backyard, she sees Gabe running back and forth at the rear of his fence, barking and growling. She walks warily back, keeping a close eye on the dog. *He can't jump this fence, can he?*

When he sees her, he runs up to her, then runs back to the end of his yard, continuing to raise an alarm. She skirts the outside of the pen, being sure to keep all extremities close to her body. Turning the corner of the fence, she sees the grass beyond had been flattened, noticeable because of the remaining dew. In the trampled area, she sees a fresh, albeit cold, slice of pizza—Chaney's breakfast of choice. At the edge of the depression is Chaney's backpack, papers spilling from its half-opened zippered top.

Extending from the crushed grass are two parallel paths leading back through the field where it appears a car or truck has driven through. Lily's heart fills with dread and fear for Chaney. She takes off through the field, following the tracks. The smell of wet grass and damp soil wafts in the air. Her sneakers become soaked and squelch from the dew, and her jeans are soaked up to the knees, but she doesn't care. She has to get to Chaney. It might already be too late.

Lily's heart thunders in her chest, matching the rhythm of her footfalls. The uneven ground beneath her feet conspires against her;

hidden dips and snarls of grass cause her to stumble and fall. Each time she goes down, she claws her way back up, her hands grasping the slick blades and unearthing clods of mud and bundles of roots. Moisture seeps through her clothes, clinging to her skin. The world around her seems to blur as she fights to regain her footing.

Ahead of her, she sees the rear of a barn. Coming closer, she hears a female voice shouting and drops into the grass to conceal herself. Gasping for breath, she inches forward until she sees a run-in shed added to the back of the structure. There, sitting by the back wall, is Chaney with duct tape over his mouth and his wrists and ankles bound. He's found a nail in a board of the shed and is trying to cut the tape around his wrists. His eyes widen when he sees Lily.

Lily creeps up to him and removes her pocketknife from her jeans pocket. She cuts his restraints and then carefully removes the tape from his mouth, knowing it'd hurt less if she just ripped it off, but not wanting to risk making a noise. His eyes squinch up and his teeth clench together, but he doesn't make a sound. Someone is still screaming inside the barn, and Lily places her finger on her lips in warning. Chaney nods his head and then peeks through a crack between the boards. Lily does the same.

Sitting on a bale of hay, she sees Bougie Fitzgerald. She's been bound at the ankles and wrists the same as Chaney, but there's no tape on her mouth. She's shrieking at a man beyond her who has his back turned from her. Though Lily can't see his face, she can see the shotgun crooked over his forearm. Lily can't imagine how he's ignoring Bougie's caterwauling. He stands like a marble statue, looking out the barn's side door. His stance is familiar, and when he turns, she sees Tomás Cristo.

"Let me go, you camel-faced old plod! You won't get away with this. I'll make sure you pay. I am a Fitzgerald, after all!" Bougie bellows, squirming on the hay bale.

"Well, that name doesn't carry as much weight in Cowherd as it once did," replies Tomás with a sneer. "Not since your *beloved and esteemed daddy* left this world. Such a shame."

"A shame? That man brought nothing but pain and humiliation. He wasn't beloved nor esteemed, more like despised."

"By you?" asks Cristo.

"By everyone!" exclaims Bougie. "He was wicked. I'm not a bit sorry he's dead. Still, he deserved worse than what he got that night. Far worse. A person shouldn't live like the devil and expect to have an easy death. But when an opportunity like that comes along, you don't pass it up. No shame in how that night played out."

"True, but it *was* a shame someone killed him before I could manage it—like I did your mother."

Lily reaches for her cell to call 911, but her heart drops when she realizes she's left it at her house.

"You killed my mother? She was a spiteful witch who took pleasure in cruelty and creating fear and chaos wherever she went. Her murder was the best thing that ever happened to me. I could kiss you!" says Bougie.

"Well, that would be quite unconventional, and a little creepy, considering I'm your half-brother," replies Tomás.

That shut her up… for about 15 seconds.

"Wait… what are you trying to say?" asks Bougie.

Tomás sits on a hay bale across from her and places his gun atop his knees. "My daddy and your momma were married—for a whole day. Your mother tricked my dad into marrying her on prom night. When your grandmother found out about it, she had it annulled. Funny how someone who wasn't married in the church and isn't even Catholic can have a marriage annulled, especially since they had consummated the marriage, as *you* obviously prove. Just one look at your eyes and anyone can see the truth of that. It goes to show that with enough money and power, a person can make his own law, especially in Cowherd."

"And just how do you know all this?" asks Bougie.

"It's a good story," says Tomás, removing a leather-bound book from his jacket pocket. "It's all written right here. There're some newspaper articles from back in the day that partially explain, but truth and lies are all mingled together in those. My grandmother, my mom's mother, died last year. When my cousins cleaned out her house, they found this journal that belonged to my dad. He'd left Cowherd in 1976 to live in Conners after a painful time, which he detailed right here. When he moved back, he left it at my grandmother's.

"It's a long story, but I'll give you the short version. Like I said, your mom and my dad went to prom, and she tricked him into getting married. He knew she didn't love him, but she somehow convinced him Frank Fitzgerald had taken advantage of her and that she was carrying Frank's child. Lies, of course. But Dad believed her and wanted to do the honorable thing. Still, he was scared witless, so he kept downing the drinks your mom fed him. As it turns out, he had good reason to be afraid. She, Frank, her parents, Frank's father, and the Timmons' were about to ruin his life.

"See, Frank had taken the new preacher's daughter, Andrea Gibbons, to prom..."

"Gibbons? As in Niles Gibbons?" Bougie asks.

"We'll get to that. Evidently, Frank was worried the girl wasn't going to show him what he considered a *proper* good time, and so he bought some drugs and slipped them in her drink. Then he brought her to this very barn, where he raped her and choked her until she died. He murdered her."

Bougie makes a hiss and a hiccupping noise like she's trying to hold back a sob and whispers, "I told you he was evil."

"In that, we agree," says Tomás, stretching out his legs and crossing them at the ankles. "Dad surmises that after Frank killed her, he called his best friend Timmy Timmons, who happened to be the son of the sheriff. They cut her hair off and then took a posthole digger and busted her head with it. Dad remembered Frank had seen him using the digger earlier, and so Frank knew his prints were on it. It was all part of the plan to set him up.

"They stole a shirt out of Dad's room and planted it here. Frank convinced Penelope to lie and say she was with him, which theoretically gave Dad an opportunity to kill Andrea. And in Cowherd, theory is as good as fact if it benefits the right people. The sheriff framed my dad and charged him with the girl's murder. Only after that reporter interviewed the motel clerk and other individuals was evidence found to prove his innocence, leading to his release and exoneration. But we all know that once it's in print, there will always be people who believe it, and suspicion and fear will follow the accused person their whole life."

"What happened to the hair?" asks Bougie, her voice shaky.

"Dad received a package in the mail a few weeks after his release. Inside was her hair wrapped in a T-shirt, a note that said, 'You're welcome' and a dead mockingbird. No signature and no return address."

He's wrong about that, thinks Lily. *The dead mockingbird was the signature.*

"Ew! Why a dead mockingbird?" asks Bougie.

Tomás shrugs. "He was doing a class project on *To Kill a Mockingbird* with Penelope, Frank, Jeanie Badger, Timmons, and Andrea. They'd dubbed the group "The Mockingbirds." You remember the warning in the book, right? It was a sin for someone to kill a mockingbird because the birds do no wrong and only fill the world with their beautiful song. They're innocents. Ironic that's exactly what they did: killed one innocent and set up another.

"That was just the beginning of the vile things your family did to mine. They practically stole our land, nearly bankrupt my grandmother, and there's not a doubt in my mind that they're responsible for the arson that killed my daddy, and for Luís' death, too."

"Luís…"

"Yes, your *paramour*. You tried to hide it from everyone, but some knew. Including your father. I think he ran Luís over to keep you two from being together, marrying. *Procreating*. He hated our family just because we were honest and honorable, and he and all his kin were far from it. I think there were others—yourself included—who knew it was him. Especially since Frank was gone just weeks after Luís."

"I didn't just *think* he killed Luís. I *knew* it. He bragged about it to me. I promised myself I'd avenge his death," says Bougie. "Divine retribution."

"Ah, but see, only God can mete out *divine* retribution. That's one of the many ways you Fitzgeralds differ from the Cristos—you think you're God," says Tomás.

"But *you* killing my mother wasn't playing God?" asks Bougie.

"I might have been *playing* God, but I have never thought I *was* God…there's a difference."

"I don't see the difference," says Bougie. "So, all of this is the reason you killed my mother?"

"That, plus her trying to take my farm from me. A month ago, I got a letter from Penelope's lawyer informing me she was going to petition the courts to declare you the legal owner of all Cristo land and assets as my father's first-born child. She had filed an affidavit of heirship and was going to invoke Heirs' Rights to take everything—my home, my land, my business, everything. That's when I knew I had to kill her.

"I planned for weeks. I had worked out every little detail until that woman ruined it by dying of the poison before I got inside the house. The poison was supposed to just incapacitate her. My plan was to strangle her with the scarf—your scarf if you remember."

"How did you get my scarf?"

"Niles took it from Norma Jean at the taproom for me. I wanted that particular Hermès scarf, the one Penelope was going on about in her column. I thought it would be a poetic gesture and lead the sheriff to believe *you* to be the murderer.

"When I sneaked in, she was sitting ramrod straight in her chair, but she was already dead. I realized it the moment I wrapped the scarf around her neck. She wasn't breathing or struggling. I had arrived mere *seconds* too late. I have to admit, it made me crazy mad, and that's why I threw her head down into the gravy. A slight departure from the plan, but it gave the townspeople something juicy to talk about."

He leans forward on the hay bale, elbows on knees, and flashes her a smile that doesn't bother pretending it's sane.

"You're mad," Bougie whispers.

CHAPTER 33

November 13, 2024 – Wednesday
Cowherd, Mississippi

Lily's thighs and calves are burning from squatting, but she doesn't dare move. Yes, he is mad. He reminds her of the villain in Poe's *The Tell-Tale Heart*—

Now, this is the point. You fancy me mad.

Madmen know nothing.

But you should have seen ME.

You should have seen how wisely I proceeded...

"So, Niles was your accomplice," says Bougie. "Not Pastor Carothers."

"Oh, they both were," he says with a smile. "I'd convinced Niles we were just going to scare her. I'd told him about Penelope's involvement in shielding Andrea's killer, and he wanted revenge. It's why he came back to Cowherd after all. He wanted to find out who had killed Andrea, confront them, and bring them to justice. He had been writing Penelope threatening letters for years, all to no avail, of course. I told him it was impossible to put the fear of God into someone who thinks she *is* God. He was very naïve. He had no idea how politics and justice works this town.

"So, he took the scarf, then he went to Norma Jean's shop and stole the shears. I told him to watch for when you went in and go that same day, once again, to throw suspicion on you, or possibly on Frank's true daughter, Norma Jean. If it caused the sheriff to suspect you both, all the better. I used Norma Jean's shears to cut off her hair, just like they hacked off Andrea's. Stabbing her with the shears was impromptu. I was still mad the poison had killed her before I had the chance to choke the life out of her. But I thought both added a sinister vibe. Niles' other contribution was to lure the dog away so he wouldn't raise a ruckus when I went in.

"As for Carothers, I saw him pocketing the money from the offering plate, so I blackmailed him. I'd seen that he visited Penelope most mornings. The morning of the murder, all he had to do was unlock the French door before he left. That was it. He thought it was a bargain until he realized I'd killed her and that he was an accomplice."

"And then you killed Carothers?" asks Bougie.

Tomás shrugs. "Carothers told me he was going to leave Cowherd, but I didn't trust him. Before he could take off, I went to his house and forced him into his car at gunpoint. I drove him to Raven's Roost, shot him, and then pushed him and his car into the lake. Then I called Niles to pick me up. I told Niles I'd been hunting, had laid down for a rest, and fell asleep, and when I awoke, it was dark. The body surfacing wasn't part of the plan, and when Niles saw it, he worked it out that I'd lied to him and had killed Carothers."

"Then you tried to blow him up. Your best friend!" shouts Bougie.

"Oh, I knew that measly bomb wouldn't kill him. It was just a warning. One I'd say he got loud and clear."

"But where did you get the poison?"

"I got the idea from Sam, unbeknownst to him. He used Paraquat—the legal kind—for weed control. I researched it and found that in Mexico you could buy it without the dye and emetic and bad taste. Me and him went down to Mexico to talk to migrant workers and look for land. I smuggled an empty bottle under a tarp in his truck, then bought some off a farmer there and put it in the old bottle."

"But how'd you get her to ingest the poison?" asks Bougie.

"Well, that was simple. I just added it to the milk in her morning bottle delivery."

"How did you know your aunt wouldn't drink it? You could have killed your own aunt!"

"Mary is lactose intolerant. Isn't that funny? A dairyman's daughter being lactose intolerant," he replies with a deranged laugh.

Lily is worried about what will happen at the end of this maniacal story time. The man is obviously insane, and hysteria is building in his voice. Anger and bitterness and hate have beat on his psyche until they've broken through and conquered his soul. She's reminded of Poe's *Raven* and the lamenter's spiral from a sound mind to utter madness fueled by lost love and overwhelming grief.

"I'm done with this game," says Bougie. "Why have you brought me here?"

"Why, to kill you, of course," he replies, standing up and raising the shotgun.

"No!" screams Chaney, dashing through the shed door to the barn.

"No!" Lily screams, reaching out to catch Chaney. But she's a fraction of a second too late, and Chaney runs to stand between Tomás and Bougie, arms raised just as when he tried to protect his dad from Sheriff Timmons.

Tomás lowers the gun a fraction, confusion on his face, which changes to anger when he sees Lily. Lily runs in front of Chaney, pushing him behind her back. He struggles to get out in front of her, but she keeps him firmly shielded with her body.

"Mr. Cristo, you should put that gun down. The sheriff is on the way," Lily bluffs, praying God will forgive this lie, just as she's asked him to forgive the dozens of other lies she's voiced since becoming a WISPER.

"Let him come, though I doubt he'll try to save any of you if he does come. By now he will have figured out you're snooping into Andrea Gibbons' death. He won't want to stand in the way of someone else taking care of his problem, especially when he can keep his own hands clean," says Tomás, once again raising his shotgun.

"Wait! Please let Chaney leave at least. He's an innocent child," says Lily. "Why did you bring him here?"

"I grabbed her at her mother's house and dragged her to the back field where I'd parked my truck." Cristo says, pointing at Bougie with the barrel of his gun. "He saw me trying to throw her into the truck. He ran over full steam and knocked me over and kicked me in the face, too. So, I had no choice but to bring him along. And now that he's heard everything, I'll have to do away with him as well. I don't like it, and I'm not proud of it, but it's just the way it is."

"Just let me say goodbye to him first," says Lily. And not waiting for permission, she turns and kneels in front of Chaney, pulling him into her embrace. "I'm going to distract him," she whispers in his ear. "You run to the house and call for help. You'll know when." She barely perceives his slight nod.

Turning back around, she takes a step toward Tomás and lifts her arms with her hands facing palm out.

"Mr. Cristo…" she begins but gets no more out. She hears him release the safety, raising the gun to his shoulder.

Without hesitation, Lily rushes toward Cristo. She grabs the fore-end of the gun and pushes it violently to the side. A shot rings out, hitting the side of the barn. Chaney knows this is his cue, and he takes off like lightning through the door to the run-in and out through the field.

CHAPTER 34

November 13, 2024 – Wednesday
Cowherd, Mississippi

Eamonn Kelly had booked a flight to Natchez as soon as he got Lily's voicemail.

It's too unsafe for her to remain in Cowherd. I'm bringing her home—well, at least to D.C. until I can find her another placement. Maye I should have called beforehand, but I'm afraid she'll try to talk me out of it.

Arriving at Lily's cottage, he pounds on her door but doesn't get an answer. He sees her car is in the driveway, so he goes next door and repeats the process there with the same result. Hearing a dog barking crazily in the backyard, he skirts the side of the house and heads to the back of the property to see what's upset him. Seeing the trampled grass and truck tracks, he kneels to inspect them. That's when he hears the shot.

Eamonn bolts upright, laying his hand on his firearm, and turns toward the field. Scanning the horizon, he sees nothing, but then he hears the whooshing of grass and running footsteps. Taking some steps forward, he sees a boy running toward him full tilt. He rushes out to meet him.

"Whoa!" he says, grabbing Chaney by the shoulders. "What's going on?"

Chaney sees the badge on Eamonn's belt and wastes no time in filling him in on what's happening at the barn.

"Come on! We gotta' go now!" Chaney entreats Eamonn, and without waiting to see whether Eamonn is following him, Chaney turns and flies back through the field. The boy's speed impresses Eamonn, and he knows it's fueled by desperation, as is his own. Unable to see tussocks and holes, they both stumble several times, but determination and fear push them on. When they are in sight of the barn, Chaney pulls up and holds out his hand to caution Eamonn to do the same. Eamonn hears the strident, ear-splitting outcries of a woman he knows isn't Lily, and the fear spreading through his body intensifies. They hunker down and make their way stealthily across the farmyard.

⊂⊱⊰⊃

Upon Lily's assault, Tomás had hit her with the stock of the shotgun, propelling her across the dirt floor. She landed hard on her belly, and the impact knocked the wind out of her, leaving her gasping for air. Feeling like she was suffocating, she tried to push to her knees, but dizziness made her lower herself back to the earth. Rolling onto her back, she stared up through the barn's rafters to the metal roof, forcing herself to take slow, deep breaths, willing her diaphragm to relax and help her breathe normally again.

Bougie had fallen silent when Cristo first raised his gun at her, either from shock or because her survival instinct had finally kicked in. Now, she's screaming loud enough to raise the whole town. Threats and curses and pleas issue from her mouth in an indecipherable tirade. Tomás leans his gun against a hay bale and grabs his roll of duct tape. Using his teeth, he tears some off and slaps it on Bougie's mouth. Then he grabs two shotgun shells out of his jacket pocket and puts them slowly and decisively into the gun's chamber.

Lily again tries to rise but can only make it to her knees. She half crawls, half drags herself across the floor to sit with her back against Bougie's legs, trying to put herself between Tomás and Bougie.

"Woman, you just keep getting in my way. I'd hoped that little whack on the head at the graveyard would knock some sense into you or at least instill a need for self-preservation. You should have just left everything alone. I didn't want to hurt you then, and I don't now, but you leave me no choice."

"Mr. Cristo, I know this really isn't you," says Lily, rising to sit on her heels. "Everything I've heard about your father says he was an honorable man. In fact, Pastor Meadows said he'd never met a man more honorable than Mattias Cristo. He said Mattias believed, like his mother before him, that all people are equal and loved by God regardless of their race or how much money they have or do not have. And Pastor Meadows' very words about your mother were, 'she was just about as close to an earthly angel as I've ever met.' I know they must have instilled in you some of that integrity and compassion."

"I might have been like that once—before I read his journal…"

"Why do you think he left that journal with your grandmother?" Lily asks. She sees his brows knit together as if pondering her question, and she hopes her words are beginning to disarm his anger. "Could it have been so you would never read it? I don't think he'd want hatred and bitterness to fester in your soul and change you into the very kind of man as those who had wronged him. You're better than those men. You've made horrendous mistakes, but you can still make things right with God."

"How can I make things right?" he screamed. "I'm guilty! I killed Penelope and Carothers, seriously injured and scarred someone who thought me a friend, kidnapped two people, attacked you, and I'm now holding you hostage?"

"You'll have to face consequences for what you've done, but God can and will forgive you if you ask. You've got the hard part behind you: you've realized you're guilty. It's a kindness when God lets us see our sin for what it is," says Lily.

"Pfft!" scoffs Tomás. "Woman, have you listened to anything I've just said? I'm not worthy of God's forgiveness."

Lily shook her head. "You're right—none of us are. But God loves and forgives us because of who *He* is, not who we are. Think of King David: he was an adulterer and a murderer, but he repented, and God still called him a man after His own heart. No one is beyond God's forgiveness. If you truly repent, He will forgive. The only unforgivable sin is rejecting His salvation."

"I've made a vow to my father that I'd avenge him and kill all those who wronged him. Once the sheriff is dead, I've fulfilled that vow. If I give up now, I'll have failed," says Tomás, his voice is gruff as if he's fighting tears.

"You made a vow to a dead man! A vow which, from the little I know about your father, he would never have wanted you to make. Think about how he raised you, the things he taught you, the way he lived his life before God and man. He was back in Cowherd for many years before his death. In all that time, did he ever try to take revenge on any of those who were involved in Andrea's death or his imprisonment for it? Be honest with yourself. Is this about what you think *he* wants or about what *you* want? Is it *his* dignity you want restored or is it your own pride driving this bloodlust?".

Lily sees Tomás's chin go up, and he levels her with a fierce look.

Have I gone too far? I'm speaking the truth, but most people don't want to know the truth when it doesn't affirm their own desires.

Just then, Lily notices a movement from the side door, and Sheriff Timmons nonchalantly steps inside. His revolver is in his hand and aimed at Tomás. *How long had he been there? How much had he heard?*

"Well, I'm plumb hurt, Cristo. Why would you want to kill me?" says Timmons, coming further inside the barn. "I tried my best to keep your old man out of jail."

"You're lying!" yells Tomás, pivoting his gun toward the sheriff. He's getting antsy, shifting his weight from foot to foot and darting his eyes between Timmons and the women.

"Well, I admit I was there while the others planned his down-fall. But when my dad asked me to hide that girl's hair in your pa's room, I couldn't do it. I hid it at my house instead. It was only weeks later that Frank realized what I'd done and made me give it back to him. He told me that he later returned it to Mattias with the dead mockingbird. Frank always had a flair for the gruesome. Of course, that was learned behavior, behavior that was beat into him. He wasn't bad all his life—pompous and conceited, sure—but it wasn't until later that he turned nasty. Beatings and brutality, all that does something to a kid. I mean, how would you have turned out if you discovered your dad killed your mom but told you she'd left and it was your fault? He was primed for badness."

"If all that happened to him as a child, I'm sorry for that kid, but there comes a time in a person's life when they have to quit blaming their parents and their past and take responsibility for their own actions," says Tomás.

"Maybe so, maybe so. But that's not why we're all here, is it? You've come to kill these two, and I've come to kill you—and I guess I'll have to get rid of them, too. Sorry, ladies. It's a matter of being in the wrong place at the wrong time," he says, as he cocks the hammer of his revolver and points it at Tomás. Lily turns her face and lifts her arms to cover her eyes as shots ring out.

Lily hears Tomás fall. She grabs Bougie and pulls her down with her behind the hay bale. Peeking over, she sees the sheriff lying in a pool of blood, shot cleanly through the head. *How did Tomás accomplish that with a shotgun?* Just then she hears steps and turns her head to see Chaney rushing over to her. He wraps his arms around her and buries his head in her chest. Looking past his shoulder, she sees Marshal Kelly holster his gun and rush over to where Tomás lies clutching his shoulder.

It seems the sheriff's shot at Tomás wasn't as accurate as Eamonn's. Did Cristo even fire his shotgun?

Eamonn moves the shotgun out of Tomás' reach and takes off his shirt, using it to apply pressure to Tomás' wound before removing his cell phone. His eyes lock onto hers as he speaks to the 911 dispatcher, calmly advising them of the situation and requesting an ambulance. Throughout the conversation, his eyes never stray from hers; in them she sees a gravity that speaks volumes, an intensity that seems to belie the calm exterior he maintains. Those eyes, usually so steady, betray a flicker of something—an emotion too complex to articulate, but unmistakable in its sincerity.

For a moment, the world outside seems to dissolve, leaving only the two of them in that fragile space. But then his eyes soften at the edges, a hint of sadness crosses his face that seems to convey regret and an echo of unspoken words hanging in the air.

And rightly so, because beneath it all, we both know these types of feelings are not ones we're meant to share. Besides, it's highly likely I've misread the exchange. It's not like I'm well-versed in romantic expression. He's concerned because he feels responsible for me, that's all. A relationship with a person under his charge is forbidden. As I've told myself countless times. Yet, in spite of the truth of these thoughts, she can't suppress the rush of happiness that engulfs her. *He came for me.*

With insistent squeaks, squirming, and elbowing, Bougie shatters the moment. Lily releases Chaney's hold and takes out her pocketknife to cut the tape on the woman's wrists and ankles. Chaney takes a corner of the tape on her mouth and rips it off, taking a step back at Bougie's howl.

"It's the best way, Miss Bougie, I promise you!" he says, slightly grinning through his tears.

In the distance, Lily can hear sirens already making their way to them. But not to save them, for God had sent two angels to their rescue.

∞

Chaney and Lily edge away from the flashing police cars, shouting officers, and the constant crackle of radios. Across the field, they see Bougie surrounded by several officers, her arms flailing as she talks, clearly in the middle of giving some kind of statement. They know their turn will come soon enough.

Slipping behind a couple of trees, they find a fallen log to sit on, a little shielded from the chaos, but still close enough to hear the commotion. They sit side by side, shoulders close, but quiet, watching as Eamonn confers with the other officers. After a few minutes, Chaney finally breaks the silence.

"What are we going to do about Bougie? She said she killed him. Her dad."

Lily takes a deep breath. "She didn't say it outright."

"She didn't say it plainly, but she didn't deny it either." Chaney picks up a small twig and tosses it. "She made it clear she's not sorry he's gone. Said he got what he deserved. Still, it was fourteen years ago, and the sheriff ruled it an accident, right?"

"He did," Lily says. "But that same sheriff covered up a lot of things, did a lot of bad things himself."

Chaney's gaze flicks away, like he's gathering his thoughts before speaking. Lily looks through the trees toward Bougie and says, "Brother Meadows told me that a lot of horrors went on in her house—abuse—for years. You don't grow up like that and walk away unscarred. Then her father killed the man she loved." She pauses. "If she did it, it wasn't right. I can't say I don't understand it, but if she did it, she still needs to be held accountable."

Chaney shifts uncomfortably. "So what do we do? I mean, do we tell someone? Or do we just keep quiet?"

Lily is quiet for a bit before she answers. "Like you said, it's been fourteen years. She didn't *technically* confess. And without a confession or proof, I don't know what anyone would even do with it after so much time has passed."

"But it still matters," Chaney says.

"It does," Lily agrees. "It still matters. And God saw all of it. Even the parts no one else did. I believe He's just but also merciful and wise. As for me, I believe there's a right answer somewhere, I just don't know what is right now."

Chaney gives a small nod—like a boy who understands more than most people twice his age.

CHAPTER 35

November 15, 2024 - Friday
Cowherd, Mississippi

They are gathered in the backyard of Lilliputian Cottage on an unseasonably warm November day. Pops, Percy, Chaney, Pastor and Mrs. Meadows, Lily, and Eamonn have united for a Thanksgiving feast. Bougie appears at the gate, likely having followed the sound of laughter, and without missing a beat, joins them in the yard as if she'd been invited. Lily welcomes her with a quick smile. No surprise, no fuss. *That's just Bougie.*

It's not yet Thanksgiving, but Lily knows she'll be gone by then, and she has much to thank God for. She'll soon be leaving Cowherd to live another lie in another town, leaving these friends she never wanted, but are so thankful for.

Looking at Eamonn, her heart fills with gratitude and joy as she remembers how he'd protected her. True, that was what he had promised to do as a WITSEC Marshal, but the look in his eyes afterwards whispered of a different commitment. It's possible she's mistaken. It may just be self-delusion and a fool's dream.

That's something I'm very good at, after all. Why would a man like Eamonn Kelly allow himself to have feelings for a fugitive? The question applies equally to myself: How could I allow myself to have feelings for him or anyone while I'm a hunted woman? I must constantly push people away for their safety and mine. I live a lie every day. Yet isn't this the reality I've walked in for the past 12 years, just with different secrets, different lies? Eamonn has a keen intuition, and he knows I have secrets that run deeper than WITSEC. What he doesn't know is that I've made a promise to never reveal the truth of what happened that day in 2012 when my father was killed, and the weight of this unspoken confession tears at my heart. Yes, he knows I am keeping secrets. Still, he came for me.

ᨦ

Eamonn watches Lily mingle, speaking with each of her guests. Which of these is the special friend she had mentioned? The only single man that's her age is Percy, so he must be the one. Eamonn feels his throat tighten, and this time he can't pretend this disquiet is mere protectiveness or worry over her safety. He sees Lily walk toward Percy and Chaney, but it's not Percy whose hand she takes and pulls aside.

Lily and Chaney go to the back fence and sit on the grass. They talk for what seems like an eternity. When they return, he can see they both have been crying. So, Chaney was the mysterious new friend who had aroused this jealousy inside him. He feels an acute, yet unwise, sense of relief. Not only unwise, but unprofessional, unethical, and unforgiveable. These feelings for Lily should not be warring inside him, but the events at the barn made them undeniable. He never understood the Pascal quote, *"The heart has its reasons which reason knows nothing of"* until this moment.

ᙂᙓᙂᙅ

Elton Jacks brings the binoculars to his face. He's lying on a hillock in a field behind a small cottage, watching the crowd in the backyard. He's traveled long and sundry paths to make it here today. Yet, he knows he would have gone to Hades and back to find her.

He had scoured the Lexington accident reports and finally found an anomaly. Backtracking to the day of the accident, Elton had located the hospital where they took her, through much trial and error. "Accidentally" running into various U.K. Med Center Security members at local bars until, after countless days filled with lots of leading questions and too many bottles of beer, he was rewarded by making the acquaintance of Officer Mark Jessup—a good ole' boy who liked to talk. Jessup led him to Marshal Eamonn Kelly. He had been watching and tailing Kelly for weeks now, and he had just about decided it was a fruitless endeavor. But then he followed him through D.C. to Natchez. Followed him to Lizzy.

ᙂᙓᙂᙅ

The flash of the cell phone took Lily by surprise as Bougie put her face next to hers for a selfie.

"Oh, Bougie, please don't put that on…" begins Lily, reaching for the phone.

"Too late!" says Bougie, turning her back and clacking out some characters on the cell. "I've posted it. See: 'My rescuer and best friend, Lily Jordan'," she says, showing Lily the Facebook page. "You're way too reclusive, Lily. You know you'll never get a man like that!"

Lily thinks of the man at 854 Janson, black boots, black jeans, black heart, and a shiver goes down her spine. She remembers the warning Eamonn gave her about the dangers of social media—he'd warned her about a predator who knew her face and would stop at nothing to find her. *What has Bougie done?*

ᢀᣞᣝᣜᣟ

The flick of light again blinks in the field. Eamonn squints his eyes to discern what's making it. *Is there someone out there with binoculars? Are they being watched?* He rises from the table, intending to walk out and investigate, but Chaney grabs him.

"I just wanted to thank you again for saving Lily, for saving all of us," Chaney says. Eamonn flicks a quick look back to the field, but the light is no longer there. *I probably imagined it.*

"You're the one who led me to her," he tells Chaney. "Without your speed and courage, I would have never even made it to the barn. You're the actual hero here."

"Will Mr. Cristo be in jail for a long time?" Chaney asks.

"Yes, he will, probably for the rest of his life," answers Eamonn.

"I think he was good at the end, don't you? I mean, he had that shotgun but didn't use it. I think he's sorry for all he's done."

"I hope you're right," says Eamonn. "You know, that was an impressive murder board you made. You've got a very analytical mind."

"Thanks, I saw one on TV." Chaney leans toward Eamonn. "Lily told me about *you know what,*" he whispers. "Do you really have to take her away?"

"I'm afraid so. I need to be sure she's safe," replies Eamonn. He reaches for his wallet, pulls out a card, and hands it to Chaney. "This is my personal number. If you need anything, just call me. I mean it."

"Thanks, Marshal. I'll keep it safe; I promise. Oh look! She's putting out the desserts. Gotta' go!"

Eamonn turns and walks into the field to the crest of the slope. He turns around, scoping out the field and peripheral area, but he sees no one. Sure that he's imagined the flashes, he pivots to return to the house, but something on the ground catches his eye. Kneeling and picking it up, he sees it's a postcard. A card with a single heart on it.

Epilogue

The dark room reeks of cigarettes, rancid body odor, and the stale scent of cheap cologne. In one corner, a worn-out couch sags under the weight of countless restless nights. Nearby, a coffee table is littered with empty beer bottles, half-eaten Mexican food containers, and overflowing ashtrays.

A flimsy table sits in the center, cluttered with multiple computer monitors showing surveillance footage, facial recognition software, and encrypted messages. A handgun lies within reach of a large muscular man, his bulk threatening to collapse the spindly chair he's fallen asleep in, his body slumped, and his neck crooked in an unnatural position.

Thick curtains attempt to block out the daylight, casting the room in shadow. The silence is heavy, punctuated only by the distant sounds of the outside world. This is a place of waiting and watching, filled with the anticipation of violence and the inevitable arrival of fate.

The facial recognition program has been running for months without a solid, identifiable hit. He had tweaked the algorithm several times after the software misidentified two other women who looked nothing like the witness. When a notification chimes, shattering the stillness, the man startles and throws his arms out, nearly toppling the chair. A Facebook photo taken near Natchez,

Mississippi, fills the screen. He fears this is another mistake, but when he looks closer, his eyes light up and a predatory grin spreads across his face. Picking up his cell, he dials his boss.

"Sí, soy yo. Dile Padrino Diablo que hemos encontrado a la gringa."

The End

Acknowledgments

Writing this story has been a collective effort, and I want to take a moment to recognize the wonderful individuals who have played a role in this journey.

To my friends and family—my own kith and kin—your unwavering support, encouragement, and understanding have been a crucial source of strength for me. Thank you for believing in my passion and cheering me on every step of the way, especially during the moments of self-doubt, of which there were many.

A special thanks to my fellow writer and friend, Elsie McKenney, author of *Eve's Covering*, for generously sharing insights and experience. Your guidance has been invaluable throughout this process, and I'm truly grateful for the inspiration and accountability you've offered.

To my beta readers, your thoughtful feedback has been essential in refining this story. I truly appreciate the time and energy you invested in reading my work and offering your perspectives, helping me shape it into the best version it can be.

Thanks to my sons-in-law: Nick, who provided this sheltered woman with vital, descriptive information about wounds and weaponry, and never tired of bizarre and unsavory questions; and Andrew, who has more faith in me and my abilities than I do myself.

Thanks to my daughter-in-law, Katie, for her fashion advice and reminding me precisely how a beauty salon smells, and my son, Ryan, for embodying the qualities of a true Protector, which made it a joy to capture that spirit in my writing.

And to my daughters, Rachel and Regan, who inspire me daily with their love of story and keen insights into life—thank you for being my Ideal Readers. Your excitement fuels my creativity and encourages me to write, reminding me of the joy that storytelling brings.

Lastly, I am grateful to the Lord, whose faithful, ever-abiding presence has provided strength and clarity throughout this process—a comforting reminder that I'm never alone in my endeavors.

Again, thank you to everyone who contributed to this story; each of you has made a significant impact, lending your insights, kindness, encouragement, and unwavering belief in me and my story. I love you all.

Author's Excuses and Other Useful Explanations

Folks and Where They Came From (Or Didn't)

This is a work of fiction. The events and most of the characters in this story are entirely imagined, though a few of the places are real enough to find on a map. That said, two characters were inspired by real people no longer with us—but remembered with deep respect and a bit of storytelling license.

The first is my father, a Southern Baptist preacher for forty years and the inspiration behind Pastor Meadows. He was a big man in both heart and stature—steady, compassionate, and wise. Week after week, he sought the Lord and then wrote his sermons, shaping each one with care, clarity, and conviction. From him, I learned to love both God and the written word, gifts that continue to shape the way I think, speak, and write, for which I am deeply grateful. Though not mentioned in the book, my mother was the first to spark my love of story. When I was a child, she read to me nearly every night, opening worlds I might never have found on my own. Together, they sparked a lifelong love of reading and writing that has never faded.

Any Readers who attended LaRue County High School in the 1970s or 80s may recognize a loose depiction of Garland Blair in the character of Mr. Keith. Mr. Blair was my English teacher during my senior year. He was brash, sharp, and unapologetically direct. He didn't hand out compliments easily, so when he said what you wrote was *"pretty good,"* you believed him. He was the first person who made me feel like I *could* write, not with flattery, but by calling things as they were and pushing me to meet a standard I hadn't realized I could reach. His voice, unfiltered and unforgettable, has echoed in my head ever since. I learned a lot from him, and I'm thankful for the tough love that shaped my confidence as much as my writing.

The rest of the cast is fictional. Any resemblance to actual persons, living or dead, is purely coincidental. If you think you see yourself in these pages, rest assured: it's not you. And let's both be grateful for that. Who'd want to be stuck in a mess like this?

What The Marshals Would Neither Confirm Nor Deny

As you might expect, the inner workings of the Federal Witness Security Program are not exactly public knowledge (which is probably for the best). I did my best to dig up what I could, but WITSEC and the U.S. Marshals were, as one might hope, tight-lipped. That left me to fill in the blanks with a mix of educated guesses, storytelling instincts, and a healthy respect for plausible deniability.

Much of what I did learn came from *Witsec: Inside the Federal Witness Protection Program* by Pete Earley and Gerald Shur—a book so chilling it took me three attempts to finish. If I've bent the truth, I promise it was only enough to keep you reading and me sleeping at night. Any mistakes, inaccuracies, or wild leaps of logic are entirely my own.

Want more small-town suspense? Sign up for my newsletter for exclusive bonus chapters and sneak peeks:

www.KayeBrownstone.com

COMING NOVEMBER 2026

Whispers of the Blessed

You first met her as Lily Jordan in *Whispers of Kith and Kin*, but when her cover is blown, she's forced to run once more… straight into a web of lies, betrayal, and deadly secrets.

A remote mountain lodge was meant to be Holly Joseph's sanctuary. Now, it's her prison—and a killer is locked inside with her.

For Holly Joseph, living under a new name in the Witness Security Program is a constant, lonely battle. Hiding from a ruthless drug cartel, she arrives at the historic Hawthorne Lodge in the mountains of West Virginia, praying for a quiet place to disappear. But her hope for a safe haven shatters when she finds the lodge locked, the town's businesses closed, and the streets eerily silent. The only place with warmth and life is the Baptist church. Drawn to the light and voices, she slips inside, inadvertently becoming part of the service. As she takes in the scene, she realizes she's stumbled into a funeral. And the man in the casket is her host—the owner of Hawthorne Lodge.

When, at the center of the gathering, a mysterious Native American elder steps forward, a hush falls over the mourners, the silence stretching as the elder's gaze sweeps across the church. Her eyes then come to rest on the grieving family, and she casts a chilling curse upon them—a prophecy of vengeance for sins buried deep in the land.

As the elder's words still echo in the church, outside snow begins to fall, pale flakes drifting across the mountains, each one a subtle omen of the chaos stirring beyond.

Soon, a record-breaking blizzard descends on the town—ruthless, furious, and swallowing all in its path. With the lodge cut off from the outside world, the curse's chilling prophecy starts to unfold. Tensions rise, trust erodes, and the line between superstition and reality blurs. When death strikes, a terrifying truth becomes undeniable: a killer is walking among them, and their sanctuary is anything but safe.

With fear spreading as fast as the storm outside, Holly knows she can't wait for a rescue that may never come. Teaming up with a brilliant but quirky historian, she must untangle a web of family secrets, buried betrayals, and the Hawthorne family's shadowed past to uncover the truth before the killer strikes again. But in a place where everyone has something to hide, trusting the wrong person could be deadly.

A Little About Kaye...

Kaye Brownstone is a Central Kentucky-based author who shares her home with a mischievous little black demon dog called Finn. With a wide-ranging background that includes stints as a summer camp counselor, bank teller, homeschool teacher, school secretary, transcriptionist, appraiser, ASL interpreter, and over 20 years working with youth and college students at her church, Kaye brings a wealth of life experience to her writing. Her devotional writings have appeared in *Daily Devotions for the Deaf* and various homeschooling publications.

When she's not writing, you can find Kaye binge-watching British crime shows, reading, watercolor painting, or attempting to keep up with her children and grandchildren, who are equal parts chaos and inspiration. Her dream? To retire to a well-lit hobbit hole in the Shire, where she can live as a hermit among rolling hills... though Finn would probably chase anything that moves, so peace might be optional.

Her family says Kaye loves like none other and is fiercely loyal, forgiving, and caring—though they also caution that she can wield a hairbrush with surprising skill if provoked (word of advice: do not interrupt her while she's reading... although she's positive her brother wasn't nearly as maimed as he claimed to be).

If you were to ask Kaye what she considers the most important thing about herself, she would say that, though her feet are firmly planted in Kentucky soil for now, this world is not her home. She is a beloved child of God living in hope and confidence that one day she'll be called home—her true home—the place her heart has always been homesick for.

Connect with Kaye

Thank you for stopping by! I'm so grateful for your support and would love to stay in touch after today.

Scan a code below to follow updates, share a review, or find your next read.

Amazon Review

Leave a quick review to help other readers discover *Whispers of Kith and Kin.*

Website

Visit my website.

Goodreads

Share your thoughts or add the book to your shelves.

Newsletter Sign-Up

Facebook

Follow my author page for updates, news, giveaways, and events.

Cozy mysteries with an edge— somewhere between cookies…and carnage.

www.ingramcontent.com/pod-product-compliance
Lightning Source LLC
Chambersburg PA
CBHW030640260626
47157CB00007B/2417